*Two royal brothers must balance duty with love
when they unexpectedly find romance!*

A brand-new duet from author Heba Helmy

When Lady Olive asks her best friend, Elise Clifton,
to correspond with her royal match, Prince Saleem
of Egypt, Elise obliges... After all, what harm can
exchanging a few letters do?

The two young women leave England
and embark on a ship to Alexandria,
but Olive decides to run away, leaving Elise alone
with the captivating prince and fighting their
forbidden attraction!

Meanwhile, Saleem's brother, Prince Adnan, is
tasked with retrieving Olive, only to find himself
drawn to the stubborn, beautiful lady and
determined to uncover her secrets...

Daring to Fall for the Prince

Available now

Look out for Olive and Adnan's story, coming soon!

Author Note

This book is a love letter to my birthplace. Looking out over the sea in Alexandria, Egypt, is a magical experience. Everything seems possible: one's wildest dreams for themselves or peace for everyone. When I was writing, peace wasn't happening and it made working on this difficult. I took solace from the characters: sunshine Prince Saleem, who pushes down his melancholy to take action when it's needed, and Elise with her struggle to not feel alone. She was so deserving of love and security, family—and I wanted her to have it, just as I want the same for others.

I made a concerted effort to showcase Alexandria as a mishmash of civilizations, a way that generous, committed people can work to live together in harmony, to treat all their members—no matter their religion, color of their skin or socioeconomic status— as part of a collective human family. Every place here is real and a few can even be visited today. While Raseltin Palace is still, I believe, used for state affairs, The Lodge is based upon El Montazah, and its gardens and beach are open to the public. You can still ride the trams across the city and explore the Catacombs of Kom el Shoqafa. I did, however, alter the anniversary date of a particular donkey's fall. It proved too good of a truth—too good of a metaphor about how love can sometimes happen—to not include in the fiction.

DARING TO FALL FOR THE PRINCE

HEBA HELMY

Harlequin
HISTORICAL

Harlequin®
HISTORICAL

Recycling programs for this product may not exist in your area.

ISBN-13: 978-1-335-54016-4

Daring to Fall for the Prince

 Harlequin Enterprises ULC
22 Adelaide St. West, 41st Floor
Toronto, Ontario M5H 4E3, Canada
www.Harlequin.com

Printed in U.S.A.

Egyptian born and Canadian raised, **Heba Helmy** holds an MA in English literature and a PhD in language and literacies (both from the University of Toronto). She is a former high school teacher and current part-time university professor. Her academic practice focuses on culturally sustaining narratives—and her creative one is all about storytelling that centers love. She lives far too much in her own head, but you might find her online at linktr.ee/hebahelmywrites.

Books by Heba Helmy

Harlequin Historical

The Earl's Egyptian Heiress
A Viscount for the Egyptian Princess

Look out for more books from Heba Helmy coming soon.

Visit the Author Profile page at Harlequin.com.

*For H., heir, spare and all-around best oldest son
a mother could ask for. Love you.*

Chapter One

Alexandria, Egypt—March 1883
Saleem

The sun rose from the gloomy clouds so splendidly that Prince Saleem Ahmed Ali *had* to drop the newspaper he'd been perusing and stick his head out from the carriage he'd been waiting in to bask in its smile. It sparkled over the Mediterranean's sapphire waters and brought another gift with it: a glorious span of rainbow.

What a wonderful day to meet the woman who might soon be his bride!

'A reminder that summer is on the horizon.' Saleem sighed happily, wilfully ignoring the sea's salt to imagine the air tasting like toffee on his tongue.

'Summer is always on the horizon in Egypt. It's winter that struggles to get a foot in our country's door.' His brother, Prince Adnan Ahmed Ali, sitting opposite Saleem, did not stick out his head to see the sun or the rainbow. He probably wouldn't have noticed either even if he had.

Saleem and Adnan did not share mothers, but that fact alone was not enough to account for their starkly different dispositions. Still, Saleem would not fault his brother for his irritable mood. Adnan had arrived in Alexandria only a short while ago, his train from Cairo still cooling on the tracks a few metres away.

'Before summer there should be a wedding,' Adnan continued. 'You understand the preparations involved? The wooing?'

'Yes, Mr Ostaz-ever-reminding-of-my-duty,' said Saleem. 'Have I thanked you for coming—despite concerns about your mother—and for your patience as I wait for my soon-to-be-wooed to disembark?'

'Your smoothness in changing subjects is unrivalled.' Adnan covered his grin with a teasing shake of his head. 'Perhaps, if you did not need frequent reminders of your duties?'

Saleem chuckled. 'And your smoothness in returning to subjects I am attempting to change rivals mine.' He crossed his legs. 'Rest assured, Brother, I am a new man. One who is committed to learning the ways of international politics as our father is asking. And though my instincts tell me that Egypt will not find her salvation in foreign entities, I have made a schedule to educate myself on the topic.' Saleem picked up the *Telegraph* newspaper he'd set aside when his brother arrived and fanned the air with it. 'I start every morning by reading on the world's affairs.'

'And what have you learned?'

'That the object of my wooing is running from crime-ridden London. I wonder if her father's house is near Soho? Talks about a man—a wealthy industrialist, one Mr Clifton—found dead. His brother thinks the fellow's daughter conspired with her lover to do the deed!'

Adnan countered, 'There is crime in this country, too, Brother.'

'I hate that I cannot stop it.' Saleem wished he could, at

least, do something about it. Were it up to him, no Egyptian would ever suffer.

'Because you are next in line to rule and must be protected from it.'

Any who did not know the two brothers, an heir and a spare, would be hard-pressed to guess which was which. Adnan was, in fact, older and, Saleem would be the first to admit, the wiser. He would have made a most capable khedive, or viceroy of Egypt, but machinations of the harem as they were meant that Adnan's mother, an Egyptian woman from an insignificant family whom their father had married and divorced quickly after a spat with Saleem's mother, a Turkish princess, could not claim any rights for her only son.

Saleem's mother, the khedive's first and only official wife, had had daughters before he was born, two years *after* Adnan. But the two did not get to know each other until his fifteenth birthday. Saleem grew up with older sisters who, along with his mother's coddling of her only son, babied him. The khedive, realising his heir did not understand the ways of the common Egyptian man, brought Adnan to court in order to harden Saleem.

What actually hardened Saleem was the fact that his father had lied to him about Adnan's existence. Both he and Adnan had experienced their father's betrayal and they grew close over that fact. It had taken a while, but now Saleem could barely imagine a life without his brother's friendship and counsel.

Yet, try as he might to carry himself with the severity owed to his title, Saleem's cheery disposition did not make it easy. It wasn't his brother's fault, but there were times he believed his father would have rather Adnan been his successor. He hated feeling jealous and, in actively trying to counter it, to prove to both of them that he was fit to be heir, Saleem stumbled sometimes.

He needed Adnan to help with any binds he'd get himself into. That mix-up with Iranian and Iraqi envoys? How was Saleem supposed to know that the grain was being imported from Iraq rather than that their tea was being exported to Iran? It was a natural mistake, no harm had been done—and Adnan had changed the subject quickly so that it was only as if they'd misheard him all along.

Then, there was the time that, under the influence of opium in a public den, he'd agreed with a journalist that Egypt had misjudged English interests in the Suez Canal project. In Saleem's defence, he did not think a drug could make him speak as if he did. Adnan had had the wherewithal to ensure the article would not be published when he'd come to collect his brother and saw who his companion was. How he'd exactly done that, Saleem wasn't sure.

Needless to say, he would never take opium again—but such was Saleem's mantra: *Try all things at least once!*

It was a mantra he regularly goaded his brother with, but Saleem was secretly glad Adnan did not subscribe to it. He'd missed a boyhood with a responsible older brother and felt as though he was making up for the years they had spent apart.

'Besides,' Adnan said now, leaning forward to tap on the date beneath the article, 'this newspaper is a few months old.'

Saleem shook his head good-naturedly before stepping out of the carriage to wave over a boy wearing tattered trousers and shoddy slippers. He handed him the *Telegraph* and gestured to the man opening a nearby falafel stall. 'Charge him more for it because it's from England and the ink quality is better.'

Saleem's gaze followed the grateful boy as he skipped
to where the corniche dipped towards the shore. Dock la-
bourers were lining up for their pre-midday breakfasts.
They'd have left their homes at the crack of dawn on tea
and biscuits and their upcoming meal would need to carry
them until the late afternoon when they'd finish their work
for the day.

The cook's helper cut the newspaper into triangles and
folded them into cones to soak up the hot oil from the bean
fritters as they came out of the vat. Soon after, the cori-
ander-and-green-onion-scented smoke insinuated itself in
the air, vying with the sea's brine.

Falafels were not typical fare in Saleem's home in Alexandria—or any of their royal palaces for that matter. Most
of their chefs had been trained in European cuisines and
while his mother might sometimes call on a traditional
Turkish breakfast with all its varieties, a crispy falafel
stuffed between pickled turnip slices in *balady* bread—
that was a rare treat.

Adnan knew exactly what Saleem was thinking. He
stuck his head from the carriage, 'You want your breath
to smell like *ta'ameya* when you meet your bride for the
first time?'

'She is not going to kiss me! Plus, we are not even officially engaged yet. Recall that I am still wooing?'

Saleem noted the set of Adnan's jaw, stubbled with the
beard he had to shave daily to keep it at bay. He didn't
mind not having that problem, nor did he think himself
less handsome for it, but he'd heard said that some women
liked facial hair.

'Besides, the smell may force Olive to pay me more attention than you.'

He was teasing, but Adnan frowned. 'Marriages should

be sacred, Saleem. Lady Olive Whitmore is not going to fall in love with me instead of you. That is *if* she finally graces us with her presence. Her ship has already docked!'

Adnan's impatience was because he'd left his sick mother alone in Cairo—which made his being here a particularly gracious act. It was why Saleem had arranged for a few days of fun in Alexandria, giving his brother a little respite before the four of them——Lady Olive had brought a travel companion——were scheduled to take the train back there.

'You know how ladies can be. They want to make certain they're not missing anything as they gather their things. She does not know I am waiting and the servants sent to help them disembark were told to not say anything that would spoil the surprise.'

Saleem frowned. Perhaps he should be more apprehensive.

'Ladies can be exasperating!' Adnan came out of the carriage to stand next to his brother. 'No matter, I am glad to meet the woman who managed to be deemed a satisfactory option to you *and* our father. It is quite the accomplishment.'

Saleem was proud of it, too. Olive Whitmore was the only child of Lord Whitmore, a political man who also happened to be one of Egypt's wealthiest foreign investors. When his father first suggested that theirs would be a smart match, Saleem had taken it upon himself to write to Lady Olive, inviting her to spend time in Egypt this year.

He'd not expected her letter back to him to be so warm. Their exchanges had begun in earnest thereafter. He enjoyed writing her letters and eagerly awaited reading her responses.

'We are *friends*, I suppose.'

Adnan grinned. 'You once told me that you wished for a sordid love affair with the most beautiful of women before you were tasked to marry. A forbidden romance, an adventure you could look back on when your wife by arrangement bored you.'

'And you responded by saying that friendship is most important. That if we had it, my wife would be my life's partner and she could not bore me.'

'Did I? What a wise brother you have!'

'I have had no very sordid love affairs, but...'

'You are ready to settle,' Adnan finished the thought. 'While I have not your experiences in that department, I do still believe that friendship is the first step to love, but other things help it along, too.'

Saleem lifted a brow, teasingly elbowing his brother. 'What specific "other" things?'

'The British Consul visited us last week and mentioned that Lady Olive is exquisitely beautiful, that she—and these are his exact words—"dazzles at first glance".' Adnan grinned, 'Were he a younger man, I'd have clocked him on your behalf.'

'I did not show you the portrait folded into her last letter.' Saleem hadn't had much time to study the miniature, it was only received two days ago, but something about it didn't feel quite right. He admired the artistry certainly. He wasn't a painter himself, but it had him wanting to go back and explore the finer details in the extensive art collection held at his family's Cairo palace.

Saleem pulled the portrait from his coat pocket and handed it to his brother. Rather than comment on Olive's beauty or compliment the artist who'd captured it, Adnan frowned. 'If she responds positively to wooing, keep your admiration for her close to your chest, protected. Don't let any come between you both. Not your mother or sisters. Not me or our father.'

'How could *you* come between mine and Olive's relationship?'

'You can trust me, but you are kind-hearted, Saleem. Optimistic to the point of not seeing the realities that can mar a relationship. What if you learn that the real Lady Olive's character is dissimilar to that of the young lady in her letters? People can write who they are not.'

Saleem knew Adnan was concerned for him, but he hadn't read their letters. Didn't *feel* the honesty in them. 'Did you not just say that I am the one with experiences? Lest you forget, Adnan, between the two of us only one is a virgin.'

'And only one takes matters of Islamic law more seriously, Brother! And though I will not preach to you as a *shaykh* might, premarital relations do fall into the forbidden haram category.'

'Oh, *you* wouldn't preach to me?'

Adnan handed back the portrait with a grin. 'Do you carry it on your person for a reason?'

Saleem sighed. 'Maybe you're a bit right. Olive *looks* different than the girl I imagined from her letters. I cannot describe exactly how, but I want to compare this miniature to whom I meet when she gets off that ship.'

They stared out at the vessel in the distance. The buzz of all manner of people descending and crates and luggage being hauled out was chaotic. Saleem spied two of his own servants hoisting a trunk.

Adnan faced his brother, adjusting his collar as if he were a tailor ensuring the fit was right. 'Whoever *she* is, she is sure to be instantly captivated by you, for there are no men as handsome and ridiculously charming as my brother! The two of you will spend time together before your engagement. Your time together will propel you from the friendship found in letters to the love gained from face-to-face interactions.'

'Not sure how "together" we will be considering she will be accompanied at all times by a chaperon as is the English fashion. Her travelling companion is likely a spinster type, probably one with eyes at the back of her head.'

A contemplative look crossed Adnan's face. 'Lady Olive has no mother. It must be hard on her. She would need to maintain her maiden-ness until her father makes the trip over, leads the engagement arrangements on her behalf.' He turned away, likely reminded of the inevitability he would be losing his mother, too.

Saleem gave him a minute, then aggressively sniffed the air, forcing his brother's attention back to him with a jubilant, 'Smells as though our falafel sandwiches are ready!'

Chapter Two

Elise

Miss Elise Clifton would have been angrier over Olive's disappearing act if it were not for two things. The first was her hunger. Elise needed to eat, could barely stand upright on an empty stomach. The second was knowing that when she was satiated, she was very good at dealing with her emotions—and devising plans to counter whatever negative consequences they might induce.

Rather than speak to Prince Saleem's servants come to collect their luggage about 'the Lady Olive's' whereabouts, Elise slipped off the ship they'd crossed the Mediterranean in to make her way to a food vendor along the path where the sands ended and the city began.

Elise's father used to do business in Alexandria, it's where he met and fell in love with her mother, the daughter of a Greek merchant visiting the city at the same time. For that reason alone, she'd always thought fondly of it and hoped to see it for herself.

'We'll go there together some day, Kythoni.'

Her father's voice was an echo within Elise, one getting more and more distant.

Now that both her parents were gone, this trip would

have felt necessary even if she hadn't come on a secret mission beyond simply being Olive's travelling companion. Elise hoped that when her mission was complete, she'd get closure about her father's death and work out what the next phase of her life would be. Work out what she would do and where she belonged.

What Elise hadn't accounted for was doing it without her best friend by her side. Her anger at and simultaneous worry for Olive threatened to bubble over as the man selling food called boisterously, 'Falafel! *Gahis el* falafel!'

A horde of dock workers began forming a line. Elise had never eaten falafel, but the smell was enticing enough that even the staring men couldn't prevent her from joining them.

In England, Elise was ever conscious of people's gazes. She favoured her mother in colouring, rather than her paler father. She was twelve years of age when her mother died, but had grown up acutely aware of how others treated her when she was not with her husband. A finely dressed brown-skinned woman demanded attention and rarely for innocent reasons. It had hardened Elise to witness the bigotry of perfect strangers. Frustrated her, even as a child, that they should make assumptions about her mother's virtues or use her to their advantage, believing her easily dupable.

Dressing plainly meant that Elise would be overlooked, blend into a crowd. *Be unmemorable.* This had been to the chagrin of her father who gifted her fine gowns that remained, for the most part, in her closets.

Yet, here I am, she thought, *half a world away from said closets and still drawing attention.*

But it was not for her darker skin, since most were similar shades, nor was it due to her clothing, a modest green gown in a style she'd been told was suited to Egypt.

The eyes on Elise now, she realised, were because she was the only woman among the gathered men. She was pleasantly surprised to see that the workers were kind, making room for Elise in the queue, urging her forward by moving out of her path and gesturing with their hands when she did not respond to their words.

Since Elise knew no Arabic—she should have studied the language books Olive had spent the trip poring over—she wondered if she should thank them in English? Would they treat her differently if they learned she was not an Egyptian woman?

Even as she contemplated the questions, their attentions were drawn elsewhere. A *very* well-dressed gentleman had appeared, unwittingly proving Elise's point.

Those in line let him pass as they had her, but he left wide smiles in his wake, thanking them in Arabic. The man continued to talk animatedly as he moved forward, turning those smiles into chuckling in response to what he was saying.

He was much taller than most everyone there, his bronze face bare of hair, his straight nose and strong jaw lending him a statuesque profile. Curly brown hair meandered down his long neck to the nape of his coat—a fine design with golden button details that looked as though it should be on display in the window of a Savile Row shop.

He must have felt her staring because he faced her with warm hazel eyes. Elise noted how they contained granules of amber which caught the daylight like honey glistening in a jar.

His full lips were distracting enough that it took Elise a full minute to realise he was talking to her.

In Arabic.

She felt her face flush, despite the chilly nip of the weather.

Could Elise help it that she had a painter's sensibilities and noticed things? In this case, not a thing, but…one very handsome man. Though, in that aspect of her life, it really was better for her to merely *notice*, rather than *act* on any impulses. Elise had learned that lesson the hard way.

Around her, the workers had begun collecting their sandwiches, so when the well-dressed stranger held one out for her, a warm smile playing on his face, she shook her head. It was abrupt enough that she brought on a pinch in her neck and caused the man's smile to drop.

She'd never seen such a captivating face.

Elise actually had to resist reaching out to touch the contours.

I'm not a sculptor! It must be the hunger.

She forced herself to turn away and fished for a single piastre from her travelling purse. She held up a finger to the vendor, indicating she wished for a single sandwich.

The vendor looked at her oddly and then at the stranger. Both shrugged.

Only after the vendor had handed Elise what she'd paid for, and the gentleman left to whoops of approval from the men gathered, did it strike her he'd bought everyone in the line sandwiches.

Everyone, except Elise.

If he thought her rude for not accepting his generosity, he had not dwelled on it.

His demeanour could not be further from my own.

Elise regularly reflected on her interactions with others, whether they were intended with malice or not.

You're not here to take a lover, she reprimanded herself, *what does it matter?*

She might have found the stranger attractive, but she was done with men. *Yearning* was no longer a word in her vocabulary.

Elise found a lone boulder to sit upon, one that provided a view of Prince Saleem's men hauling her and Olive's luggage from the ship and across the sandy beach towards a pair of carriages parked on the road.

She chomped into her falafel sandwich, marvelling at the flavours of toasted coriander and cumin, the crispiness and slight spiciness for one bite, then a second. Alas, Elise's third bite came back with only bread. She opened its pocket to find the rest of it empty. The vendor must have thought her lifted finger meant she only wanted a single falafel fritter!

Elise released an exasperated, unsatiated sigh. Full stomach or not, it was time to decide what to do about Olive. She unfurled her friend's note to read again.

> *Forgive me, Elise.*
> *I have no interest in meeting the Prince and will not entertain any plans for my life that suit Papa. I need time alone and am assured that you will know how to speak on my behalf.*
> *All my love,*
> *Olive*

Elise had believed Olive was resting in her room on the ship, but after they'd left the harbour in the Nile Delta city they'd first stopped in, she'd knocked on her door and found the note instead.

'Damn it, Olive, what were you thinking?'

Elise hadn't come to Egypt to worry about her friend. She'd come to learn more about the gold bar she'd found after her father's death.

'*Yours is a pragmatic imagination,*' Thomas Clifton used to say.

He'd meant it as a compliment, said it to her when Elise offered helpful solutions to his business dilemmas. She'd once overheard him say it to a colleague who'd commented on a painting of hers that hung on his office wall.

'*My daughter possesses a pragmatic artistry. Quite unlike any other, but as masterful as the masters.*'

But it was another conversation Elise had overheard that had her fretting after his death. That had her worrying he might have been murdered—by his own brother.

She had only run into her Uncle Andrew once and the experience had been altogether unpleasant—considering what had prompted it. Or, rather, *who*. But Uncle Andrew had barged into their Manchester home the night before her father was set to travel to London. She'd been awakened by shouting. The chilling words, the slur her uncle had uttered then rang in her ears now: '*Give me the gold bars, Thomas, or you and your d— daughter will pay with your lives!*'

Elise didn't want to believe her uncle had anything to do with her father's death and so part of her was grateful that, in the end, it had been dismissed as an accident, the result of a fatal tumble. She'd have forgotten the entire incident, perhaps, but in the days after Thomas Clifton's body was found, her uncle had accused her in the papers of having something to do with it, even implying that Elise's 'lover' was involved.

What a joke that was, since he was the one who'd sent Gerald into her life in the first place!

Her father's lawyer told her that 'Andrew Clifton posed no threat' to her name or her inheritance and he was right for the most part. But the sum of money she inherited upon her father's death, comfortable as it would keep her, was somewhat smaller than anticipated. When she asked the lawyer if there'd been any gold bars among her father's assets and he said 'no', she thought that maybe her Uncle Andrew had got them and was satisfied.

But a few weeks after her father's death, Elise found a gold bar in their London town house. It was half wrapped, as if Papa had planned to ship it. It didn't have a name or a complete address, but there was a city and country destination noted on the paper: Alexandria, Egypt.

Elise would have reported what she'd found and the conversation she'd overheard to the London police, but they'd proven useless with the investigation into her father's death. And with all that Lord Whitmore had done for her, insisting that she come and stay with him and Olive, Elise did not want to burden him any further. He had a political career and a reputation always at risk by his association with her father.

Elise had been set on hiring a private investigator, but then Lord Whitmore received the invitation to visit from the khedive of Egypt. Olive became obsessed with the prospect, even though her father could not clear his schedule. Figuring out the origin and destination of the gold bar meant that Elise had her own reason to want to come as soon as possible, too.

It was decided the two young ladies would travel together. Keep each other safe.

Still, something had felt *wrong* about their journey.

Olive had been distant since Elise had come to stay with

the Whitmores. At first, she thought it was because Olive felt bad for still having her father. She was often short with Lord Whitmore in front of Elise. Elise thought the journey—just the two of them together—would allow them to reconnect, talk the way they used to. Instead, Olive spent most of the time in her cabin, studying books in Arabic in order to, she claimed, 'speak to the Prince'.

Elise reminded her that Saleem knew English and, for all intents and purposes, Olive *had* been speaking to him in the letters they'd exchanged. But that wasn't the entire truth. And Olive had herself admitted as much when the ship docked in the Nile Delta city of Rosetta.

'I should get the Prince a gift,' she'd declared.

When Elise had offered her help, Olive replied, 'You've already done too much, responding to him as me. Saleem might very well be in love with you through those letters.'

They'd both laughed it off, but Elise twinged with the same guilty feeling she'd felt since that first time responding to him.

Prince Saleem's introductory letter for Olive had been soon after Elise's father's death. Olive had come into her studio, asking Elise to answer on her behalf. She said it was because Elise had previously had a paramour, but Elise suspected it was meant to be a distraction *for* her. She thought it was Olive's way of helping Elise with her grieving by pretending to need her help.

She heartily approved of Elise's first response. But when the follow-up letters from Prince Saleem came in succession thereafter, Olive lost interest entirely, leaving Elise to continue writing him in the way she thought best.

Elise had not come to Egypt for Saleem, but she would be lying if she didn't admit she was eager to meet the

Prince. Although she'd loathed the duplicity involved, she *had* enjoyed corresponding with him.

She recalled what he had written in one letter.

> *The gardener planted hibiscus today. I do not un-*
> *derstand precisely why, but it reminded me of you.*
> *Do you believe people find their like in flora? If*
> *yes, my brother would definitely be a cactus! I jest,*
> *but he can be prickly! When we meet in person, I*
> *shall see if you are indeed like hibiscus and you can*
> *decide which I would be.*

Saleem had drawn a flowering shrub in the margins, an amateur's hand, but an earnest attempt that pressed upon Elise's sensibilities. She'd sneaked into the Whitmore estate library to look up the genus and found it was a hardy one, its perfume released when pressed or dried. Despite never meeting her, nor fathoming who he was writing to, it seemed Saleem *knew* Elise.

She had barred herself in the library that day and cried for the first time since her father's death. A much-needed release of emotions. Saleem's subsequent letters continued to act as a tonic. He wrote as if he'd magically perceived her suffering and wished to lead her through it.

Elise knew it was ridiculous to equate the two but she believed that if Olive's entry into her life helped her get over her mother's loss, then Prince Saleem's words had helped her get over her father's.

Both were her dear friends, but only one knew it.

For her part, Elise had tried to be honest with the Prince. She stopped signing her words with Olive's name. She'd not gone as far as to put her own name to them, but she'd end her letters with truths.

Yours, while sitting on the banks of the Thames...

Or,

Affectionately, as I swallow the last morsel of a cheese and cucumber sandwich...

Elise counted on the thrashing waves to muffle her loud groan. Her hunger made her extra-sentimental, but she couldn't help thinking that although Olive had acted recklessly, when she returned, tail between her legs, Saleem and she might still find a way to marry.

How would he react if he learned Elise was the person behind the letters? She'd known they could never be anything more than friends, but she'd meant to discuss it with Olive before they arrived. Impress upon her to tell Saleem the truth as soon as they disembarked so that it would not be awkward between the three of them. Indeed, when Elise knocked on Olive's door to find her, it was to tell her that much and because she also wanted to enlist her help with the quest to learn who her father meant to send the gold bar to in Alexandria. Instead, she'd found her goodbye note.

Guilt pricked at Elise now.

Maybe if she'd told her earlier, Olive wouldn't have callously chosen to break their itinerary. Lord Whitmore would compare the 'rational' head on Elise's shoulders to the 'reckless' one on his daughter's. He'd never have agreed to Olive travelling to Egypt were it not for Elise accompanying her.

She should have kept a better eye on her friend, strived to learn how she'd got it into her head to abandon ship! Did Olive not know that her father was the kindest of men, one who prioritised his daughter's happiness? Lord Whitmore would never force her to marry a man she did not want.

Elise tossed the rest of her pita to where three seagulls hovered. As they descended on it like hawks, she stood up, herself still ravenous.

Alas, she couldn't delay any longer. It was time to tell the Prince's servants that the woman they were waiting for wasn't coming.

Chapter Three

Saleem

Saleem handed his brother the falafel sandwich, pleased he'd secretly managed to buy for everyone in line. He'd always seized opportunities that satisfied the many, especially if they came at such little cost.

The many, save for that *one* woman who'd refused him. 'Do you think I should have bought for our guests? Lady Olive and her travelling companion would be hungry, certainly.'

'Delicate, pampered English ladies prefer finer things,' Adnan disparaged between bites. 'And do not lead with thoughtfulness, Lady Olive may take advantage. Letters are not enough to know a person, Saleem. Even this informal visit of hers before an engagement is announced is suspect. Eshra is the only marker of whether a marriage can succeed. Eshra is the process of living with one another, understanding each other's small and big habits in order to foster and grow true, lasting companionship.' He held up a finger. 'And before you tell me again that you two are already friends, know that friendship and companionship are two different things.'

Adnan reminded Saleem of a recent conversation with

their father. The two of them had said his optimistic disposition would not permit him to be a strong king, but Saleem countered by saying he'd trust his instincts, that they
came from his awareness about people, his empathy for
them. Their father had scoffed, stressing Saleem needed
to learn to lead with his mind, while his brother had regarded him with near pity.

Saleem had a hard time deciding whose reaction bothered him most.

He could be a good leader *and* trust his own instincts.
He was determined to prove as much to both his father
and brother.

The servant who'd been loading the last of their guests'
luggage approached, a worried expression on his face. He
looked up to Saleem's personal guard, Mustafa, sitting
beside the carriage driver, before getting a nod to speak
to him.

'Everyone has disembarked, my Prince. The ship Captain said there *were* two English ladies on board, but one
got off in Rasheed. The other, upset at the news, demanded
they return, but he had a schedule to keep and—'

Before he could finish, the young lady Saleem had seen
at the falafel stand came running from the beach. She
shouted and waved her arms in a distressed manner. And
he, disliking to see a woman in such a state, instinctively
moved towards her.

Then Saleem heard her, not just shouts—but the En-
glishness of them.

He'd believed her mute earlier, yet here she was with
the most compelling of voices. He could almost hear the
timbre of it in a sad song, a sultry smokiness.

When she saw him, her face shifted into a look he could
not quite read. Was it embarrassment at their encounter?

'You are Prince Saleem,' she exclaimed.

'I am.'

She dipped in a curtsy. He'd have stopped her, but she rose quickly as if she was not used to niceties anyway. She held his gaze when she straightened. Her eyes were a deep-set green beneath a mass of thick knotted lashes and full but finely arched brows. Her skin was a darker shade of olive with a smattering of freckles along her upturned nose. Her long raven hair was tied in a low braid that whipped in the breeze. Additionally, her simple maroon galabia was decidedly Egyptian-looking. Saleem couldn't be blamed in having assumed she was, too.

'Those are my things,' she said. 'I thought they might take them without me.'

'Yours or Lady Olive's?' Adnan had come to stand next to his brother and, though he sounded rude, it was a reminder that the woman they were waiting for had not arrived. And Saleem should be more concerned rather than focusing on the one before him who was clearly *not* Olive.

'*Ours*. I accompanied her. My name is Elise Cl... Er... *Thomas*. Elise Thomas.'

Next to him, Adnan bristled. Where others avoided conflict, his brother actively attracted it. Their sisters called him the 'goat' because of his propensity for head butting.

'And I am Prince Adnan. Can you let us know where Lady Olive is? We are surprised to learn she disembarked earlier, in a city she does not know. Is your mistress always this foolish?'

Adnan's tone was clipped, but before he could apologise on his brother's behalf, Saleem caught the moment when Elise's face relaxed. She was not bothered by Adnan. In fact, she looked as though she was about to trust him with something important.

Saleem clamped a pang of jealousy. Why should he care about any woman's reaction to his brother, let alone one he had only just met? Adnan inspired confidence in people regularly. The very air around him seemed to shout of his capability.

But Elise wasn't cowering. 'You have it wrong, Prince Adnan. I am not Olive's maid, nor is she my mistress. We are, in fact, as close as sisters might be without sharing blood. Lord Whitmore was unable to accompany her, so she and I came together.'

Saleem watched Elise's haughtiness with curiosity. There was something quite striking about it. When he had interacted with her in the falafel line, he believed her almost pitiful and proud. He'd been right about the latter, but wrong about the former.

'To address your question,' she continued, 'Olive can be reckless, but she is not a fool. Nevertheless, I will only rest when she has been retrieved.'

'You tried to get the ship Captain to return. He should have listened.' Saleem's mind raced. What might he do to ensure Lady Olive's safety?

Adnan nudged him, his head tilting towards the servant waiting. It was a warning. Although their command of English was weak, if news of Lady Olive's premature departure were to get out, they might have a problem on their hands. Saleem did not want it getting back to his father that he'd lost the daughter of a good friend *and* political ally before she'd arrived.

And Allah forbid anything bad should happen to her!

But these servants were Saleem's recent hires and he'd used his intuition. He believed them good and trustworthy. Although their loyalty had yet to be tested, they did answer to him.

'Excuse me, one moment,' he said to Elise, then marched to the eldest of the servants.

'Take the ladies' things to the Lodge, have the staff set up their rooms. There has been a slight delay and I don't know when we will return home, but everything should be ready as soon as possible.'

'That would please you, my Prince? We do not want to leave you here, out in the open,' the servant whispered so as not to draw attention from those passing.

To alleviate his concern, Saleem pointed to Mustafa sitting next to his carriage driver. 'You know my personal guard who has followed me like a shadow for many years. What most don't know is he has a kind of djinn sense. He is able to detect threats before the threats even know what they are.'

A loud clearing of the throat from the man in question stopped Saleem from mentioning Mustafa's knowledge of what seemed like every fighting technique known to man or his aptitude for hiding a ridiculous amount of weapons on his person.

Saleem grinned. 'His hearing is good as well,' he reassured the servant, 'I am safe with him.'

'*Hather*, my Prince.'

When he'd seen the carriage carrying the luggage off, he returned to Adnan and Elise. She was showing him a note and they both didn't notice his return until Saleem peeked over his brother's shoulder. He caught a glimpse of the words before Adnan hid it away.

I have no interest in meeting the Prince and will not entertain any plans for my life that suit Papa.

Saleem hadn't brought one of her letters with him to compare, but he knew, 'That is not Lady Olive's hand.'

Adnan's face softened. 'Women can be fickle, Saleem. It sounds as though Lady Olive needs time to retrieve her lost senses. She needs me to help her *find* them.'

Saleem shook his head. 'I should go to Rasheed, there's a fellow I know who'll help. You return to Cairo, take Miss Thomas with you if she wishes?'

It took Elise a beat before she understood that he was asking her. 'No. I need to stay in Alexandria. There is something I have to do here. Besides, what if Olive were to return? She knows to come to the palace here.'

Saleem turned to his brother. 'Perhaps you can accompany Miss Thomas to the Lodge, then?'

'The Lodge is your domain, brother. You are whom people will be expecting. It will raise more questions if I arrive in your stead. Let me go to Rasheed. Whoever hears from Lady Olive first informs the other, although I'm not sure what the most expedient way to do that would be.'

'I can arrange that through my contact, it is not a problem.' Saleem put a hand on his brother's shoulder. 'I don't want your return to Cairo to be delayed.'

Adnan switched to Arabic, 'I can take out my annoyance on the Lady Olive. Lecturing reckless people soothes my soul.'

'It is unlike her,' Saleem rationalised, with a glance in Elise's direction. 'The Lady Olive I got to know would keep to her itinerary, her appointments.'

When she didn't confirm it, he held out a cupped hand to Adnan. 'Let me study her note,' he demanded. 'You know my pride is not so easily bruised and why I cannot abide a lie.'

'Very well.' His brother reached into his pocket to retrieve it, but Elise spoke before he could.

'It is Olive's hand and while you may think you know her, with all respect Prince Saleem... *I* know her better.' She sighed with exasperation. 'I should have been more vigilant. Lord Whitmore entrusted me. Were he here, he'd be beside himself with worry.'

'We should be grateful he is not. The khedive would...' Adnan didn't need to finish his thought.

Saleem knew it would be a disaster if something *were* to happen to Olive. But what sort of man would he be if he fretted over political ramifications while a young lady was alone in a city she'd never been? He took a deep breath, letting the sea air fill his lungs and pushing down the sense of being a disappointment.

Along the corniche, a pair of girls—siblings by the look of them—kicked a ball close to their carriage. One laughed shyly, egging the other to retrieve it.

Saleem sent it back and thought of how, were there not a crisis, he'd have liked to join their game as he often did when he spent time with his family. He thought he and Olive had that in common because in response to his naming those he grew up with—all the cousins!—she had written about the loneliness of being a single child, her longing for the bustle of big families.

Why would she choose to be alone now?

No marriage had been arranged; she was visiting with the understanding that this was merely a meeting of friends. Then, and only *if* they both agreed, would they discuss an engagement. She hadn't given him the chance to woo her, to show her they could be good for each other. Yes, his father wanted a political and financial boon for Egypt and Saleem wanted to prove his worth as heir, but if Olive decided she did not want to marry him at the end, Saleem could have handled it. He'd have spoken to Lord Whitmore, found a way to help his country without making her his wife.

She should have at least gleaned that much about him from their letters.

Saleem turned to Adnan. 'My contact in Rasheed is named Yasser. He owns the Rosetta Carriage Company. Their office is by the railway station and he has knowledge of the city like no other. He'll have a man at the mailing post and access to a telegraph machine with a direct line to my office there.' Saleem pointed to a building at the Raml Station across the street, away from the sea. 'Through him, we can contact one another expediently.'

Adnan's brow furrowed, 'How do you know this Yasser?'

'We collaborated on engineering matters related to the tram project.' Saleem tsked at his brother, 'Our guest will think me a useless prince. Must you embarrass me before Miss—' he was arrested by Elise's impossibly thick lashes and momentarily forgot the last name she'd given '—Thomas.'

'"Elise" suffices.'

'Elise,' he repeated slowly, his tongue hitting the back of his teeth as he did. It was a pretty name and suited her well. 'If you call me Saleem, I shall call you Elise.'

She nodded, her glance falling downwards. She did not strike him as bashful, but she was proving to be quite a mystery—one that was distracting him from the mystery of where and why Olive had disembarked prematurely. He turned back to Adnan. 'Yasser will make quick work of finding Lady Olive. Nothing happens in Rasheed without his knowledge.'

'I will tell him that *Prince Saleem* sends his regards.'

Adnan was reprimanding him for asking Elise to do away with his title.

Maybe, too, it was because of her that Saleem didn't push the matter of going to Rasheed himself instead of his brother. Adnan could be a rough host and she clearly felt upset over her friend. Saleem had no desire to cause Elise further distress.

'The next train leaves shortly,' he said, 'you should not miss it.'

Adnan grabbed the pack he'd come with from the seat of the carriage.

He asked Elise, 'It should not be so hard to find an English lady in such a small city and my brother showed me a portrait she sent, but does she have any other distinctive marks?'

It occurred to Saleem that if he'd been wrong about her hand, her picture might be as well. He pulled it from his pocket and held it out to Elise. 'Is this Lady Olive?'

She blinked a few times before answering, 'That is her. Flawless. No distinctive marks.'

'You keep it, you might need it. To show people in order to look for her.'

Saleem watched Adnan tuck the portrait away.

His brother stuck out his hand, but Saleem went for the hug, a gesture that always seemed to surprise Adnan, though he did it often. *Ma'asalama.'*

After bidding him farewell in turn, Adnan whispered, 'This is not your fault.'

Was it not?

Saleem's innate optimism would return soon enough,

but, lately, in the time before it did, he had begun to wonder if it only existed to distract him from facing his feelings of inadequacy, the ones he could not seem to shake.

Chapter Four

Elise

Elise's heart had clenched to see Saleem's face drop when he looked over his brother's shoulder and saw that Olive had left because of him. She was already feeling guilty over not watching Olive better and now that was compounded. Saleem didn't know Elise had been writing the letters. Nor that she and Olive were entirely different people.

Even if he weren't disappointed, he'd have been surprised by the words he'd read. Saleem had proven himself as having an astute understanding of Elise's character, but he'd unwittingly attributed that character to Olive, rather than her.

He said he cannot abide a lie.

Deciphering her feelings towards noblemen was complicated for Elise, but thinking of Saleem as merely a generous and attractive man in a falafel queue made her want to tell him the truth right then. In the end, it was frustration at Olive that stopped her. Fear, perhaps, that, without Olive there to admit her part in the deception over the letters, Saleem would lay all the blame for it at Elise's feet.

She wouldn't let Olive's selfish runaway act distract her from what she had come to Alexandria to do.

Saleem's back was to Elise as he silently watched his brother's train leave the tracks. It took a beat after it had departed for him to face her and that was only when she'd called his name.

Elise called it mostly because she needed to stop admiring the breadth of his back, the taut muscles there that stretched his coat.

Saleem met her gaze, 'Adnan will find your friend.'

'I trust in your trust of him,' she said, 'but I fear there may be more going on with Olive than that note would indicate.'

'What else might there be?'

The intenseness of his stare, the suspicion in it, staggered her tongue. Saleem was a young man who strived to know others, his charm honed on his ability to understand them. Hadn't she surmised as much from his letters?

But Elise had spent her honing skills on the exact opposite. She had learned to hide her emotions, present an unreadable, even enigmatic, face to others. Although the sentiments in her letters had been authentically Elise's own—most likely, a response to Saleem's honesty—she had not believed he'd magically recognise her as the author upon first glance.

Why, then, did the expression on Saleem's face now sting more than she cared to admit?

When she'd anticipated their first meeting, she imagined it being focused on Olive. That he'd take one look at her and immediately fall in love. That was why Elise had painted her portrait and sent it to Saleem. She'd planned ahead in order to not feel inferior when the Prince was rendered speechless by Olive's fair beauty.

But that had nothing to do with his question. How could

she explain what was wrong with Olive when she'd not spoken to Elise about it?

'Olive has been upset. She might have had an argument with her father—'

Before she could say more, a man jumped from the carriage. He pushed Saleem back so abruptly, the Prince stumbled into Elise. He grabbed her elbow with one hand and took her hand in his other. Saleem was ensuring she wouldn't fall to the ground, but when she was upright and he'd let go of her elbow, he kept her hand in his.

'Mustafa!' Saleem admonished the fellow right as a howling dog running after a screeching cat passed them in a whirlwind.

Elise caught the flash of a pistol holstered onto the man—Mustafa's—belt as he and Saleem exchanged words. Even though she could not understand them, she tried. Better to channel her concentration on that than the sensation of Saleem's palm enveloping hers.

The contrast of smooth skin with a firmness of grip weakened her. She felt sure she'd flail if he let go, which was precisely why she had to break the connection.

It must be her frustration with Olive, the disruption to Elise's careful plan. Her lack of a proper meal.

Saleem barely noticed when Elise eased her hand free.

'Mustafa is my guard,' he explained with a smirk, 'who likes to prove he's quick on his feet for a middle-aged man.'

'We have remained too much in the open.' Mustafa spoke in a heavily accented English for her benefit. He held open the carriage door, cocked his head to the Prince as if he were a teacher punishing an errant student and fired off what sounded like a proper chiding. Saleem chuckled, the affection between the two men clear.

'He tells me I have dressed too conspicuously to meet Lady Olive and will attract the wrong kind of attention.'

Elise decided she liked Mustafa and gave him an agreeing nod. 'Well, I am sure Olive would have appreciated it.'

'Would she?' It was nearly a scoff said under Saleem's breath. One that proved gratifying for Elise because it validated her anger towards Olive.

When she was in the cab seat, Elise leaned back and closed her eyes, spent. The cushioning was a lush turquoise velvet, cooling. The carriage certainly boasted eminence, but it did so in a surprisingly soothing way.

Saleem took the seat opposite and she could sense him watching her, the questions he had on the tip of his tongue. He remained silent, however, letting her rest.

She cocked open an eye and explained, 'I do not function well on an empty stomach. The ship provided sustenance, but since Olive disembarked, I tried to get them to go back and…forgot to eat.'

The left side of Saleem's mouth quirked. 'Did you know that an entire falafel sandwich has at least five fritters in it, made with hearty ground beans, stuffed with pickled turnips and a ground sesame tahini. It is quite filling.'

Saleem's curly hair bounced with his laughter, so heartily at his own quip, she could not help but do the same.

'And to think I wanted to get two extra sandwiches for Lady Olive and her travelling companion, but Adnan was sure the two of you wouldn't like it, that English ladies had more refined palates,' he said.

'Your brother was wrong about that. Though she doesn't need food as much as me, both Olive and I have what would be better termed as "experimental" palates. We love to try new things.' Elise smiled sadly.

A memory of her and Olive at age fifteen came to mind.

She'd bought prickly pears that had been imported from Greece as a kind of joke and in honour of Elise when she heard their name. Not knowing better and before Elise could warn her not to, Olive picked one up with her bare hands. Elise had spent hours tweezing out the minuscule slivers from her friend's fingertips, but in the end, Olive declared it her favourite fruit.

'Not too sweet and under the skin, the fruit is perfectly balanced in texture.'

'I blame myself for not convincing the ship captain to go back for her.'

'He had to keep a schedule. Others to consider. Don't blame yourself. And as you say, if Lady Olive had a disagreement with her father, then,' Saleem said with a sad smile, 'that could be a cause for any irrational decision.'

They fell into a comfortable silence thereafter as the horses plodded through the city to what was called 'the Lodge'. In his letters, Saleem had described the recently constructed home, how it was an enclave meant for the family away from the stately palace on the other side of Alexandria, the Raseltin Palace that would have welcomed Olive if she'd been accompanied in a more official capacity with Lord Whitmore.

Elise could not tell him how charmed she'd been by Saleem's claim that if the Mediterranean was a poem, then the Lodge's private beach was 'its best canto'. Nor could she say how excited she was to explore its gardens at dawn and dusk, since he'd written that the nuanced shades of orange and pink in the sky were impossible to count.

When they'd ridden past the palace gates and descended from the carriage into the courtyard, Elise saw the Lodge as Saleem had described in his letters. The main house was three-storeys tall, with red tile detailing in parts, arched windows and long balconies. At either corner of the building were two tower-like structures, one taller than the other, and both ending in what looked like a cross between domed minarets and square-shaped gazebos.

The architecture was brimming with details Elise couldn't quite categorise.

Saleem supplied, 'The Lodge is a distinct palace by virtue of how it combines key features from a number of different styles. While the Byzantine dominates, you can see the towering needles are Gothic, and with the straight columns and pillars you have a more Classic look. But then, the geometric patterns and arches are from the Islamic era. Inside, you'll find the building further makes use of Baroque elements. And, certainly, modern-day amenities were and continue to be added. There are even a few rooms upstairs that are insulated with cork—lest a baby be sleeping and does not want to be disturbed.'

Elise hadn't even stepped inside yet but she appreciated the attention to detail. The way Saleem had thought of the future. He'd not said outright in his letters that he wanted children, but she'd assumed as much. And she'd not asked either since talk of family was a painful reminder of what she'd lost.

Before she'd been devastated by her 'paramour', Elise had wanted a brood of her own. After learning Gerald had come to her via her uncle and only for her inheritance, Elise doubted she'd ever trust a man enough to fall in love ever again, let alone start a family with one.

'You would think the different styles and traditions would clash with each other, but it works seamlessly, magnificently. It is a marvel, Saleem, deserving of accolades. Truly.'

'Alas, I cannot take the credit,' he said even as he looked

pleased at her comment. 'My grandfather saw the potential, the way the topography features outcroppings, grottos, even a small island.' He pointed to a pair of cannons to their left. 'Because the area is elevated and sits on a hilltop, decades ago it was used as a lookout point for dangers that might reach the city's shores from the sea.'

They walked up the staircase to gaze out on the lush gardens, but before he could say more, servants emerged from the main house to welcome them.

Saleem spoke to one in a rapid Arabic and Elise found herself being pulled inside by an eager young woman, who was much too fast, for the palace decor blurred. All Elise knew was that she was being led somewhere.

She ended up in a fairly intimate dining room. It was a table with a setting for six, the walls adorned with airy landscapes and the space endowed with a window so large, it felt as if anyone eating here would be doing so al fresco.

The young woman indicated Elise should sit in the chair she held out to her. When she had, all manner of breakfast foods followed. Plates of cheese and olives, fried eggs served with juicy tomatoes, clotted cream with honey.

It was meant for Elise, surely, but she wondered if she should wait for anyone else. Though she was used to eating alone, she rather disliked it.

Perhaps Saleem will join me, she thought, before her stomach countered with a clenching rumble.

While she was deciding if it was from hunger or something *else* concerning the Prince, the servant returned with what was clearly the main course: a type of meat.

Seeing that Elise hadn't begun, the young woman tsked. She took it upon herself to fork a portion of the meat on to a torn piece of the bread and brought it to Elise's mouth.

Only after she'd accepted it did she realise what kind
of meat it was.

Liver. Elise loathed it back home and would have
clamped her lips tight if she'd known, but the preparation was lemony and garlicky and was spiced with toasted
cumin seeds.

'Utterly delicious,' she remarked and the maid nodded
as if understanding the English.

When she left thereafter, the floodgates were opened.
Elise supposed it was a good thing no one was present
to witness her indulging as a bear might. Two and a half
loaves of bread and three wiped-clean platters later—
including the entirety of the liver—she reached for the
pitcher of water just as Saleem rapped on the wall beneath
the arched entryway and made his entrance.

He'd changed his formal suit for a pair of casual trousers and a short-sleeved chemise in a shade of taupe that
was extremely suited to his skin tone.

She tried not to stare at the muscles on his upper arms
and the way they bulged as he lowered himself into the
empty seat next to her.

Elise gulped her water down quickly, only barely avoiding a coughing fit.

He is a prince, she reminded herself, *who might one
day marry Olive.*

It was easier when she had considered Saleem as a
friend through correspondence, but seeing him now as
the generous Egyptian man she'd met and found immediately handsome made it harder to remember.

*He is a prince who might one day marry your best
friend,* she repeated as he pushed the empty plates to one
side.

He wiped the last of the clotted cream with his little

finger, putting it to the slight gap between his upper front teeth and sucking.

The satisfying sound he made and the way he looked at her now had Elise imagining what else he might enjoy… *sampling*.

Saleem had not noticed the effect he was having, but he'd soon guess if she did not manage to wrench her eyes from the lonely curls of chest hair, taunting her from the top of his shirt. She clasped her legs together in an effort to prevent her body's involuntary and inconvenient responses to him.

'Satisfied?' he asked.

It took Elise a beat to realise he was talking about the meal.

'Quite, yes. Thank you. Your staff, the kitchen…they are most talented. The liver, incredible. All of it was delicious.' She took a deep breath. He couldn't know what she had been feeling, she needn't be nervous.

What she needed was a clear head. And now she'd eaten, she should have one. She could plan.

Saleem said, 'I wanted to ask about Lady Olive's state. You mentioned she fought with her father. We were surprised that she did not wait for him to accompany her. Do you think that is the only reason she did not want to meet me?'

The line that formed in his brow was strange, as if it knew it didn't belong there. He'd told Elise not to worry about Olive, but that didn't mean he'd taken his own advice.

Perhaps he is smarting from being spurned.

Prince Saleem believed, as Olive did, that Lord Whitmore wanted them to marry. That this trip was meant to end in an engagement, if not an actual wedding ceremony. In his introduction letter, he'd said that his father talked often of his friendship with hers, how beneficial it had been on a personal level and for Egypt. As heir, Saleem wrote, he wanted to honour that as best he could.

'I don't know what is going on in Olive's mind. Truth told, my mind was occupied with my own father's death.'

Elise had spoken abruptly, but when she saw the frown in Saleem's brow deepening as though it was getting comfortable, she felt sorry she had.

'My condolences for your loss.'

She didn't want to cry, not in front of Saleem—even if she didn't think of him as a stranger, he still believed she was one. 'Thank you. I mention it only because I'd gone to live with the Whitmores afterwards and believe that Olive distanced herself from her father because she didn't want me to feel bad for not having mine.'

'Considerate, yes. She sounded like a sensitive soul. In her letters, I mean.'

Elise wanted to shout that he didn't know Olive. That she was the sensitive one from the letters. And it wasn't exactly 'considerate' of Olive to abandon ship with only a scribbled note, was it?

Elise clawed back her annoyance. 'If I'd been honest with Olive about why I wanted to come to Egypt, Alexandria in particular, she'd not have disembarked before we'd arrived. Olive would have wanted to help me with it.'

Saleem leaned forward, folding his arms on the table, close enough she had to move her own so they wouldn't touch. 'I can help in her stead. What is this personal matter? If you're able to share it, I am listening.'

He was, with his whole body and being.

And maybe she was missing Olive's presence more than she was aware. Missing a friend, because in that moment, he was the man in his letters, the one who'd unwittingly helped in her grieving. Saleem was the friend Elise believed she could confide in, longed to do as herself. Openly and honestly.

Just as she'd taken in the meal, Elise released her story in a torrent. About her father's death. How she'd been in Manchester, declining to accompany him to London for a week-long excursion and being devastated when her papa did not return. How his death was ruled to be a result of a blow to the head.

'Whether it was an accidental fall or whether he was pushed on to the pavement in a scuffle, coroners could not say. Or rather, they did not care to investigate further. My father's business did not start in the most savoury of manners. He had never been arrested for anything illegal, but he had no allies in Scotland Yard. Papa had been selling his business shares, was ready to retire. He wanted to secure my inheritance, but I am an only daughter and with the laws the way they are, well, it was…difficult.'

'Why, if you are his only child? You *are* unmarried, I assume.'

Elise shivered to think of her 'lover' then, how he had nearly been a son to her father.

'A titled, noble suitor of mine named Gerald turned out to be the worst sort of cad. He'd come to know of me via my father's estranged brother, Andrew. Papa…well, he was a changed man thereafter. It is why he decided to sell his businesses, ensure his wealth would always be mine.'

Elise took a deep breath before continuing, 'The night before Papa left for London, Uncle Andrew paid us a surprise visit in the dead of night. I overheard them arguing. It was ugly, to say the least. My uncle demanded "the gold bars", threatened that if he didn't get them, Papa and I would pay with our lives.'

She lowered her head. It dawned on Elise she'd not talked about that night with anyone. Even Lord Whitmore had not asked for details when he invited her to stay with them or when that awful article about her came out in the papers.

And Olive, who Elise used to talk to about anything and everything, would change the subject if anything to do with fathers was brought up.

'It must have been devastating. Is your mother well?' he asked.

As far as he knew, only Olive was motherless.

'She died when I was a girl.'

Elise lifted her eyes to his and caught the look of sadness there. *For her.*

If she were not careful, she might get attached to Saleem in the flesh as opposed to the friend in correspondence she'd known the last few months.

Elise wouldn't fault herself for experiencing physical desire for a man—such yearnings were sometimes against one's will. But to give her heart to a man thinking they could *belong* to one another, have a life together?

Elise had made that mistake with Gerald. She'd never make it again.

She would not dare to fall for a prince.

'Do not pity me,' she warned.

'That wasn't my intent.' Saleem scraped a finger at his temple. 'Adnan said something earlier, made me see how I take my own mother for granted, try to escape her at any chance. I should be more appreciative of her.'

'She dotes on you.' It was something he'd said in his letters and, though it gladdened Elise to match his words to the man sitting in front of her, the confusion in his face was further reminder that he did not know he'd been corresponding with her rather than Olive.

A moment later, he shook his head. 'Never mind me,' he said. 'Let us return to your matter. Is it possible your uncle had something to do with your father's death? That he wants the gold bars because they should have been a part of the wealth that came to him?'

'I'm unsure. My father never mentioned anything regarding gold bars to me or his lawyer who filed an inventory of his assets. Upon his death I received a sum of money and, though smaller than anticipated, it should keep me comfortable, but it did occur to everyone that Papa might have taken more drastic measures to protect the rest of his wealth. Knowing his estate would be scrutinised because of his *past* with Scotland Yard.'

'Nobody found anything to prove it?'

'No. But, after he was buried and the case into his death closed, I was finally allowed back into our London town house. I found a gold bar beneath Papa's secret floorboard. It was wrapped as if he'd meant to ship it, but did not get the chance. No name or address. Only a city and country.'

'Which were?'

'Here.' Elise shrugged, trying to make light of it. 'Well, not here as in the Lodge, but here as in Alexandria, Egypt.'

'Odd.' Saleem leaned back in his chair, deep in thought. 'Did your father have connections in the city, people he knew? Business associates, perhaps?'

'None I am aware of.' Elise sighed. 'I would have hired a private detective in England to look into it, but then Lord Whitmore received the invitation from your father, the khedive, and Olive…well she insisted on coming without delay. Having me accompany her was a solution that suited me, too.'

Saleem smirked. 'You came here to investigate.'

'What is humorous about that?'

'I'd assumed Lady Olive's companion would be an elderly spinster, a shrewd sleuth. In one way, I was right.'

She pouted, jesting as if offended, 'I am not that *old*!'

'You most certainly are not old.'

Elise was *really* starting to enjoy the music that was Saleem's laughter. The way he navigated the serious and the light was admirable and she hated to put an end to it, but asked anyway, 'What if my uncle learned I have one of the gold bars he mentioned? Or thinks I have knowledge of where others might be if there are more? If he found out I travelled with Olive, if he gets her alone in a city she's unfamiliar with…what if he hurts her?'

'Why would he hurt Lady Olive?'

Elise scrubbed her face before answering. 'To hurt me? To demand I give him what he wants?'

'You think him capable of that?'

She didn't want to burden Saleem with irrational fears. The truth was that she didn't know what her uncle was capable of, besides his plot with Gerald that didn't exactly go to plan.

'I don't know, honestly. He should be busy with his own life in England. A noble family he married into, a small estate. Influence. I doubt he'd be gallivanting after me, but when I found Olive's note, I worried…well, I just want to be cautious. Make sure she isn't hurt.'

'My brother will find Lady Olive, not let any harm come to her. She, too, must be worried about you.' He seemed sure, but Elise had her doubts. 'Until she returns, I will take it upon myself to see you are safe here. No more fretting or imagining the worst scenarios, all right?' Saleem nodded, then waited for her to do the same. 'Do you have the gold bar?'

'It's in my carpetbag, the brown with the leather handles.'

Saleem called a servant to retrieve it. While they waited, the young woman who'd brought Elise's attention to the liver entered the dining room and spoke to the Prince in Arabic.

He turned to Elise to translate. 'She is named Khayria and has been tasked by our housekeeper to take care of your needs while you're at the Lodge, but she is afraid you might find the language barrier insulting. She therefore asks if you'd like us to hire a girl from the English school nearby instead?'

'It is nice to meet you, Khayria,' Elise addressed the maid first and shook her hand as if they'd just met. Then, she turned back to Saleem. 'She would risk her own job to suggest it? What a brave young woman. Tell her there is no need, I appreciate her very creative methods of communicating and was not at all insulted earlier.' The two women shared a knowing wink when Saleem translated that part.

When Khayria left, Elise dared to add, 'May I also not depend on your language skills?'

Saleem answered with an enthusiastic, 'Absolutely.'

'You'll be relieved of your duties when Olive returns. She brought books and spent her time on the ship learning Arabic.'

She hadn't wanted to admit it then, but the truth was that Olive's dedication to the language, how it kept her confined to her cabin, bothered Elise. Saleem knew how to speak English, but that her friend should want to learn it for him meant Olive was looking forward to the role she might soon play in Egypt: Princess bride of the heir apparent.

*But that cannot have been right, given Olive's decision
to not meet Saleem at all.*

'Not only relieved, but pleased as well.' He smiled,
but then qualified his comment, 'Learning any additional
means of communication or what might facilitate it between people is admirable. Not that it should surprise me,
Lady Olive is a wonderful letter writer.'

The servant brought in her bag and Elise was grateful to
have something in which to conceal her face until any guilt
that may appear there passed. She pulled out the gold bar,
tucked into a lacy handkerchief, and handed it to Saleem.

His eyes lingered on the lace for a beat before trying
to get a sense of the bar's heft. 'It is average size and cannot be worth that much. Why should your uncle threaten
lives over it?'

'I thought I overheard him say *"bars"*, but perhaps I was
wrong.'

'Perhaps this one is one of many more,' Saleem mused.
'If we discover who your father meant to send it to, that
person can tell us.'

We. Us. A sensation of relief filled her, catching Elise
unawares. She was glad she'd confided in Saleem. 'How
to find them—without a name or address?'

'Will you leave it with me for a day or two? I'll have
Mustafa make enquiries with the police.'

'Thank you, Saleem. For listening and trying to help it.'

'No need for thanks.' He leaned closer, his eyes lock-
ing on hers. 'You have been through much and I am glad
to be of service.' If she thought there was warmth in his
eyes, just then they seemed to catch a fire, hotly raking
over hers for a long moment before he cleared his throat.
'It is the least I can do for Lady Olive's travelling compan-

ion and good friend. I know this is what she would want, besides which, you are *our* guest.'

The 'our' sounded different to her. Before, he'd been talking about him and Elise; now, it seemed as though he was referring to himself and Olive. As if they were already a couple, as if this home was already hers.

She fought through an internal flare of disappointment.

'You must need a rest,' he said, rising to stand by the dining room door. 'I'll have someone show you to your room.'

It was Khayria who answered his call. She spoke in a flurry, then looked to Saleem to translate. 'They should like to draw you a bath, but are wondering what scent you prefer. Jasmine or rose, for example?'

Before she could think better of it, Elise blurted out, 'Hibiscus.'

Chapter Five

Saleem

Planning and expectation were strangers, eluding Saleem even as he tried to know them better. He'd *planned* to woo one woman, but Olive had run off. He'd *expected* she'd come with a prim travelling companion, but Elise was a beautiful young woman. A confounding one whose lashes were most...alluring.

His exhale was long and drawn out.

Saleem had to maintain the 'new man, responsible khedive-in-training' he'd vowed to be. Keep his focus on and hopes for a meaningful relationship with Lady Olive alive, despite her not wanting to meet him. Saleem trusted that when she did, she'd remember the friendship they'd fostered in their letters. That Olive would believe, as he did, that it could lead to so much more.

In the meantime, Saleem was pleased that Elise trusted him with her dilemma.

He twisted the gold bar, holding it close to his eyes and then at a distance. He examined each of its corners, pressing a hard thumb to every millimetre of surface. All to find any clue.

Then, the perfume of roses filled the air, distracting Saleem from the task. It was rose mixed with a headier scent. Elise had asked for hibiscus, but the flower was more decorative, scentless. Hibiscus was dried, used to make the *carcaday* drink. Khayria must have added some of that to the more pungent and commonly used rose petals.

Do not picture Elise getting into the bath.

But as soon as Saleem thought it, the picture flooded his mind. Her slipping out of that dull dress and whatever was worn beneath to enhance her figure as Englishwomen were wont to wear—though her body looked quite perfect and needed no enhancement. He saw her dark skin lapping the water, letting it wash away the weariness of travel.

Saleem knew where the bath was set in her room, that her colouring would glisten like gold in the sunlight that streamed into it at this time of day. Elise would push back her onyx hair, straight and slick as tar, and then when the work of being clean was finished, she might relax a minute. Close her eyes. Would her upper and lower lashes be entangled when she did?

There was an engineering marvel he'd relish examining.

Saleem might have blamed the house for his wayward thoughts because it wasn't the palace in Cairo where the ladies' *hamam* was secluded in a separate harem wing. However, he could not think badly of the Lodge.

When he'd arrived in Alexandria to oversee the city's tramway expansion project, because his father was not interested in it and Saleem thought it a good way to prove his worth, he'd not expected to love it so much himself. He quickly realised that his visit would be longer than expected and decided to stay at the Lodge because of its proximity to the tram's central station rather than the sprawling Raseltin Palace on the other side of the city where his family usually stayed and hosted dignitaries. He'd draw attention any time he left there and was sure to not get any work done.

Having resided in the Lodge since then, Saleem was glad of that decision. He intended to make this home his mainstay the year round. He'd hired his own staff, ones who did not need to confer with his father on decisions. Here, at the Lodge, Saleem was his own man. King of the Castle.

He'd hoped Olive would like it, too, having described the Lodge and its grounds at length. She'd written she was looking most forward to exploring the gardens and beach.

Clearly not enough.

'My Prince.'

Mustafa stood at the door, shaking him from his thoughts. 'The gates have been secured for this evening's guests.'

'Guests?' Saleem threw back his head. He had entirely forgotten about the dinner he'd planned for Lady Olive's arrival and Adnan's visit from Cairo. Without the guests of honour, it was unnecessary. 'Is it too late to cancel?'

Mustafa took the seat Elise had vacated, his grin large when he announced, 'Yes, my Prince, it is much too late. Even if we were to send out notes asking them not to come at this very moment, the guests may already be on their way. Would you have us refuse them at the gates?'

Mustafa had not liked the prospect of the party when Saleem first suggested it. His guard was the one who had had to spend the hours painstakingly going through the guest list with the police office. He'd kept beseeching Saleem to keep it small.

'You were right, I admit. There is no purpose to it now and I fear I may not be a gracious host.'

'As I recall, this gathering was meant for you, too. You convinced me of it by saying it would establish your network in the city, work towards your very noble goals for Alexandria.' Mustafa's voice softened when he added, 'And, you are always a gracious host.'

The guard had been by Saleem's side for nearly five years, devoted as any security detail could be. Saleem considered Mustafa like an uncle.

'The guests will be expecting to meet Lady Olive.'

Mustafa nodded. 'If you're concerned about having to explain her absence in any formal capacity, recall we did not provide too many details on the invitation. We stressed that you wished to know your neighbours better in an intimate gathering.'

'Good foresight on your part. I will hobnob to the best of my ability and control the damage that might occur if the gossips among them question her absence.'

Mustafa studied Saleem. 'I heard what transpired at the harbour. Are you upset about Lady Olive's note?'

'More surprised than upset. I thought a party in this romantic, lovely setting would be the first chance to woo her, to make a positive, private impression—before we headed to Cairo and our fathers' endeavours to arrange our marriage were begun in earnest. I was confident the lady would, at least, be open to me courting her.'

'Any lady should be open to that. You are a prince in soul and status. Even when women do not know who you are, I am at your back seeing *how* they look at you. The chiselled chin attracts them most.' When Saleem grimaced, Mustafa held up a hand. 'Don't let my compliments feed your ego.'

'Since they only come when you feel sorry for me, trust me, I do not.'

'Feel sorry for a prince?' Mustafa joked. 'Or feel sorry for my lack of chiselled chin?' He angled said chin to the gold bar. 'You should put that in the safe.'

Saleem pointed out a corner of it—a minuscule flaw in the otherwise standard Bank of England mark on it. 'What does that look like to you?

Mustafa leaned forward to examine it closely. 'The drachma sign. Greek currency.'

Saleem caught the pensive twist that crossed his guard's face. 'What are you thinking?'

'It is probably nothing.'

'Another dog chasing cats,' Saleem quipped. 'Come now, I want to hear it.'

'There is a Maltese businessman named Portelli coming tonight. He insisted on bringing a guest, a female companion. I would have declined the request, but since he is the most powerful man in the European quarter and she is but a woman who would not likely pose a threat, I allowed it. My contact at the police station said Portelli keeps a mistress, a *Greek* woman named Stephania who has lived alone in Al-exandria for many years, even before he arrived. Some believe it is her wealth that actually finances his speculations.'

'Why does he not marry her?' Saleem was genuinely interested, but also asked, 'What do you think she has to do with a marked gold bar?'

'I don't have the answer to either question, it only came to mind because she is Greek.'

'There are many Greeks in Alexandria,' Saleem added.

'True, but my cautiousness is ever on alert. Where did you get the bar?'

Saleem told Mustafa of Elise's father's death and the

threat she'd overheard her uncle make before it. 'She found it hidden after he died, packaged as if to send it here—but there was no name or address. She's come to learn whom her father meant to send it to and why.'

'*Miskeena...*' Mustafa expressed sympathy for Elise's predicament, her loss.

Saleem handed over the gold bar. 'Put it in the safe for now, as you said. Tomorrow, see what you can find out with the police. Maybe the Anglo-Egyptian Bank, too. Ask whether it is normal for a Bank of England stamped gold bar to be marked with a Greek currency symbol. Maybe there is a clue there. If we can help Elise with it while Adnan searches for Olive, then the Princes of Egypt will have done both young ladies a service.'

'*Hath'er.*'

Mustafa made to leave, but Saleem had one last question. 'Do you think I should invite Elise to join the gathering tonight?'

Was that a smirk on his guard's face? 'If the Maltese businessman is an example, having a woman on your arm is necessary.'

'She would not be on my arm. Until an hour ago, I'd expected to be courting her friend, not talking to you.'

Before he left, Mustafa sniffled in an exaggerated manner—a gesture he did when disagreeing with Saleem. Unlike his father who'd tell him plainly when he was wrong, his guard was paid to be compliant.

Regardless of what Mustafa thought or the distraction that had come from the beautiful but sad Elise, Saleem *had* to keep his mind on Olive Whitmore. He had to trust that when they did finally meet, their letter exchanges would prove a precursor to a relationship built on mutual admiration.

*A connection to the British House of Lords with
a wealthy friend in this age of turmoil and strife?
My son, you would be saving me and the country in
a way befitting a true leader of Egypt. You needn't
love her. Your love of country would be enough to
keep you happy.*

Saleem could still see his father's face when he first suggested a marriage between him and Lady Olive. He wanted
to please the khedive, he always had, the way Adnan did.
Even though his father tried to curb his admiration for his
older brother, it was always there, written on his face like
a secret he believed only he knew.

But Saleem had learned it long ago. That look of his
father's had gnawed on his optimism like a dog with a
bone. Even when the khedive's commands for Adnan were
harsh, his dismissal of his brother's ideas biting, that look
of admiration remained. It was one of pride, one that knew
Adnan was the khedive's equal and was up to any challenge. With Saleem, the khedive's looks were around limited hopes, their implication was 'this is the best I can
expect from you'.

Saleem had determined to not only please him, but ex-
ceed his father's expectations through realising his own
ideals and strengths. His marriage was supposed to be the
first act to prove this. Him marrying Olive might benefit
his father, but it was also supposed to fulfil Saleem's desires for a loving relationship.

He'd hoped Lady Olive would want to get to know him
face to face.

She might yet, still.

In the meantime, Saleem would help her friend Elise figure out the mystery of the gold bar—and if that endeared him to Olive, then that couldn't be a bad thing either.

There were many paths to love and hadn't he always favoured the roads that were unknown, full of surprises?

Planning and expectation could be delayed for a bit more.

Saleem spent the afternoon overseeing decorations and tasting the sampling menu for the gathering that night. When the housekeeper expressed nervousness at it being her first such event, he told her it was his as well. That, at home in Cairo, it would be the realm of his mother or sisters. 'But I have every confidence we will both be a riveting success!'

Inspired by the bath smell that resulted from Elise's hibiscus, he chose chilled *carcaday* drinks with which to greet their guests, a beet salad course, a dinner of lamb okra with the ripest tomatoes 'for the fresh red colour'.

Saleem decided that for dessert they'd forgo the cake pre-ordered from a local Parisian-styled bakery with a welcome message for Lady Olive and instead have *basboosa* with a rosewater-infused syrup.

He suggested his chef should 'decorate it with crushed pistachios and serve it with bitter Turkish coffee. Don't waste the cake, either. Have one of the drivers take it to the orphanage near Raml Station immediately.'

Fresh flowers would be arranged in all the places that mattered and the curtains and cushions in the large salon would be changed to the damask set.

The housekeeper had one last question. 'And our guest? Will Miss Elise be attending the evening? I believe English ladies would require help dressing.'

Saleem remembered Khayria's earlier suggestion. He'd never thought to employ female servants who spoke

English, even though he'd planned on Lady Olive and her travelling companion, to stay for a few days here en route to Cairo. It had been an oversight.

'She doesn't know it is happening, but I do not want to disturb her if she is resting. Give me a few minutes and I shall return with a note for you to slip beneath her door.'

Sitting down at the desk where he'd written many a letter in the last few months, Saleem put ink to paper.

Elise,

I hope you enjoyed your bath and that you have had an opportunity to rest after your journey. I should like to inform you that I have tasked Mustafa to look over the matter we discussed. Hopefully, we will have more answers in the morning when he returns from his visits to the authorities.

Earlier, I failed to mention I'd arranged a get-together to welcome the arrival of Lady Olive—and you!—and in celebration of my brother's visit from Cairo. In truth, it had slipped my mind, what with all the fuss at the harbour this morning.

As it is with only a select few of Alexandria's business leaders and politicians and as it is quite late in the day, I cannot cancel.

All this to say I would be honoured if you would join us. If you are tired or otherwise not feeling up to it, then do disregard this invitation. In that case, I will send a dinner tray up later this evening. I will also send writing materials with this note. If you require any translating assistance from me, then please send word—any time of day or night.

Most sincerely,
Saleem

It was silly to write Elise such a long letter while she was in the same house, but somehow it felt natural for him to do so.

Chapter Six

Elise

Seeing Saleem's familiar hand, his words addressed to *her* directly for the first time, brought Elise an odd and rare pleasure. It felt like a victory, but one she knew she shouldn't celebrate. Adnan might have already found Olive. If she were to return and apologise for her rashness, Saleem would forgive her. It was who he was.

And if he forgave her, then he would want to begin his courtship of her in earnest.

Elise *should not* harbour any yearning sentiment for the man who might one day be her best friend's husband.

Sleep or wait for the dinner tray? she questioned herself. The bath had been incredibly enjoyable and invigorating.

She stepped past the shuttered door and on to the balcony of her room. Spreading her arms wide across the sturdy waist-level railing, Elise leaned into dusk's sea breeze. It swept through her loose hair and warm body, chilling her in a way that was further energising. She took in the scene below, the unbelievable greenery of the gardens.

Her father once told her that Alexandria was an array of blues from the sea and browns from its sands, but he clearly hadn't been to this part of the city.

The Lodge's grounds were a tropical paradise, a romantic painting come to life. Numerous trees and their various leaves, catanias and palms, shrubs and anthurium might have made it more jungle-like, and, although they weren't manicured too heavily, there was a pattern to them, one of something new and magical, but balanced between two extremes. Saleem's gardener must be very talented.

Bursts of bright flowers and fruits coloured the scene: yellow lemons and purple hyacinth. Pretty birds flew about, their song a jolly whistle in the air. And there, in the far left corner, a patch that seemed to be moving until Elise realised why. *Peacocks!* Saleem hadn't said anything in his letters about them. Perhaps they were a new addition.

With the sea behind it all, it was glorious enough to make Elise believe that all was well with the world and she could be…happy.

There was enough space on the balcony for her easel—it would be lovely to paint during the day, an awning for the rain. She could paint in the gardens, too, or on the beach. The possibilities were endless.

You'll not be in Alexandria long enough to settle, she admonished herself.

All would be settled with Olive and Elise would find whomever her father had wanted to send that gold bar to. Get her answers. Then it would be time to figure out what the rest of her life would be.

How I will manage my aloneness.

Her things had been arranged well, as if Saleem's staff were expecting her to stay a while. Her easel and paints were next to the armoire with her toiletries. And after her bath, she'd opened the closet and saw that Khayria had unpacked her gowns and hung them.

From her angle on the balcony, Elise could not see the

main gate, but the tail end of the road where coaches would turn to make it to the house was visible. It was empty now, but when the first guest arrived, she heard the distinct sounds of horseshoes clopping on cobblestone. It prompted her own bare feet to fathom the cold cement and go back inside her room.

She was overcome with a desire to thank Saleem and started writing a note, but a blot of ink on the page seemed insufficient. And, at the last minute, she realised that he would recognise her hand, realise the ruse devised by Olive.

Elise would not disguise her script—enough of a lie had been told. She could not use his notepaper, nor write to him again until he learned the truth of who he was corresponding with.

You cannot leave him without an answer. He will think you ungrateful.

If Elise had doubts about attending his function, when her eyes landed on her dark rose gown, they were alleviated.

She'd *show* Saleem her gratitude.

Uncharacteristic of her, really, but what other choice did Elise have? Also, if Saleem's guests had been invited under the pretext that the party was for Olive, Elise did not want to leave him alone to account for her absence. She could put on a brave face and represent Olive as she'd asked her to do in her departure note.

She'd have to get past her annoyance at Olive and remember that her friend *had* trusted Elise.

Indeed, it was Olive who'd encouraged her to try on the gown when they'd spotted it while shopping in preparation for the trip. She'd said the colour would suit her, but Elise bought it because it couldn't have fit better if it been tailored specifically for her by a skilled seamstress.

The gown had burgundy lace detailing throughout, the bosom sitting perfectly on Elise's chest, the waist cinched so she'd not even need a corset. The short puffy sleeves enhanced her long arms perfectly and the full but light skirt made walking in it feel as if she were treading through a cloud.

Elise brushed her hair, lifting it from her face and pinning it in a high bun atop her head.

Her eyes had always been dramatic and could not take too much enhancement, so she applied kohl with a sensible hand in order to balance their largeness with the symmetry of her face. Over her lips, she applied a crimson rouge.

The trip had taken its toll in terms of the gauntness of Elise's face and the dabbing of freckles on her nose and cheeks that were made more prominent from the sun exposure, but she was satisfied enough with the results when she slipped on her shoes and twisted in the mirror.

Were Olive here, she'd be pleased.

Her friend had tried for years to get Elise to attend balls with her, but she'd resisted. Even for Olive, there'd never been much opportunity. She used to dream of her debutante ball, but without a mother or female relative of esteem to plan for her, her Season never alighted. She'd cried to her about it once and Elise had tried to comfort her.

'We might not have mothers,' she'd said, 'but we are sisters. And one day, we will meet our Princes and dance to our hearts' desires.'

Why did you abandon me, Olive?

Elise brushed away the angry thought and made her way to the dinner party. The entire third floor where her guestroom was located was empty of Saleem's staff, but she easily found a staircase that took her two storeys down, following her ears to the bustle.

She had a moment to herself at the edge of the parlour door to observe the scene. Only a few people were mingling and all of them were around Saleem. He was telling a story that had them riveted.

Unaware of her presence, Elise was free to marvel at his. He was a bright light against the more sombre decor that matched the darker gown she wore. It was almost as though Saleem had known and arranged his outfit to match her dress.

His smile was remarkable, all sparkling teeth, and genuineness. As he spoke, he was innately conscious of those around him, laying a hand on one man's back who'd drifted off or turning to face with his entire body whoever was responding to him.

Finally sensing he was being watched, Saleem turned to her and his smile dropped for a split second, confused, his brow strained, as if he didn't recognise her.

When it returned, however, Elise fancied it was wider than it had been. His steps towards her were long strides and, in seconds, he was standing before her.

'You came.' Saleem stated the obvious, then took her hand without thinking, enfolding her arm into his and crossing his other one to keep it clutched in his.

Elise had not worn gloves.

She *should* have worn gloves.

Did he not feel the shock as she did?

'Ladies and gentlemen,' he declared as if he were a herald announcing her arrival in a most enthusiastic manner, 'may I present my guest, visiting us from England, Miss Thomas!'

The surname she'd first given him was not Elise's legal

name *Clifton*. It was her father's first name. Though she'd meant it to conceal her identity, given her mission of finding out about the gold bar, Elise supposed it was accurate due to something that Olive had mentioned before their voyage.

'Did you know that most Egyptians take the name of their fathers as surnames—even in the case of adopted children? It is part of the Muslim faith.'

Saleem introduced Elise to the guests, a mostly older crowd whom he charmingly admitted to having met for the first time as well. But they were forgiving, perhaps because of his truthfulness, and quick to supply any information he did not know. Following his example, the guests were gracious enough to speak in English for Elise's benefit, apologising when they could not and asking Saleem to translate.

At some point in the small talk, Saleem saw he hadn't let her hand go and, when he finally did, he looked at her sheepishly.

His grin could almost make Elise believe it was intentional.

'Pardon my liberties,' he whispered close to her ear. The thickness in his voice touched her as an aphrodisiac might. She was glad he wasn't holding her hand any longer because he'd have felt her digging her nails into her palms.

He is a prince, meant to woo Olive, she reproached herself, even as she whispered back, 'You are pardoned.'

There must have been something in her voice, too, because his grin disappeared and his Adam's apple bulged in his throat.

Before Elise knew what to make of that, they were interrupted by a middle-aged couple: a stout man who wore nearly as much jewellery as the taller woman on his arm.

'Sinjur Portelli,' Saleem introduced him. 'He is originally from Malta, but has made quite the name for himself in Alexandria over the past few years.'

'My friends call me Portelli,' he replied to Saleem.

'Though he does not have many friends.' This from the woman on his arm. She was pretty enough, but in a tired-looking way. If her comment was made lightly, her close scrutiny of Elise said otherwise.

The woman *inspected* her. Head to foot, in a manner as though accusing a maid of being caught playing dress-up with her mistress's clothing. Because of how she'd grown up with strangers' reactions to her mother's finery, Elise deplored any looking at her now. She tried to avoid it at all costs, but this gown was not the kind that would allow her to hide. And being on the Prince's arm, too? What had possessed her?

Saleem stiffened next to Elise. On alert. 'English ladies are not so accustomed to people staring,' he addressed the woman, his voice sharp enough that he forced her gaze away from Elise to him. 'Miss… Dimitri.'

The woman schooled her face and smiled. 'Please call me Stephania. I was only surprised at the English background and thought you might be from some other European background but your surname, it is Thomas? May I know your given name?'

Elise lifted her chin, met the woman's gaze. 'Elise Thomas is my name.'

Before Stephania could react, a servant came in to announce dinner was ready. They led everyone to a different dining room than she and Saleem had been in earlier. It was larger, made for welcoming guests more formally.

Still, it was warmly lit and set for casual service with people choosing their seats at will, save, of course, for Saleem's. It was held out for him at the head by one of the servants. Before he sat down, Saleem gestured to the servant to attend to Elise first. She was placed to Saleem's immediate right, thankfully, and kept away from Stephania.

The dinner served was utterly delicious and Elise busied herself with enjoying what she was eating while Saleem was immersed in a conversation with the man to his left, the head curator of the city's libraries.

At the first lull in their conversation, Saleem bent his head towards her. 'Is everything to your liking?'

'I did not think I could eat after that huge lunch,' Elise said, smiling, 'but I could not resist the party…be here on Olive's behalf as well.'

'You proved the most exquisite distraction from me having to explain her absence. Thank you,' Saleem breathed. 'Hibiscus befits.'

Something about the way he spoke the last two words, the throaty repetitive 's' sound in tandem, caught in Elise's chest. She dared not meet Saleem's eyes lest he see evidence of the storm brewing inside her. Instead, she focused on the back of his hand nearly scraping the edge of hers. The strength there.

He tugged his hand away and continued as if he'd not said anything at all blush-inducing, 'We shall throw another party when Lady Olive arrives in Cairo. My mother and sisters are likely planning a series of them at this very moment. It is their favourite pastime.'

Elise gulped down her drink, a frothy chilled and sweet wine. Or perhaps not wine at all, it tasted more like a strong cold tea. The glass confused her. She felt flustered. Had Saleem meant to imply anything with the hibiscus comment? Had he guessed the truth of her involvement with

Olive's letters and was ascertaining whether or not she'd continue the lie?

Elise was normally more level-headed, especially on a full stomach.

She gathered her wits. 'Tell me about your mother and sisters. Your family?' And then the last question that she wasn't sure she wanted the answer to, 'Were they hoping to plan yours and Olive's wedding as well?'

'Yes. They're aware that a marriage between us would benefit the country. On a trip to England my mother met Lady Whitmore before she passed away. She found her to be most hospitable and declared that such a fine lady would birth a fine daughter. My father has long held that the best an heir can do is marry strategically—or perhaps that's the best he thinks *I* can do.'

Saleem frowned and Elise was starting to see now how it was such a rare thing for him to do. Perhaps it was because he felt sad that Olive had delayed his family's joy. His father's pleasure.

She'd have asked more about him and his father's relationship, but Saleem had already brightened,

'Besides which, they like to plan *any* party! My eldest sister is married with a host of little ones. They're all excitable by nature, but one in particular, Maysoon…we call her May…is definitely counting on one so long as it happens *after* her birthday. She already has dresses chosen for each event—her birthday party, of course, has the prettiest of the two. Oh, and she tells everyone she meets, "My *khaloo* will marry the second-most beautiful woman in the world."'

'Second?'

He tsked in mock reprimand. 'She would forgive you that question since you have yet to meet her and see that she is, in fact, *the* first most beautiful.'

Elise's burst of laughter surprised even herself. 'I admire her confidence.'

'She would claim it is not confidence, but candour. Facts.' He smiled. 'May is our greatest joy, Allah protect her. She is the only one who can make my surly father, who practically breathes the country's well-being, forget he is the khedive and only her grandfather.'

'I should have liked to see May's effect on my father.' Saleem sobered. 'Was he a surly man, too?'

'He was a good father, but complained about every little thing. It took me a while to understand it was so he wouldn't burden me about the bigger ones, the dissatisfaction he felt with his life. I don't remember how he was when my mother was alive, she was my entire world, and after she died, we were both mourning in our own ways rather than healing together.'

Elise looked down at her plate. Why were her words less measured around Saleem? What was it about him that loosened her tongue so?

'It must have been hard for you, living with a parent who was always sad.'

'I appreciate happiness, but it was not my father's sadness that bothered me. People will feel what they feel and, even as a girl, I knew that his sentiments were not a reflection on me. What bothered me most was how he always hid *why* he was sad. I could have helped him if he had trusted me rather than trying to shield me from his woes, cover it with his surliness.'

Saleem said no more as the main course dishes were removed from the table by the staff, but she got the sense he was mulling over what she'd said, as if it had resonated with him. Elise wondered if he'd wanted to speak more about the relationship he had with his own father.

Maybe, like Olive, he, too, was conscious of her lack of one. Was Elise's aloneness coming to the surface, giving others the impression that she was to be treated with sensitivity?

The table was soon loaded with dessert plates. Elise declined the coffee offered her, despite its decadent rich smell. 'I will not sleep were I to drink it this late.'

Saleem lifted a teasing brow, 'Only older travelling companions fear sleepless nights.'

She quipped, 'They must rest their eyes, better to watch their wards during the days.'

Their banter was easy, natural, but then Saleem raised the coffee to his lips and it took all of Elise's strength *not* to gape at how their fullness overwhelmed the thin-lined golden rim of the demitasse. Tried to ignore the tightening in her chest as she imagined those lips on hers.

Saleem mused, 'There is such a thing as a late-morning start.'

'Do you have them often?' Elise hadn't *entirely* meant to imply anything untoward, but Saleem took it that way.

He answered mischievously, 'Late nights lead to late mornings. The best fun to be had is in the evenings, when the sun isn't there to bear witness. Or chaperons with eyes at the back of their heads.'

Beneath the table cloth, Elise clasped her fingers together. Saleem had the kind of mannerisms that were dangerously disarming. Couple them with his handsomeness and even the most restrained and contained women would lose sight of who they were in his presence.

She was no exception. 'Ah, but, Prince Saleem, you are the sort to bask in the sunlight.'

Were they flirting with one another?

'You've looked into my soul, Miss Elise, and got the

mark of me.' Saleem's chuckle came effortlessly. 'Lucky for me, this is Egypt and we get much of it. Even with the latest of mornings, we do not miss out on the sun.'

Then, before she knew what he was doing, he'd taken his fork and lifted a piece of the dessert on it, then held it out to her. 'If you will not drink coffee with me, you must try the *basboosa* at least, infused with rose syrup. My idea. Cook wasn't too sure, so your honest opinion is required.'

She could not say she actually tasted it, but Elise savoured the sensation of it. The fork, having been in Saleem's mouth, on his lips, and now being in hers and on hers felt...dangerous.

Passion, not restraining her natural desires, was what had led to Elise's mistakes with Gerald. Though the two were different, the latter a cruel cad and Saleem a generous man—both were nobles. The Prince was more elevated in society and, therefore, had the power to hurt her. A power she did not have upon him.

And even if she were not put off by that reality of life, Saleem was still likely planning to court her best friend when Olive returned.

Elise *had* to keep her reactions to Saleem in check. Distract herself from feeling them.

She swallowed the bite of *basboosa* and tried to think about a neutral enough opinion when Stephania shouted from her end of the table, 'Do you play any musical instruments, Miss Thomas? Ladies learn to play in England, do they not?'

In fact, it was Elise's Greek mother who had taught her all she knew of them, but rather than say anything contrary, she sighed and stood.

Music was as good a distraction as any.

Chapter Seven

Saleem

Elise had played the pianoforte beautifully.

It was the last thought Saleem had before he finally slept after the party and the first he had when he awoke.

He stretched in his bed, savouring the memory of Elise at its bench.

At first, he'd been afraid the piano was out of tune and that fact would be fodder for Stephania, who acted as if her greatest wish was to catch Elise in a lie. But if it was out of tune, he did not notice. He'd been mesmerised by her fingers, long and graceful upon the keys as if they were working to lull the room into a spell.

It was a song Saleem didn't know and might not hear again, but last night, the musical notes of it passed through his entire being, at once lulling and invigorating.

Her playing had him forgetting there were others in the room besides the two of them—and the absence of *who* should have been there. His guests must have experienced the same. In fact, as soon as she'd entered the room, they'd forgotten that the party was meant for Olive Whitmore in the first place.

And Elise's look of genuine surprise when everyone clapped, Stephania's loudest of all, filled Saleem with joy.

Strangely, it was the same feeling he would get when his father was impressed by something he did. Which was to say it was very much a rare feeling.

'Breakfast, Prince Saleem.'

The rap on his bedroom door reminded him it was late. His hours had been disordered since coming to Alexandria, but the staff intuitively knew exactly when to deliver his tray, no matter the night before. In Cairo, the servants cared only for the khedive's rigid schedule.

Saleem jumped up quickly and let the tray bearer inside. 'Did someone see to our guest?'

'Miss Elise ate an hour ago. She then walked to the peacock patch, my Prince.'

'Very good. I shall join her there shortly.'

'Shortly' might have been better termed 'momentarily'. Saleem rushed through his morning routine, downing the milky tea as he ran a comb through his hair.

When he slipped outside, he was glad to see it was a bright day, warmer despite the winter month, and not a cloud on the horizon. Saleem had spent time in different countries, witnessing snow on mountain tops, ice crystallising upon tree branches, serene lakes reflecting pink and white cherry blossoms. Although such scenes made him feel less a prince under the weight of a father's expectations and more a mere creation of Allah, it was here in Alexandria, by this side of the sea, that Saleem's heart felt at ease.

Here, the rains were quick to end, the nips of cold temporary, the sea constantly working to regulate the air, keeping it temperate and moist throughout the year. Cairo was pleasant enough in the winter, but in the summer, the heat could be unbearable during the daytime. Now he had spent the winter in Alexandria, Saleem never wanted to spend another away from it.

He would normally walk slowly on days like this, appreciating the smell of the dewy grass, the sound of the mellow swaying of the waves, the vision of butterflies dancing between flowers. Today, Saleem found himself sprinting. The peacocks were kept at the furthest corner of the Lodge's grounds because the gamekeeper insisted the noisy birds would be disruptive. Saleem had agreed with the decision, but regretted it now.

Why was he so eager to see Elise again?

He'd hoped to be like this in Olive's presence. Saleem couldn't feel attracted to her best friend in her absence. That would make for a mess.

He needed something besides the question of the gold bar to occupy their time alone. Saleem determined to use it to ask about Olive. Her likes, dislikes. Favourite colour. Most hated food. He thought he'd known Lady Olive from her letters, but he'd clearly interpreted them wrong, so getting the answers from the woman who knew her best would be...a way to stop thinking about Elise.

Saleem compiled a list of questions, but forgot them instantly when he saw her.

Elise had set up a canvas and easel to one side along with a bowl of seeds in the centre of the space. As the pair of peacocks called and wailed around it, she set brush to canvas, her fingers working as deftly as they had the pianoforte last night. Saleem had to cover his ears with the peacocks' racket, but the noise did not hinder her focus. She wore a large white apron cinched tight at the waist and heavily used, it would seem, with all the paint stains. Her thick hair was caught in a ponytail behind a yellow kerchief to keep it from her face.

Elise, herself, made for a beautiful painting. One he would have enjoyed basking in for much longer than he did before she noticed his presence.

'Good morning.'

Saleem read her lips, rather than heard her say it, lowering his hands from his ears too late.

The peacocks quieted when he crossed the space to stand before her. Saleem noted the lavender frock that peeked from beneath the neckline of her apron.

Was it a simple dress like the one she'd travelled in or lavish like the one last night?

'You're a painter,' he said. 'A woman of multiple talents.'

'If you mean along with my eating,' she answered with a teasing quirk of her brow, 'then I agree.'

'I meant the music last night, actually.' He pointed to her canvas. 'May I look?'

Elise stepped aside, her cheeks reddening in a manner he should *not* be finding so alluring.

Saleem concentrated on her work, the lines of the peacock, the arrogant look that stared back at him from the stretch of canvas. Elise had chosen dark colours, a cacophony that made for a harsh background. She'd concentrated on the broken limbs of the trees, their drooping leaves, the cracked earth beneath the bowl of feed. It was as if the peacock was reprimanding the observer, asserting his domain, no matter how others might disparage it.

'You don't like it,' Elise said after he'd been quiet for a few minutes.

He turned to her, hoping she might see the awe in his face. 'It's masterful, the lines, the blended shades, the details in the feathers, the magenta and turquoise. You've captured the peacock in a moment where he seems ready to jump from the flat surface and proudly shake out his plumage. And there, the claws digging into the earth, incredible! And in so little time.'

'You don't like it,' she repeated.

He didn't *not* like it, but tried to answer truthfully, 'It *unsettles* me.'

Elise hadn't fathomed the compliments he'd paid her. Chin lifted, she asked, 'Did you expect whimsical? A tame bird?'

'Peacocks are noted for their arrogance, they know they are beautiful and they like to flaunt it. So, no, not really that.' Saleem was eager to explain himself properly. 'Is that anger in his face? Why? The day is bright and ahead of us, encouraging us to chase it. The peacock is a bird noted for its splendour, the patterned symmetry of its train, the points that look like eyes there and there—' he pointed to the spots without touching the wet paint '—they are a miracle for us to contemplate.'

The expression he read on Elise's face told him that she was listening to his opinion, even if she was also offended by it.

She appreciates truth, he thought, and it encouraged him to go on.

'To me, your peacock looks angry, he knows he will be perceived, but he believes it inevitable that people will misunderstand him. It is a dichotomy because he both wants to be praised, but hates that people have to see him in order to do so.'

Elise nodded. She could see what Saleem was saying.

'Tell me that look is not him daring the voyeur to his magnificence to even *think* about looking at him?' He used two fingers to indicate the peacock's eyes, which he then turned to his own. 'Tell me he is not about to gouge mine out.'

'I think you're safe.' Elise grinned, putting a hand on

his arm in what seemed to be a conciliatory gesture...but then her face looked as though she needed reassurance. She reddened, pointing to a smudge of paint on his forearm. 'I did that.'

Dipping her finger into a cup of water next to her palette, she worked to wipe it free, but it proved harder than she expected.

Touching me is making her nervous. The thought pleased Saleem more than it should.

'My paintings frequently turn out darker than I intend them to, my experiences infusing them in a way that is guttural. For me painting is so misaligned with the control I seek in real life. The fact that Olive disembarked ship, for instance, when she should have been here. Maybe also a thing to keep my mind off my worries...well, the point is that if I don't plan the pieces enough before starting, my brush has a way of taking charge, in my absence.'

'Your brush has a mind of its own,' he said, trying not to pull his arm away as she worked on the smudge. This close, Saleem could smell Elise, an intoxicating blend of turpentine from her paint and the rose-hibiscus blend from her bath.

'Precisely! The brush's spirit consumes me, demands to be set free.' Her laugh was a small thing that Saleem didn't know what to make of. 'Mine is a wanton brush, but it is why I love painting so much. It harnesses my passions.'

That last word was not the one she'd wanted to use, Saleem thought.

And by the time she'd started explaining, it was already too late. Behind those lashes of hers, she considered him and he stepped closer as if drawn by a magnet.

She'd stopped talking, but her last word had the blood

coursing through his veins and it made him ask, 'What sort of passions run through your veins, Elise?'

They locked gazes for a long moment before he mustered the will to finally step back.

She dropped her fingers from his arm. He'd no idea if the smudge remained, but he knew he needed to rein in his desires. Channel Adnan's grumpiness.

He was supposed to be courting Elise's best friend, after all. How many times did he need to remind himself of it?

He turned back to her painting. Then he recognised the same sentiment of surprise he'd felt in the portrait card he'd given his brother. 'You painted Lady Olive.'

'Yes, that was me.' Elise frowned, 'Saleem, there is something more you should know.'

But before she could tell him what it was, Mustafa appeared.

'My Prince, Miss Thomas, pardon the interruption.'

Saleem wanted to tell him that, in fact, he did not pardon it.

Mustafa was normally more discreet, but perhaps he sensed, if not the danger, then the folly of leaving Saleem alone with a woman he was not supposed to be wooing. A woman he was only supposed to be helping figure out whom her deceased father meant to send a gold bar to.

Remembering the reason *why* Mustafa might interrupt him was fortuitous. 'Did you learn anything?'

Mustafa said, 'I returned from the police station now. My contact mentioned that they recently learned of an Englishman in the European quarter who is looking for gold in Alexandria, but he has been picky about the manner it comes in, insisting it must be in bars. Rumour has it he will pay handsomely for them as long as the bars meet his demands. What those demands are, no one knows, until they try to sell them and he refuses.'

'You think it's my uncle? That he is here in Alexandria?' Elise's worry twisted in Saleem's gut.

'They've only started investigating now and do not yet have a name,' Mustafa said.

'Wouldn't there be a record of landing? We should investigate that to learn if he is here. Regardless, Elise, you are safe at the Lodge.'

'There would be a record,' Mustafa agreed. 'But without a crime to follow up on, the police will not open up a case. They wouldn't look into the ship manifests with the border authorities unless there was one. My contact says that if this Englishman is doing anything nefarious with the gold bars, "a well-placed bribe is hard to trace".

'So even they don't have a name, only the name of the shop those looking to sell are supposed to go. It is in the European quarter.'

Saleem noticed the deepening line in the other man's cheek. He knew that mark. 'What aren't you telling us?'

Mustafa grinned. It was a look of pride Saleem wished he'd see more often from his father. 'Yesterday, the female companion to Portelli? Stephania? She was…er…*focused* on Miss Elise throughout the night.'

'I am used to behaviour of that manner, happens in one way or another when I wear a gown,' Elise dismissed.

'Because other women may be jealous?' Saleem wondered aloud, stopping himself before adding if said jealousy was due to her beauty.

Elise only offered a shake of her head in response. He'd remember to ask her the reason later.

Mustafa continued, 'You will recall, my Prince, how I thought it strange that Portelli insisted on answering the dinner invitation with the insistence on bringing a guest. I observed Stephania's behaviour from the shadows last night. She was fixated on Miss Elise.'

'Maybe she wondered how I could be an English-woman.'

'Some people do not realise when they're being rude,' Saleem offered.

Mustafa countered, 'It was more than that. Before Miss Elise even came down, I heard her asking one of the maids about Lady Olive specifically. She wanted to talk to her. Your arrival took her by surprise. Plus, now we know her full name, I asked more about her today. It turns out that before he died, Stephania's father Dimitri was one of the wealthiest merchants in Alexandria. He was a Greek who also happened to be a jeweller.'

'Why does that matter?' Elise asked.

Saleem explained, 'After you left it with me, I noticed markings on the gold bar—it looked like the Greek drachma sign.'

Elise's eyes widened. 'Oh. My mother is of Greek origin. Do you think that has anything to do with it? That perhaps Papa was sending it to someone from her side?'

'Do you have family here?' Saleem asked.

The question clearly tore at her. Her whole body seemed to sink. 'Not that I know of, no.'

'And if your father wanted to send it to anyone from your mother's side, why not to Greece directly?' Saleem asked.

It was difficult to tell now what Elise was feeling about the investigation—more pressing, however, was the question of what danger she might be in if her uncle were in the city.

'My last stop this morning,' Mustafa concluded, 'was

to the Anglo-Egyptian Bank, but I couldn't find anyone to answer my queries about why a bar of gold might be marked other than with its standard. Their man, one Mr Patterson, is currently in Cairo, but returns on Thursday.'

'If my Uncle Andrew *is* the stranger buying the gold bars, he must believe Papa already sent it and means to find it or if there are others like it. Or, he has followed me to Alexandria and hopes to find it before me. There must be more.' Elise folded her arms together. 'At least now we know it isn't likely that he's bothering Olive.'

Saleem could almost see her mind working through the possibilities and, were the situation not urgent, he'd have enjoyed studying Elise's process. 'You are not in danger either. Not with me here.'

'I think you, my Prince, should visit the police station,' Mustafa suggested, 'open an official, royal investigation into this Englishman.'

'I'd rather you did not,' Elise answered. 'If it is my uncle, he may cause additional problems for Lord Whitmore, who has already had to deal with much on account of him.' She looked at Saleem. 'Nor do I want you, as a prince, to be associated with my uncle. He may have married into a noble family, but he is a man with no scruples. I cannot impose further on your generosity towards me.'

'Say no more about imposing, Elise, for you insult me when you do.' Saleem did, however, see her point about Lord Whitmore and how such an investigation brought up with local authorities might irk his father.

This was not the first time Saleem had sent Mustafa to the police station with a task since arriving in Alexandria, but they had managed to accomplish what they wished to through discreet contacts within it. It was precisely because Saleem didn't want to make things so official it would reach the khedive and risk being interfered with or dismissed. 'We will hold off until Adnan returns safely with Lady Olive. Has there been word from him?'

'I did not go to the tram station yet. This took up my morning and I rushed back to tell you. I do have an...idea I wanted to check with you, but it would require careful planning.'

'You wish to draw the nameless collector out with the bar of gold currently in our possession.'

Mustafa grinned. 'I know how you think, my Prince, knew you would suggest it. As it happens, the shop taking the gold on the foreign Englishman's behalf is near the tram station.'

'We will go together then,' Saleem decided. *Ya'Allah.*

'What if we find this Uncle Andrew in the shop or if he has hired reinforcements? I have yet to scope the area and it could be dangerous.'

Saleem didn't want Mustafa to be burdened unnecessarily. He understood his guard's need for precautions and allowed them when he could. 'Then I will go to the tram station and you to scope out the shop area first. We can devise the details of our mission on the way.'

'I wish to come,' Elise interjected, 'play my part.'

The idea of her in danger was troubling, but Saleem knew what it was like to be left out of actions or decisions which directly concerned you. He'd not push Elise towards the same peripheries as his father tried to do with him.

'And if we were to find Andrew?' he asked. 'Are you ready to face your uncle?'

Chapter Eight

Elise

Elise wasn't ready to face her Uncle Andrew and she doubted she would ever be again. His constant interference in his quest to have her inheritance, the slur and threats she'd overheard him make, the fear he was responsible for her father's death—if she let it, it would consume her.

When he had first spoken to the papers, she'd wanted to give her own interviews in response. Tell a journalist how Andrew Clifton had married into a family of rank and shunned his own brother until he needed his money. How he had put his wife's nephew in Elise's path in a bid to ensure he'd always have access to it. How Gerald played on her affections and took her virginity in order to ensure she'd marry him and the inheritance would go to them.

Her father's lawyer had said that doing so would only ruin her own reputation.

'Best to ignore it. Public opinion will favour Andrew and Gerald, who is a nobleman.'

'I will have to be ready,' Elise assured Saleem. She twisted her arms around her back and tugged on the strings of her apron to pull it off.

Saleem warned, 'If he is capable of murdering his own brother, then—'

'Then I want the truth!' It was hard to claw back the anger nipping like a hound at her feet.

Saleem squared his shoulders. 'Tell me, Mustafa: should a foreigner buying gold under nefarious circumstances, without any business licence, be allowed to on our soil?'

'There must be a law against it.' Mustafa inclined his neck towards Elise. 'People have been known to rot, forgotten in some of our jails.'

'And our prisons have officers uniquely qualified to determine guilt over a crime.' Saleem held up both hands. 'Not to make light of a serious allegation, or to say Andrew wouldn't get a fair trial if such a determination were to occur. We would be under legal and moral obligation to bring our findings to the proper authorities. In England as well.'

'Thank you…thank you, both.' Elise felt a rush of gratitude despite the nagging voice that that told her he was using her situation as a distraction. That, when Olive returned, he would resume his wooing of her as he'd planned to do.

An hour later, Saleem led her and Mustafa through a less busy hall above the central tram station to avoid the crowd. Nevertheless, he took the time to greet those he did encounter. They clearly knew and respected him, yet it was as if they'd forgotten he was a prince.

Maybe it wasn't only Elise who saw Saleem as that gentleman at a falafel stand.

He embodies the idea of a 'people's prince'.

Saleem asked a fellow to find out about messages from Rasheed while Mustafa, having ensured the Prince's safe arrival in an office he himself had opened with his own key, left them to check on the shop in the European quarter.

Alone in said private office, Saleem held out a chair for Elise, then took the one next to her. It was too short for Saleem's frame, its arms made small beneath his longer ones.

It was a sparsely furnished space but she wondered why he would not take the larger chair behind the desk.

Did he wish to be nearer to her, or was it to disaffirm the divisions between them precisely because he was a humble noble?

'Mustafa can be overly cautious,' Saleem said.

'I had not noticed.'

He nodded appreciatively at her teasing remark before sobering. 'He lost his only son soon after he came to work for me. Cancer. A type called leukaemia. I had not realised it could come to such young people. There was nothing anyone could do to save him. It was Allah's will, but for other things, or so Mustafa likes to remind me, "there is a watchful eye and guarded limbs".'

He changed his voice to mimic the guard, but then seemed to notice the swell of sadness Elise felt with the knowledge of the man's loss.

'I tell him that human beings have instincts, too. We can trust them, hone them so we know when something *feels* right or not.'

Sounds from the busy level below filtered upwards: the pinging of telegraph machines, the raised voice commands of managers, the rushed patter of shoes along tiled floors.

'Where do you lie on the matter, Elise? Vigilant, unwavering caution no matter the circumstances or having faith in an internal barometer?'

'I would say that I agree with Mustafa, but you've seen me paint.'

'Yes.' Saleem crossed one leg over the other and adjusted himself so his body leaned more towards her. 'You are a woman of plenitudes. I noticed it upon your arrival. You seemed familiar to me, a friend even, and yet I had only just met you.'

Elise noticed how carefully he chose his words, as if he wanted to ensure he didn't upset or insult her. She'd been close to telling the truth about her being the one to write Olive's letters while they were in the garden earlier and even now she thought she should. Yet she held back, unsure. While Saleem's criticism on the painting she'd titled *Peacock at First Light* was provocative and appreciated, it had dismayed her.

At the back corner of her mind and when all was resolved with her uncle and the gold bar, Elise believed that the next chapter of her life could involve gallery showings of her art. Elise understood that art was personal and viewers of it would have their own experiences by which to view it, but she was not sure that she could stand others gawking and perceiving hers. Just as she avoided a rich woman's clothing that might attract people's unwanted attentions, her painting felt *too* personal to share with others. What if it were rejected, told it didn't belong among the other artists' works in any given gallery?

'Tell me about Mustafa's son. How young was he when he died? Does he have other children, a family? When does he see them if he is always guarding you?'

Saleem threw her a look that said he knew she was avoiding talking about herself, but he would oblige her questions. 'He'd been divorced for years before his son got sick. The boy was twelve when he died. There is an older daughter, too, but she recently married and will soon start her own family. Tragedy strikes and life continues for people.'

Elise agreed with that sentiment on one level. She was living proof of it. But… 'Spoken like someone who has *not* experienced tragedy. I don't know if "continuing on" with a life is akin to living it.'

'Is it not a start?' he asked, defensively. 'I cannot imagine the devastation of losing a child, but being lied to as one? And by someone I loved more than any other—that was a tragedy I am still learning how to continue on with in my life.'

He'd said he wouldn't abide a lie to Adnan that first day and Elise guessed from then and from his facial expressions that he was talking about their father.

Saleem didn't love her, certainly, but the fact remained that Elise had—*was* lying to him and she felt terrible for it.

'Assalam alaykum.' A man entered and Saleem stood from his seat to shake his hand.

They walked around the desk in an awkward dance. She wondered why the man didn't sit behind it so Saleem could assume his seat next to her, but it occurred to Elise that this wasn't the man's office.

'This is your office!' she exclaimed.

Saleem nodded unpretentiously while the other man very enthusiastically declared in what little English he had, 'Prince Saleem, master man of tram trains in Alexandria. First in all Africa. Smart Prince. He is owning best vision. Central communication here from this office but spread to whole city. Cairo will be jealous of how we take no taxi, no *hantoor*, no walking-only jump-on tram stop and, like a cable car, we ride fun. In twenty or thirty minute we are in one area and travel to other, quick. Prince Saleem tram project shall make Alexandria best city in whole country!'

Having exhausted his English, the man switched to Arabic and kept on talking.

Although Saleem listened attentively, he did not lose awareness of Elise's presence either. Gerald would constantly forget she was in a room, even when there was only one language being spoken.

'He says there has been no word from Adnan yet, but wants to discuss a matter concerning the tram project. Do you mind?' Saleem asked apologetically.

Elise checked her disappointment. She should *not* want to constantly be alone with the Prince. 'By all means, we need to wait for Mustafa anyway.'

Saleem ushered the man to a table in the far corner of the office, bright from the sunlight streaming in from a large window. A pillar blocked her view, but, from afar, the table looked as though it held a model train set.

Elise followed the conversation between the two men. Not that she understood any of it, but Saleem fascinated her. He was different than he'd been at the gathering last night. More studious, his brow knitting as he spoke, animated. The man with him seemed truly impressed at the points Saleem was making, not as he would a prince, but as a respectful colleague.

When the man finally left and they were alone in the office again, Saleem didn't resume his seat. Rather, he came around the pillar and leaned on it with the left side of his body. Then, crossing his arms in a manner that stretched his shirt so that the muscles of his abdomen were contoured, he considered her for a minute while she tried desperately not to gawk.

'Join me,' he invited, his tone almost *seductive*. 'Let me show you what we do here.'

Elise obeyed, mostly to disrupt that stance of his that

was making her weak in the knees, despite being in a sitting position.

When she neared the table, she saw it wasn't only a miniature train set, but a map of the city with meticulously detailed streets and quarters. She immediately noted the signature of a French cartographer on one side of the canvas—the artist, she supposed—but superimposed on the entirety of the table map was a pane of clear thin glass, marked up in Arabic and with further lines. She could not read the latter, but it looked as though plans were being made for expansion.

'What do you know of trams and tram lines?' he asked.

'Not very much besides knowing them to be a means of getting from one point to another? My father and I had our own carriages or could hail cabs in Manchester where we spent the bulk of our time, but I believe there are trams there, more like horse carriage trolleys—nothing like what I saw on our way here.'

Saleem nodded. 'I haven't been to Manchester, but what you describe is the same as in other European cities. In California, there is a man named Hallidie. His father was the inventor who patented "wire rope" in England and when Hallidie emigrated during the gold rush, he used it to haul the ore from the mines and over bridges. Then, seeing how the horses were whipped to climb the hilly streets of San Francisco and being aghast at the cruelty, he created a system of trolleys that moved people instead. I believe our first tram actually pre-existed his and that our expansion project may even outdo his.'

'*You* are leading this project entirely. From this office of yours.'

Saleem acknowledged the truth therein with only a slight tilt of his head.

'Alexandria has only ever been seen as a port. A port which is often written about as a backwater. This, despite the fact that in ancient times, the city was the gateway, the cusp of civilisation, learning. A bridge between empires.' He wiped at specks of dust on the pane with the back of his thumb. 'When the project first came to my father's attention, the khedive wasn't interested. I had to cajole him to let me take it on. I wish that others could better see the city's potential now. And for the future.'

Elise had hoped to spend time in Alexandria not only to find out about the gold bar, but because of her parents' connection to the city. But now she recalled how Lord Whitmore fretted over the itinerary Olive had tried to set.

'There is nothing in Rasheed. Even Alexandria is barely worth the stop.'

Remembering the conversation now, Elise wondered if that was why Olive disembarked in Rasheed. Why had she been so adamant in defying her father?

She forced Olive from her mind. 'Why is Alexandria's potential not recognised?'

'For a few reasons, but the one we are tackling here has to do with the European quarter—' he pointed to a shaded area on the map '—being secluded. For too long it has been a prime part of the city and resentment over that fact has spread to other parts.'

'How?'

'You'll see for yourself soon, but it is well maintained, wealthy, clearly only for the very rich who also are mostly *not* Egyptians. What surrounds the quarter is terribly neglected, maintained insofar as to what benefits those within it. Garbage, for instance, is picked up regularly lest the smell carry into the nostrils of those who aren't accustomed to them.' He smiled, muttered that he was 'starting to sound like my brother'.

'Anyhow, the locals see the inequity. I know that where the Lodge stands and where the primary palace, Raseltin, is situated are removed and are not yet part of the problem. But we are associated with royalty and so Alexandrians do not complain.'

He qualified, 'Although, according to my friend at the Rosetta Carriage Company who Adnan must be with as we speak, the masses do not complain *yet*. Yasser believes a revolution against the khedival system is brewing. For now, it is easier to blame outsiders. Occupying forces or foreign influences. Europeans, in their fancy quarters.'

Elise followed Saleem's finger, as he pointed out the Lodge and the presidential palace, both opposite sides of the city. 'I saw a few of the tram lines below—do they not connect to all major quarters of the city?'

'We are in what is called Raml Station and it is the hub because it is close to everything, but, no, it doesn't connect to all the quarters. We have started building upon what we have, but there is work to be done. We are designing it so that this will be the middle of the city and extending the whole system to the different parts in order to unite the quarters and even to the palaces. The tram system would run parallel to the sea here via a beautiful promenade we've yet to build.'

Saleem went on to paint, in words, his vision for Alexandria. He spoke about how the tram system would soon run via electricity as it did in Berlin and Toronto. He angled his arm above his head and chuckled at the ridiculous stance but explained why. 'The cars use pantographs, current collectors which are mounted to wires high above the trolley cars. Those wires will distribute electricity over the larger system.'

Saleem went on to explain that they'd determined to build more inland. 'The tram cars will use paints and metals less susceptible to humidity due to our proximity to the sea.'

He adjusted the glass pane reverently as Elise watched, moved. She had no knowledge of engineering or planning principles, Saleem did not make her feel ignorant, answering her questions with care and consideration. She was particularly impressed by the details he and his team had considered: who rode the tram at what times, how the seats would accommodate those with unique needs like the elderly or the ill.

'Ultimately, my objective,' Saleem said, 'is to bring the city together, to have people not feel as if Alexandria is divided and not of one mind.'

'Not just a port,' she repeated what he'd said earlier. 'Bravo, Saleem. It is most impressive!' Elise clapped her hands. 'Did I tell you my parents met in this city, that even if I didn't come to find who the gold bar was sent to and for, I would have wished to see where they fell in love. My father talked of bringing me one day, showing me all their favourite places.'

The vulnerability in her own voice caught Elise by surprise. Saleem must have heard it, too, because he stepped closer. He looked into her eyes with a kind of intensity that made her feel as though her very soul was naked, exposed.

And Elise couldn't look away.

She almost didn't hear him when he whispered a minute later, 'I do not know where your parents' favourite places were, but if you would do me the honour, I will show you mine.'

Elise wanted nothing more than to see the places he loved. She told him as much, even as the spectre of his words loomed in her mind. Even as Mustafa appeared and told them that the area had been secured and they could head to the shop, gold bar in hand.

Saleem had written exactly the same sentiment in his last letter to Olive.

Chapter Nine

Saleem

The tram project excited Saleem on its own, but to have Elise be interested in it was vindicating. If she, an English visitor with no future stake in the city's planning, could appreciate his vision, then surely his father should be proud as well.

Pride didn't mean Saleem expected the khedive would hand him the funds to ensure the expansion happened as he wished. On that, his father had decreed Saleem needed to marry rich. Egyptian women didn't provide dowries—it was the other way around here. But British women? Whenever he broached the need for funds for his tram or other projects, his father said Saleem should be grateful to him for facilitating the courtship between Saleem and Lord Whitmore's daughter.

But Saleem had never wanted to marry a woman for her money, he wanted to marry for love. *Marriage and business should not mix.* He'd repeated it until he could no longer bear the pitying look the khedive tossed him whenever he did.

And when Saleem changed tactics, hoping to convince him that the tram in Alexandria, like the Suez Canal project, was an investment in the country's future, his father countered by saying that the latter served Europe—not just a small population of people in a port city.

The next phase of Saleem's work involved finding local partners, people like Sinjur Portelli, to convince them of the project's viability. They would have ideas about how to raise funds or connect him with potential financiers.

If Elise's excitement was an indication, Saleem felt sure he'd succeed.

Unless her excitement stemmed from something more.

They'd had a moment before she'd pulled away. He'd been looking into her eyes, wondering if it was her face he admired, or the admiration he saw there that made his chest swell.

Elise believed in what Saleem was doing and he wanted to show her that that belief wasn't misplaced. He'd show her the city as he'd hoped to show Lady Olive Whitmore.

Not that Elise was a marriage prospect he needed to woo to please his father. Nor that he only thought of Lady Olive as one because of her dowry.

What his father couldn't understand was that Saleem would never take anything for himself from his wife, English dowry or otherwise. How would he sleep with his own conscience at night if he did?

He shook his head, pushing out thoughts of marriage and the lack of sleep at night from his mind. It wasn't safe to think about those things while in Elise's presence.

'Be careful with the gold bar,' Mustafa warned. 'Don't let it go, no matter what the man offers. It is our only assurance of meeting whoever is buying them.'

'And if it is my uncle?' Elise asked.

'Then we demand he tell us why,' Saleem answered.

Mustafa walked them through a wrought-iron fence to

a shop that sat on the margins of the European quarter. It was a quiet corner and jutted from the side of a residential building. The shop itself, a ground-floor extension of the building, was easy to miss even after one walked past the fence. Potted plants lined the marbled floor, leading to its shop window. They'd been watered and were thriving, the only sign of life in the darkly curtained shop window and door.

In fact, it didn't look like a shop at all, save for the wooden sign above it that read *Antikalar*.

'It is the Turkish word for antiques,' he told Elise.

'You speak Turkish?'

'Until recently, it was the official language at court, but my grasp of it is weak. My father stresses English now.'

Mustafa looked between them, a knowing expression crossing his face. 'I'll be outside here, take no risks. No one will recognise you as a prince here, you'll look like just another of the wealthy people who frequent the area. But shout if you need me.'

Saleem took the satchel from Mustafa and walked into the shop with Elise. He was glad Mustafa hadn't put up a fuss when Saleem suggested letting them play a couple looking to sell the gold bar. He didn't carry any weapons like Mustafa did, but he had a strong desire to be the one who ensured Elise's safety.

He wanted to protect her. Why, exactly, Saleem wasn't sure, except to think he felt protective of her. She'd been orphaned and abandoned by her friend, mistreated by the uncle who should have taken care of her.

It is natural that any decent man would wish to shield her from further harm.

'*Ahlan,*' he called, while Elise perused the dimly lit space. There was a display case of jewellery, paltry of-

ferings and mostly composed of pearl and coloured gem-
stones. A curio cabinet contained a few colourful plates
and various other decorative items.

A man lifted his head from behind a desk holding a
typewriter.

He was noticeably pale despite the darkness in the room.
With a wispy beard long enough to meet the tip of his vest,
a pale blue in a houndstooth pattern, he seemed somewhat
out of place, but when he answered them, his accent was
distinctly a dialect of Arabic spoken by those from the
Levant region.

Shami. Saleem guessed he was Palestinian or Syrian,
likely descended from the Christians who'd migrated a few
decades ago to escape political conflict with the Druze.

With a glance that stayed too long on Elise, the man
asked, 'Are you the couple looking to sell a gold item?'

'If the price offered is good, we may be.' Saleem had
never actually negotiated in the market places. After coming to court, Adnan had tried to teach him how, but there
was little opportunity for princes to frequent bazaars for
practice. Especially not in Cairo where Saleem was recognised more often there than in Alexandria.

Elise came to stand next to him. Close, but not nearly
enough.

'Can you speak English for the benefit of my...wife?'
They had discussed what they would say on the way over,
so Elise knew to expect it, yet he felt her flinch next to him.

'Your wife?' The shopkeeper turned to English, but
spoke as if he didn't believe it.

It didn't really matter what he did, the point of this
visit was to get information on the mysterious buyer of
the gold bars.

Yet maybe because she felt she had to convince him,

or bad for her hesitancy, Elise leaned into Saleem. She wrapped her arms around his, then angled her neck to look up at him in what could only be described as a loving wife's glance.

She touched his jaw with a delicate hand. 'My husband.'

Saleem's heart raced, but he smiled through it, gently brushing away a strand of her hair when she leaned into his shoulder and it hit his chin. It fell back into place as soon as he did, straight enough that it had a will of its own.

Her hair is like her paintbrush.

It was a mistake to inhale so deeply then, he realised, for it left him feeling intoxicated, as if her perfume had turned into opium.

What was wrong with him?

Saleem hated lies, that was it. He could not abide them from others and never told them himself. And that was what he would explain to Elise after they left here if she happened to notice, then comment on his racing heart.

It wasn't as though Saleem was not used to being in the proximity of beautiful women. He'd never wanted a reputation for being a rake and Adnan's belief that *'It is only fair and halal that if a man is a woman's first, then she should be his, too'* had begun to resonate with Saleem.

Elise pointed out a porcelain vase in the curio. 'Is that a Meissen Marcolini?'

'It is, indeed.'

The shopkeeper brought it over and spoke as if his knowledge of the piece was under scrutiny. He flipped it to show them the underbelly first. 'Crossed swords, dot and mark in the blue, the maker's mark.' He pointed out the detailing of the three scrolled feet and the matching scroll handle. There were portraits of children painted on to it, one a child in costume looking spoiled, the other the back of a girl, her red and blue frock lending her a mysterious air. Surrounding them were green-leafed golden wreaths.

'It is a masterfully done vase,' Saleem said, disappointed when Elise let go of him in order to examine it closely. 'Do you like the artistry, darling?'

He would buy it for Elise if she did even if their cover story was meant to be that they were in want of funds. Given their conversation about her painting in the peacock patch, Saleem was interested to know Elise's opinion.

It was the shopkeeper who answered, 'With respect, sir, it is not a vase, but a jug. A milk jug, to be precise.'

Saleem was not insulted, but Elise was on his behalf. She pushed it back to the shopkeeper. 'It is decorative. Perhaps a water jug, at best. Surely none would put milk in it. Even if it was once termed that, it is no longer.'

The shopkeeper clicked his tongue and replaced the jug. 'The item?'

Saleem removed the gold bar from the satchel. 'We heard you've an English buyer looking for gold bars. We have one for sale.' He watched the man as he spoke, noticed how his gaze had immediately sought out the *drachma* marking.

It could mean anything; he'd noted the mark of authenticity on the jug. But why would it be the case with a gold bar already stamped by the Bank of England? 'Tell us about him.'

'Or any other collectors of such items you might know of here in Alexandria,' Elise asked.

Saleem wished to ascertain if her uncle was in Egypt, if she was in danger. Elise wanted to find out who her father intended to send it to in the first.

The shopkeeper, however, quibbled on what he had said. '*Him?* Who says the buyer is a him?'

Saleem could not remember a time when he was so disrespected by a stranger. He could grab the man by his jacket lapels, ask if he knew who he was.

Elise, sensing it, weaved her fingers through his. Which prompted a different feeling altogether. Saleem managed to keep his bearings, none the less.

They needed to arrange a meeting with the buyer—that was the only way to learn whether or not he was Elise's uncle.

'A female buyer would be better,' he said, returning to the story they'd planned. '*She* might appreciate our dilemma.'

'Dilemma?'

'The gold bar was a gift…from a family member who is now gone. If my husband and I were not in financial difficulty, I would not part with it for any amount.'

'The buyer will provide the highest price for it.' The shopkeeper touched the gold bar, didn't check the gold's authenticity or do an acid test to see if it would turn green or not.

That was standard protocol. Saleem knew as much from royal jewellers.

The shopkeeper took out a card and wrote a number on it. Handing it to Elise, he said, 'That is how much the buyer would offer. The currency would be English sterling or the equivalent in any other currency you'd desire. They *may* want a meeting with you as well.'

Elise showed the card to Saleem. In truth, he had no idea how much the gold bar was worth, but from her tiny nod he ascertained it to be a high amount. 'Meeting the buyer is necessary. I will not sell unless assured that the bar is well looked after.'

'This buyer is not the sort to heed demands.'

Saleem interrupted, 'Assuming you are receiving a commission from the buyer, I would offer an additional token for a meeting. The buyer needn't even know about it. We would simply appear here at the same time they are expected. It would be for my wife's peace of mind.'

He smiled lovingly at Elise and found it wasn't as much an act as her blush would suggest when she looked up to him and allowed her gaze to snag on his.

For a moment, the shopkeeper was forgotten while he and Elise stared into each other's eyes.

Does she, too, feel the pull between us?

This was the third time in one day. First in the garden and second at the tram station. It was what Saleem would have hoped to happen with Olive, having got to know each other through their letters before her arrival.

Instead, here he was acting like a smitten boy with her best friend. Elise must think him a disloyal flirt. Salem wouldn't even know how to apologise for it, address it without making it seem as though he was.

'Newly married, are you, then?' The shopkeeper's raised voice grated between them, forcing Elise to turn to him.

'Honeymoon,' Saleem said, remembering what she'd mentioned earlier about her own parents. 'Indeed, there are a few places we need to visit on our trip and my wife has not eaten since breakfast. If you cannot tell us when you are next meeting the buyer, then we will take our gold elsewhere.'

He made a show of putting the gold bar back in the satchel and a hand to Elise's back in order to lead her out.

The man stopped them right before they left. 'Wait.'

Adnan's lesson on bartering had come in handy.

Always be willing to leave, Brother. It is important to

stick to your principles in any situation, but it's an ap-
proach that especially works in the marketplace.'

'You have not told me your names,' the shopkeeper said.

Per their agreed cover story, Elise said, 'And we will
not unless you are willing to give us *the buyer's* name.'

They'd thought of fake names, but the shopkeeper shook
his head. 'No need, I am but the interlocutor here.' He
tugged at his pocket watch, examined it as if it were a
calendar and then decided. 'Saturday, then. Two o'clock.
Though the buyer may come in at odd times to pester me
and see if there is progress on the search, that is when I
next expect them, officially.'

That was three days away. Farther than Saleem expected. He pricked with irritation. He'd wanted to handle
this before Adnan returned with Lady Olive.

'Saturday it is.'

Chapter Ten

Elise

To take breakfast the next day, Khayria led Elise down to an outer terrace. The space overlooked the sea, which was calm and inviting, its waves coming in at an even pace, slow, assured.

She enjoyed it for a bit, leaning over the balcony ledge and lamenting the fact that she'd never learned to swim. How invigorating it would be in the early mornings.

With Saleem, if he was not so against waking up early.

But even as she thought it, he surprised her by entering with Mustafa.

'Good sleep?' he asked.

'Wonderful, thank you.'

She'd spent the night reliving the moments with Saleem when they'd got a bit too close yesterday and decided that it was very wrong to allow her emotions to get the better of her. She determined to resist his charms today.

Yet, there he was, smiling in a way which caused Elise to forget *why* she should.

The ongoing lie that she had been the one answering Saleem's letters to Olive was one reason. Adnan having not yet sent any word was the other. What would happen when he did? If Olive returned in her more rational mind, she and Saleem might then take up the relationship their fathers wished for them and where would that leave Elise?

Mustafa handed her a parchment and charcoal. 'We hired a man to keep the shop under surveillance for the next few days.'

Saleem explained, 'We thought if you could sketch your uncle, our man would know who to look for.'

Elise took a seat at the small table and began. 'You didn't need to hire someone. I feel terrible to cause such an inconvenience.'

'If the hired man catches Andrew in any illegal activity, he'll be arrested. If he is a threat in any way to those who live in the area, then he must be dealt with immediately. Protecting our city is not an inconvenience,' Saleem assured her.

'As long as we find out who Papa meant to send the gold bar to.'

'Who do you think it might be?' Mustafa asked.

Elise hadn't really thought much about it, but when Saleem added, 'Or who do you *hope* it might be?' her answer was instinctive.

'A family member. A person Papa thought would protect me from my uncle, his threats. Not that I have any family here. Or anywhere for that matter.'

Neither man answered her after that and she felt embarrassed to look up from her drawing to see their reactions. When she finally chanced it, she was happy to have them sitting at a table nearby, quietly playing a game of chess while she completed the task.

Finally satisfied with her uncle's likeness, she told them she was done and handed it to Mustafa's outstretched hand.

'The last time I saw Uncle Andrew was almost two years ago. It was at a horse race…'

She remembered it, how Gerald had not expected her. How he'd callously introduced her to the older man next to him, *'Elise, meet my cousin-in-law!'* and as she was shaking his hand, Papa had appeared. The simultaneous shock and realisation on his face was like a punch to her midsection even now.

By then, her father had known Gerald for weeks, allowed him entry into their home, accepted him as the husband for his only daughter. His father had even gifted him a Breguet watch, travelling to Geneva to choose it himself.

But when Thomas Clifton realised Gerald had been acting, that he'd known exactly what to say and do because he'd been coached by his estranged brother, he lost his temper.

'You arranged this!' her father had accused Andrew. *'To steal Elise's inheritance.'*

Her uncle had spat back, *'Easy to do when you've a trollop for a daughter!'*

Papa lunged for his brother and when Gerald stepped between them, Elise thought he'd meant to protect the man he'd claimed was the father he'd never had. She couldn't have been more wrong. Her suitor and uncle outnumbered her father and gave him a beating before the crowd intervened at the sound of her screams.

'Perfect, but this Andrew is an ugly man.'

Mustafa's words pulled her from the memory but it was the concern on Saleem's face that made Elise's heart soften. He didn't speak, not until they were alone, his guard gone to brief the new hire.

'What if we picnic at one of my favourite spots in the city today? It will be a brief reprieve while waiting for word from Adnan on Lady Olive. I do not want you worrying about the gold bar or your uncle any more today.'

'Where is this favourite spot?' Elise asked.

Saleem grinned mischievously. 'It is a place at once old and entirely new. Easier for you to see it than having me try to explain and spoil the surprise.'

'Very well, Prince Saleem. Have your secrets.'

He pressed his lips together in a teasing motion. Her eyes lifted to said lips and he, sensing perhaps the effect he was having on her, let his thumb glide over the dip beneath the centre of his lower lip. With his elbow bent, his forearm flexed in a way that caused the veins there to bulge.

She nearly moaned from admiration. Because he was standing and she sitting Elise rose, unable to remain at Saleem's mercy for any longer.

His eyes roamed over her, head to toe and then back again. Elise flushed—it felt nearly as though he was undressing her.

He asked, 'Do you like what you are wearing?'

It was an emerald gown, a favourite for she'd always liked for the colour. 'Do you not?'

'I do. Very much,' he said. 'Only, for our activity today, it might get dirty.'

'I don't mind getting dirty.'

He dropped his thumb and it seemed to Elise that their roles were switched. Now, he was the flustered one.

Elise guessed it might be a jaunt to the beach, but instead they went for a surprisingly long carriage ride. They moved along the sea at first, Saleem pointing out where his new promenade would be built, but when they moved more inland, he began naming the different areas that the tram project would service.

They came to a stop at a small park, far from the shores,

though the sea breeze still stirred the air. The area had been closed off with makeshift fencing, but there was a team working inside.

When Elise descended from the carriage, she realised what was happening. 'It's an archaeological dig!'

'The beginnings of one, yes.' Saleem beamed.

'Is it the Lighthouse of Alexandria you've found?'

'No, that one is most likely in the Eastern harbour. They say earthquakes caused it to fall into the sea, but some of its stones were used to build the Qaitbay Citadel fortress. We can go there another time.' He spread his arms wide. 'But this one has not been announced to the world of antiquities yet. We are not ready yet to allow non-Egyptians access, Elise. So, today you are one of us. A member of the wider Alexandrian family.'

She folded her hands over her heart, feeling privileged at the honour even though she'd no idea what was behind the fence.

'Wait for me here,' Saleem said, 'I'll find the professor leading it to give you the tour.'

He'd begun to walk away, but then turned back with a cautionary remark, 'Be wary, lest you fall down any holes.'

It was an odd warning, but Elise assumed it concerned the dig. She'd never been near one, but after a visit with her mother to Stonehenge, she had spent an entire year obsessed with finding all she could about the ones that had happened near it.

When her mother got sick, her interest in the subject waned. She felt sorry for it, however, as she watched the archaeologists patiently going about their business in the various sectioned-off areas.

Elise moved to stand under the shade of a nearby palm tree. She pressed a hand to its trunk, welcoming the sensation of rough bark. She lifted her face to the warm sun and enjoyed the tranquillity, eyes closed. In that quiet moment, Elise believed that she would one day get completely past her grief. The foreboding sense that she'd always be alone in the world.

'Miss Thomas?'

She nearly did not answer the call. She should tell Saleem her last name because every time she heard her father's as her own, it was a mild shock. And a reminder Papa was gone.

She opened her eyes to a young Black woman with a wide-brimmed straw hat shielding studious eyes and high cheekbones.

She spoke in flawless English. 'I am Aisha Sayid. Welcome to the catacombs of Kom El Shoqafa.'

Elise shook her hand. 'It is a pleasure to be here. Please call me Elise.'

Aisha smiled. 'The Prince has asked me to start the tour without him since he has had it a few times and is arranging a picnic lunch.'

Elise fought back her disappointment at Saleem's absence.

Can you not be away from him for even a short while?

Aisha guided her through the marked sections to an area that was behind a wooden door. There were a few workers quietly working, but mostly it seemed that this was where they labelled and collected their findings.

Elise spied a sarcophagus with a relief that looked to be from Ancient Rome she'd have liked to examine closer, but Aisha was pulling her towards a few steps that rose above what looked like a large round door in the cement. She called to two of the men, who lifted it to reveal a crater that delved deep into the earth.

'There are safety measures in place,' Aisha said, pointing to ladders and pulleys, 'and a path has been laid out and trod at least a hundred times by now. But if you find it is frightening, we do not have to descend. There is no shame in going back.'

'I want to see everything!' Elise insisted.

'Prince Saleem requested I give you the choice, but he guessed that would be your answer.' Aisha smiled. 'Very well then, down we go. Please watch your step.'

The two men who opened the floor board offered them thick arms to hold as they descended what was essentially a narrow staircase, curved around a tower that had been dug, rather than one that had been built in an upward direction. Sconces and lanterns were liberally hung, but even though the sun shone above them, they could not keep the darkness at bay.

Cold seeped through the satin of Elise's gown and there was dirt all over it. She should have better heeded Saleem's warning! The stench of wet earth had her plugging her nose, but when they reached the bottom step and the cave-like area opened up to an entire labyrinth, Elise had to release it in order to not choke on her own gasp.

A six-pillared shaft had been formed from rock, an entire death scene done by a stone mason on one wall. On another, snake-like creatures jutted in warning. Ancient Egyptian deities aplenty adorned others. In one alcove, the ceiling was painted with intricate green foliage and—*was that a panther sitting among the plants?*

It was not simply a burial place, it was a work of art.

An altogether breathtaking one.

'We estimate that the catacombs were in active use for at least two hundred years between the second and fourth centuries,' Aisha told Elise. 'And there is much more to explore, but it will take years perhaps. We must be careful and move slowly.'

'How many were buried here?'

'It is hard to tell, hundreds at least. There may be additional levels beneath this one or, given that crypts were built for families, some may be empty. For whatever reason, members were not always entombed where they were meant to be.'

Elise couldn't help but think of her father, buried in London far from her mother in Greece. Because the investigation had taken its time, his body with the coroner's office longer than it would have otherwise been, she'd thought it cruel to move him. He'd not stipulated his wishes like her mother had. She'd been sick for a while and wanted to live out her days in her ancestral home when the doctors said there was no hope for her survival.

Elise rarely thought of those last months in Greece with her mother because it had ended in misery. But buried deep in the crevices of her mind, there were happy times then, too. The oranges they shared, the singing at the family's gatherings while she and her mother played the piano together.

Aisha explained, 'Alexandria was a vital city in the ancient world, a port of exchange for Greek and Roman influences culturally and religiously that you wouldn't necessarily see in Cairo or other cities along the Nile, which were rooted almost entirely in Egyptian mythologies. Not that Alexandrian ancients were unaware of the culture proliferating in the rest of the country, they were—but the thinking here, for a variety of reasons, favoured an amalgamation of those three civilisations. We knew this in theory, certainly, but finding these catacombs has—or rather, *will*—prove our work. And to think we owe it all to our donkey martyr.'

'Oh?'

Aisha must have perceived the confusion in Elise's interjection. 'It's true. A short while ago, there was an incident right above us. In the street that once existed there, a donkey was casually eating from his bucket of hay one minute and then falling through the earth the next. Thank Allah no one was hurt except the poor donkey, but the area was closed off as a public hazard.'

'That's incredible.'

'Prince Saleem had just arrived in the city to oversee the tram project and heard what happened. He called my father who'd been a professor of his and commissioned him to take charge of the excavation. If it were not for the Prince, the city might have fixed the hole by pouring cement over it, then building a sturdier road above it. Kom el Shoqafa would never have been found. He is truly a hero of the field, a patron of a prince.'

As Aisha was talking, the sound of Saleem's voice followed. Anticipation hummed through Elise's being. Anticipation, followed by a twinge of embarrassment.

He's only been gone for a short time.

'There is an echo,' he said, acknowledging Elise with a nod before turning to Aisha. 'Do you not fear I will grow arrogant with your flattery?'

Aisha laughed. 'Perhaps I am smart enough to have heard your approach and meant to charm you for more funding.'

'Were it up to me, you would have all the monies you needed at your disposal. Alas, my pocket is bound and the khedive's finances are strained.'

Aisha sighed. 'I know you are doing your best. Everyone

here does. It just seems as though our labour isn't valued by our government as it should be. We do not want to end up selling what we find to the English or French.'

'I don't want that to happen either. Rest assured, I will find a solution.' He inhaled when he met Elise's gaze in the darkened space, 'How is your dress holding up?'

She didn't want to flirt with him in the presence of another woman. 'Even if it were entirely ruined, I would not care at all.'

'Pleasurable tour, then?'

'What an experience it has been, thanks to you both.'

'We are not yet done,' Aisha said.

'I expected to see your father today, Professor, but the men above tell me they are almost all your students and are here for credit. That you're an excellent leader in his stead.'

'You're a professor?' Elise knew that while women were now permitted in many universities, teaching in them was next to unheard of. 'How admirable!'

Aisha waved a dismissive hand. 'My father paved the way. Had three daughters and insisted we all be educated higher than he was. My youngest sister is applying to take classes in England actually.'

'Your sister can stay with me, my London town house is large enough to accommodate another person. Things are up in the air with me at present since I've been living with my best friend and her father, but I do mean to settle on my own when I return.' Elise asked Saleem, 'You'll help us stay in touch until then, will you not?'

It was hard to tell in the dim light of the crypt, but she thought he might be frowning despite his reply, 'It would be my honour to be in correspondence with you.'

Before she could feel guilty about having already been

in correspondence with him, Saleem walked her to a wall adjacent to the funeral scene she'd noticed.

'The Abduction of Persephone,' he said of the mural, 'done entirely in the Greek style.'

Saleem couldn't have known her mother was buried in Greece. That Elise had just recalled the time she'd spent with her there before she died.

She couldn't stem the tears that fell, but tried to keep it quiet, to not spoil the tour.

Saleem, of course, immediately sensed her sadness, 'What's wrong, Elise?'

Aisha took her hand in her own, squeezing it supportively like Olive used to do.

'It was my mother's favourite myth,' Elise explained. 'She liked to tell it to me because it is a mother–daughter tale. One in which a woman searched high and low and did not care that the earth should fall to ruin until she had rescued her daughter from the grasp of the evil Hades in the underworld.

'Demeter, the mother and goddess of the harvest and fertility, was finally able to reach a deal for her daughter, Persephone. The deal they struck was if she were allowed freedom from Hades' realm, it meant that Demeter would allow the earth to experience the spring and summer. And when Persephone was forced to go back to the underworld after her time with her mother, the autumn and winter would ensue.'

'The Ancient Greek origin story for how the seasons came to be,' Aisha confirmed.

'Yes.' Elise took a deep breath. 'We spent time in Greece before my mother died. I was only a child, but she wanted me to know that if she could, she'd have fought to be with me harder than Demeter fought to be with Persephone.'

'I am sorry, dear Elise,' Aisha said. 'Being here—in any graveyard—can be hard, reminding us of whom we have lost.'

'It is my fault, I should have known better, thought of all the grief you've endured of late.' Saleem's perturbation made Elise want to turn the moment into a happy memory.

'On the contrary, it has been perfect being here. It reminded me of a time I'd buried and the picture of my mother, it was…special. I am grateful to you, Saleem, for arranging the tour. Please, let us continue it.'

When Aisha let her hand go, Elise fancied that Saleem considered taking up the duty. But he stoically kept his own behind his back for the rest of their time underground.

The tour passed without further incident and concluded with hugs between the women after they'd ascended from the depths.

'It was a pleasure to meet you, Elise.'

'I hope to see you again soon, Professor Aisha.'

'Will you join us for lunch?' Saleem asked, but Aisha declined.

'I have much work to do before dusk,' she said. 'Enjoy it.'

When they had gone through the enclosure and were alone in the wider open space he'd first left her at, Elise confided in Saleem, 'Save for Olive in my childhood, I don't make friends easily. But I can see that Aisha and I would get along. I hope her sister is as lovely.'

Saleem considered her for a long minute. 'In the gardens the other day, when Mustafa spoke about Stephania, you said you are used to women staring, but it is not because they are jealous of your beauty. What did you mean?'

Elise didn't even consider holding back this time, simply poured out her heart to Saleem without thinking, 'Because they have a perception that well-dressed Englishwomen are light skinned with blonde hair. That they look like Olive. If they see one who does not, it raises the sort of questions that I have never wanted to subject myself to. Maybe that is why I felt at ease with Aisha. One does not see Black women like her or darker women like me rising in London society. Not that I am in any way as smart or accomplished as Aisha.'

Saleem remained on what she'd said about herself, 'You don't believe it yourself? You think that you are inferior because your skin is darker?'

Elise shook her head, but wasn't exactly sure how to put her beliefs into words. If he'd asked her the same question earlier today she might have said that it was simply her reality—and that the only thing she could control was her choice to not place herself at the centre of others' attentions.

Now that she'd been confronted with the scene of Persephone, Elise was beginning to realise she could embrace her colouring. It was her mother's, after all.

When she didn't answer, Saleem changed the subject while leading her to their picnic. 'Did Professor Aisha tell you that it was an unfortunate donkey who first made the discovery?'

'She did!' Elise imagined the animal falling and couldn't help but laugh. 'It'll make for an unbelievable story in the history books some day.'

He grinned as though her joy meant much to him, though she was starting to realise that everyone's happiness was important to him. 'It is why I told you earlier to be careful of any holes.'

'It *had* seemed like a silly thing to say, but I could feel the care in your words.'

Indeed, he'd shown her care since she'd arrived. Rather than be bothered by Olive's absence or disappointed that whatever plans he had for her visit were delayed until Adnan returned with her, Saleem had taken it upon himself to ensure Elise's situation with her uncle was solved. In his letters, he'd seemed kind and friendly, not like an arrogant noble or royal might be. Elise was seeing how he was much more than what his letters conveyed. He was a determined, talented prince.

Getting a glimpse of the picnic he'd had laid out for them near the palm tree, the smells of hot food that filled her soul and cleared her mind, she couldn't help but admire how attentive he was, too.

It was plausible that Saleem had channelled his hurt over Olive to Elise's cause. Although, from work in the tram project and all he had done for the catacombs, it was clear he had his own channels to harness his passions.

Thinking about passions was a mistake. It brought up her physical yearning for Saleem as he ushered her on to a cushion and sat opposite, crossing his legs in a manner that put her on alert.

Elise had not been with a man before or since Gerald. Their time together had amounted to two stolen nights when her father was away. Two foolishly misguided nights on her part and on Gerald's, downright despicable, ungentlemanly behaviour. The result was that she'd thought she'd never again yearn for the arms of a man around her, the feel of one inside her.

And if she did, he'd certainly not be one who came with a title.

'I do care, Elise.' Saleem gripped both his knees tightly. Did she imagine the thickening of his voice, the heft in the words as if he knew what she was thinking?

Was it possible Saleem yearned for her, too?

It would be disastrous to have an affair with him.

She knew it. Yet if Elise had never before empathised with a donkey who'd found himself falling through the earth, she could now.

Chapter Eleven

Saleem

Follow a frown with a laugh. That had been his personal motto since he'd found out about his father's lie. But even after he and Adnan came to be proper brothers, Saleem would remind himself of the motto often in the face of his father's constant disapproval.

Today, he was determined to apply the motto to Elise. He'd brought her to a place which had made her cry and now it was imperative Saleem make her forget her suffering. He was only somewhat disappointed that the feast he'd ordered was doing the bulk of the work for him.

'What is the extraordinary magic about food in Alexandria?' she asked between mouthfuls. 'The ingredients I know, the method of preparations are ones I am familiar with and yet…it all tastes much, much better. It transforms the foods into ones I've never before tasted.'

'The freshness,' he boasted, 'straight from the sea, but also the simple spices, the textures that are as they were meant to be. The crisp in the squid, the char in the grilled *bolti* fish.'

She forked a fried calamari, then followed with a spoonful of the burned onion rice. Next came a bite of the cucumber and tomato salad. Elise was methodical about her eating, rotating as if it were a plan she could not deviate from.

Saleem watched, fascinated, but soon found it frustrating.

He placed his fork as a barrier to hers, forcing her to stop her pattern. When Elise regarded him with a question in her eyes, he held her gaze for a tad too long.

He pointed to the bowl of lemon oil, dotted with sliced hot pepper, and next to it, the tiny clams piled high in a plate. 'You haven't tried that.'

'Extra dressing and a platter of small shells for decoration?'

'*Mulkhulool.*'

He set down his fork, then did the same to hers. Lifting a clam and ensuring it was open, he dipped it into the oil. Cupping any drippings with his other hand, he reached over and held it to her lips. 'Slurp.'

Her cheeks reddened and her eyelids fell—but she did as he asked. He watched the flavours dance across her face. The tumbling of spicy oil, the twisting of the lime, and finally, the shimmying of the briny sweet meat as it slid down her throat.

Her eyes widened. 'Divine.'

Elise abandoned the rest of the food and took to eating only the clams.

Saleem had successfully disrupted her pattern, but the jut of her tongue as she sucked stoked a physical desire for Elise that made him almost regret it.

And no matter how many times he told himself that he should be thinking of ways to woo Olive when Adnan succeeded in bringing her back, Saleem couldn't get Elise out of his mind.

'Mulkhulool is better than oysters!' she exclaimed a few times.

Rather than correcting her mispronunciation of the Arabic word—he found it charming and endearing, in fact—he said, 'I ate very good oysters in Paris. A place called Au Rocher de Cancale.'

Elise fluttered her eyelashes coyly. 'I have heard of it.'

'Now it is my turn to sense that you have a secret.'

Saleem was still leaning forward, still too close. The way the waning sun in the nearly twilight sky caught the dark shine of her hair was a dangerous thing for him to notice.

'Have you read Alexandre Dumas's novels? *The Three Musketeers* or *The Count of Monte Cristo*?'

Saleem shook his head.

'I love him, his novels. Dumas had quite a colourful life and talked about frequenting Au Rocher de Cancale in an interview he did.'

Although Elise was referring to a novelist she likely had never met, not the suitor she might have married still, Saleem twinged with a prick of jealousy. 'What did you like about him?'

She squinted, angled her chin endearingly as she thought about her answer. 'His stories read as belonging in *society*, that they're necessary to our survival because of the deeper morals. Yet, there is also a quality about them that feels intimately personal, frivolous. It's hard to explain, but even in translation, when I read his novels it's as though I'm gossiping with a particularly observant friend. It feels as though he's telling me about what's happened to our other mutual friends.' She took a sip of water and then asked, 'Do you believe it's possible to know a person by only ever reading their words?'

Saleem thought of Olive's letters. He'd believed he'd got to know her, but he had been wrong.

Elise didn't wait for his answer and concluded the subject with a final insight. 'Dumas was mixed race and perhaps I could identify with him on that.' Then she patted her stomach happily. 'That was a very filling meal, thank you.'

'Adnan claims that the common Egyptian man wants nothing more than to ensure his woman is well fed.'

Too late, Saleem realised what he'd said. Would she think he was implying she was his woman?

To cover his faux pas, he stood and attempted to gather their empty dishes. A thing a prince was not accustomed to doing and certainly not with plates that were more metal than ceramic. They banged together. Loudly.

Hearing it, the waiter from the restaurant which had catered their meal emerged from the near gate to relieve Saleem of the task.

'Laa sayedi. Khalee 'anak.' He bowed low, managing at the same time to grab what was in Saleem's hands and then, moving behind him, to catch Elise's.

'You're *our* guest,' Saleem said, surprised she'd followed. 'Bask in the sunset.'

'I could not stay seated another moment with all that food in me.'

A second waiter came out with bowls of dessert on a tray.

Without examining what dessert it was, Saleem handed a bowl to Elise, hoping she would not decline it even though she'd just said she could eat no more, but she must have perceived the look on the waiter's face, too, because she smiled graciously and thanked him in Arabic. 'Shukran.'

When Saleem had taken his bowl and bid the waiter

farewell, he suggested to Elise, 'Shall we take a turn within the fence before eating it?'

Elise's pace was quick, matching his own step for step. Saleem was accustomed to slowing down when he was in the company of his mother or sisters, but now he felt as if he were getting actual exercise. 'You're a fast walker.'

'My father thought it unladylike, a consequence of having no female influence in my formative years.'

'If you like it, what does it matter?'

'I love a brisk stroll, helps clear my mind. That and good food.' Her eyes danced with merriment, 'Shall I slow down for you? Surely a charmed prince's life, the ease of it...'

Saleem laughed. 'You're calling me a sloth?'

'Perhaps.'

'Fancy a race, then? Let us test the truth in your assumption.'

He set down his bowl and rolled up his sleeves. She set down hers and adjusted the band around her hair.

'We should be careful to not disrupt the workers,' she said.

'Nor drop down any holes.'

'Are you withdrawing, *Prince*?'

'Are you, *Lady*?'

'No.'

'Neither am I.'

'Very well.' She pointed to the palm tree with her right hand while touching the fence behind them with her left. 'Three times between here and there, whoever finishes first, wins.'

'All right. On the mark, go.'

Saleem gave her a bit of a head start and then set after her, laughing as he did. She ran with abandon, so determined to win, he almost wanted to throw the race and let her.

At the first lap, she touched the fence before he did and called out, 'One.'

For the second and third, it was Saleem kicking up the dirt, pumping his arms, breathing heavily to overtake her. When he called, 'Three', even though she'd barely touched the palm tree, she didn't give up. She kept her pace and he enjoyed watching her while she came to him.

It was nearly night now, but he could see the sheen on her brow, the heaving of her chest with the effort. He held out his arms, but she refused any aid with a laugh and collapsed on to the fence, letting herself sink to the ground.

Saleem was captivated by Elise's playful side and he said something to that effect.

'Not playful. Competitive,' she countered. 'You may have beaten me, Your Highness, but you had an unfair advantage.'

'Oh?'

'Actually, more than one. Many advantages.' She counted them on her fingers. 'Longer legs. Trousers. Better shoes, more awareness of the earth.' She threw back her head, then shot him a lift of her eyebrow. 'One day, we will have a rematch and I shall beat you.'

'I will await that day, most eagerly.'

They fell into a comfortable silence after that. Professor Aisha and her team were leaving for the day. Mustafa would usher them out, not let anyone bother Saleem and Elise, but for how long could they stay here, alone, their meal done, without it seeming inappropriate?

Not for the first time since her arrival did Saleem wonder what he was doing with Elise. What was this pull he felt towards her, the ease that made it seem they'd been friends for a while?

Surely it was not a problem to want to keep her safe

from her uncle and learn whom her father intended to send the gold bar to. It might even be suitable for him to want to play the gracious host as they waited for Lady Olive's return, but...

'May I ask you a serious question?'

Elise stiffened, not in a way as to announce her nervousness; rather, it was as though she had been looser with him and this stance was more natural to her. 'You may.'

'Is it appropriate, us being alone like this or you staying in the Lodge without a chaperon? Only, I know how it is in England with unmarried young ladies and in Cairo, harem rules restrict life outside of the palace for my mother and sisters.'

'Do you think I'm acting inappropriately? You do not wish to be in my company?'

Saleem heard the bite in her tone. The disappointment. 'I do not wish to compromise your reputation. You must be a respectable young lady.'

'Because I am travelling companion to Lady Olive Whitmore?'

'That is not what I meant.'

She grated her teeth. 'What does us being alone matter if no one is here to comment on it? To see us. Would Mustafa blast it in the papers?'

'Certainly not.'

'Do you not fear for your own reputation?'

'No, but I am a man, can do whatever I please before marriage and excuses will be made for me.'

'Or after marriage.' She huffed. 'You're not just any man, are you? You're one with a title.'

Now Saleem was getting miffed. 'What does that mean?'

'It is not fair that you can seduce a woman until she

gives you her heart and body, but easily drop her whenever she no longer suits because she is not a noble such as yourself.'

Night was settling, the Maghrib athan sounding from a nearby mosque. Saleem prayed sometimes, but not as religiously as Adnan, who did not miss a single prayer, even waking up for Fajr at the break of dawn. Adnan claimed he did so not only as a religious obligation, but because it helped control his impulses.

Saleem thought he should do so now—maybe he could find a spiritual means to curb both the irk and *desire* Elise was drawing from his core. 'I have been with women, yes, but not as you make it sound. They were not love affairs. I haven't and would not do what you describe.'

She shook her head. 'Men can be rakes wherever they want in the world while women must be chaste, wary in any man's company.'

'I do not disagree with you, nor am I proud of past behaviours, but I mean to honour the woman I marry.'

Elise said nothing, but the challenging glint in her eyes put Saleem on the defensive. 'I haven't been with a woman since Olive's first letter back to me and I haven't even asked her to marry me yet. I have yet to woo her properly. You had a suitor—'

'Are you implying I wantonly gave myself to Gerald? We were engaged, Saleem, I thought he would be my husband! That he loved me.'

Where had that come from?

Saleem was struck with a jolt of jealousy. Had he imagined how her voice softened when she said his name? *Gerald.*

He stammered, 'Er... I was not implying...anything untoward. I was trying to state a point.'

A point that was moot and forgotten when Elise scrambled to her feet, piqued. He reached out, brought her back down with both hands.

She landed in his lap—too near to the part of him that wasn't thinking properly. Indeed, what part of him was in her presence?

While she straightened her gown in a huff, he asked, 'Why do you insist on misunderstanding me?'

Saleem let her hands go so that he could hold her by the waist, but his hold was loose. If she tried to get up or move, he would let her—but Elise didn't budge. In fact, she turned a notch. Seemed even to get closer, but not straddling him, exactly.

Did she want to?

He believed she was trying to resist him as much as he was her.

'What is happening between us?' It was a whisper, mostly to himself.

'Saleem,' was Elise's answer, just as quiet. Just as torn. 'I have been hurt by a man before and will not be burned by one again. And I misunderstand you purposely, because I fear that when Olive returns you will turn to her. Woo her. Fall in love with her. Ask her to marry you.' She slipped out of his lap, putting distance between them. 'Olive is my dearest friend in the world. I will not interfere in your and her future together.'

'I was optimistic we might be compatible. Our fathers wanted a marriage, yes, but she defies hers and I'd never marry a woman merely because the khedive wishes it.'

What Saleem said was true, but it hid another truth: he would have difficulty disappointing his father. All that his marriage would represent for Egypt.

Elise sighed resolutely. 'Very well, then, let us endeavour to have no more misunderstandings between us.' She pointed to his other side, the bowls they'd stowed away earlier. 'Would you pass me that dessert?'

He chuckled. 'You're hungry already?'

She lifted a shoulder. 'I could eat.'

He retrieved it, holding it back longer when her fingers touched his to grab it.

'Pomegranate.' Her gaze snagged on his as she took a bite. 'The fruit plays a part in the Persephone myth.'

'How so?'

'Early on, before her mother negotiated her partial release, Persephone protested her capture in Hades' underworld by refusing to eat. Do not smirk at me like that.'

'I'm not smirking, only wondering how long you would last!' He urged, 'Tell me what happened.'

'When she found a pomegranate, it tempted her and she couldn't resist its jewelled seeds. Hades was thus able to bind her to hell. She couldn't escape because she'd eaten the fruit that grew in his realm.'

Saleem leaned forward, his chest brushing her arm, his lips near hers. He stared at them and she licked the spot as if she knew the effect she was having on him and wanted to push further. Drive Saleem completely mad for want of her.

'Have I bound you here now you've eaten the Alexandria-grown version of the fruit?'

'You aren't evil, like Hades, and this is not hell. It is paradise.'

'You know what hell is, Elise?'

She shook her head.

Wanting to touch you, to...kiss you.

That's what he would have said, but knew he could not. Around Elise, he had to consider not only Olive's absence, but his own duties to Egypt. This very spot they'd found would need to be excavated properly, so that the tram project could one day come to Kom el Shoqafa. Saleem's projects were tied, directly or not, to keeping his focus on what he needed to do and who he needed to be as heir to his father's throne.

'What is hell is that we must now take our leave.'

Chapter Twelve

Elise

The next morning, she'd only just sat down to her breakfast when Saleem came to join her. Earlier than his usual time once again, but she was not complaining. Elise was finding it very nice to be in his sunny presence. He made the day brighter. Her food tasted better.

Despite how fraught some moments were the day before, she believed they'd come to a kind of understanding. It wasn't satisfying to recognise there was an attraction between them that would have to remain unfulfilled—but there was some peace of mind in knowing it.

'Good morning, Elise.'

'Good morning, Saleem.'

'How was your sleep?'

'Restful. And yours?'

He grinned, but did not answer her question. 'You have not gone painting since that morning with the peacocks—'

And like he had that morning, Mustafa once again interrupted them. 'Good news! Prince Adnan has found Lady Olive.'

'Thank goodness!' Elise sagged with relief. She'd not allowed herself to think the worst, giving her annoyance over Olive's disappearance priority over her fear that something terrible might happen to a young woman alone in a foreign city. 'And she is safe and sound?'

'She is.' Mustafa handed Saleem the telegram, 'Your brother writes that they should be back on the Saturday train.'

Elise watched Saleem's reaction.

Was he relieved that the woman he believed he'd been writing to was well? Glad at the prospect of earnestly wooing Olive?

He gulped his coffee as he read it. 'Saturday is the day we are set to meet the gold bar buyer. Hopefully, Adnan's train arrives after so we can have the matter with Elise's uncle resolved before then.'

'Very good, my Prince.' Mustafa then turned to Elise. 'The archivist is at the bank today. Would like you to join me? We will ask him about why a drachma symbol should be on a gold bar stamped with the Bank of England mark.'

'I would like that,' she agreed. 'He may give us a clue as to whom my father meant to send it to. Maybe then the meeting with the buyer would not have to happen. Or at least, we could go to it more prepared in terms of knowledge and what we might face there.'

Saleem tilted his head at Mustafa. 'Elise goes with you to the bank, not me?'

The guard stared pointedly at the coffee and put his hand on Saleem's shoulder. 'You've forgotten about the Sham el-Nessim festival in Kafr el Dawwar? Is that not why you've woken up so early this morning? The khedive has sent a caravan of gifts to the city and his mayors. He expects you to represent him there. His servants are waiting for you at the doors.'

'No, that is not why I woke up early.' Saleem rubbed his eyes.

Elise held her breath, she'd not seen him so irked.

But rather than answer why he had, he asked Mustafa, 'Why would the khedive not just send someone from Cairo?'

'Fareed, your sister's husband, took the train directly, I am told by the khedive's servants,' Mustafa relayed. Saleem turned to Elise—that mischievous smoulder on his face set her insides aflutter. 'Will you join me?'

'My Prince, I would advise against it,' Mustafa objected. 'Word will reach your father that you *were* accompanied by an English woman. Plus, it will be all men there, traditional foods. Miss Elise will not enjoy herself.'

Saleem wasn't heeding Mustafa's advice. He was lifting a brow in her direction, challenging her as he did with the race he had proposed last night. 'Elise said herself, she doesn't look like a typical English woman. She is half-Greek and Sham el-Nessim has roots in Coptic Easter traditions. I'll keep introductions to a minimum, talk to Fareed so he will not say anything to my father.' He wagged a playful finger in her direction. 'Also, our guest has an adventurous stomach and may enjoy sampling fesikh and turmus.'

'No one enjoys fermented mullet fish and barely cooked lupini beans, my Prince.'

'And I do believe there is a difference between Greek Orthodox and Coptic Church traditions.' Elise backed Mustafa, but the truth was that she very much wanted to go with Saleem for the simple reason that she was starting to dislike spending any of her waking moments apart from him. That little bit in the catacombs yesterday proved as much.

A very dangerous thing to get used to now that Olive would soon be back.

'You'll come with me then?' Saleem asked enthusiastically.

She laughed because she'd said nothing of the sort. 'Presumptuous of you.'

'I can be presumptuous.'

Elise looked at Mustafa. 'What about the bank?'

'It is not an appointment and tomorrow the three of us will go together,' Saleem answered on his guard's behalf, putting a hand around the man's shoulder and shaking till he'd coaxed a conciliatory smile from him.

'Na'em, we can do that,' Mustafa addressed Saleem. 'I aimed to spare you the khedive's disappointment, but especially Miss Elise's. If you insist on torturing our guest in the heat of a city with nothing to do that is any fun, then she should know I am the better friend to her.'

Elise laughed at their easy banter, puzzled that they were not family by blood.

'*Ya'Allah*, then,' she said, borrowing the word from them which she took to mean that she was ready to go.

The caravan the khedive had sent was two coaches, much like what Saleem had brought to pick her and Olive from the harbour, but the team that came with it were very unlike the Prince's servants at the Lodge. They wore starched maroon uniforms that were reminiscent of those sported by the Queen's Guard at Buckingham Palace, save for the bear fur hats. And it seemed as though they'd taken lessons in stoicism from them. They moved stiffly, as if marching in a parade, and their faces did not betray any emotion whatsoever, even as they spoke to Saleem.

Mustafa had declined to join them and Elise understood why. He did not want to spend any time with such guards who presented themselves as if they never went off duty.

'You're in good hands, my Prince.' He closed the doors

to the royal coach, giving her a wave as Saleem teased him, 'Enjoy your day off.'

'I will!' Mustafa grinned, then pounded on the door to send them off.

It was a smoother ride, the wheels seemingly padded for longer journeys, or perhaps it was the plushness of the seat. But try as she could to enjoy it, the way Saleem kept sneaking glances at her, that smile on his lips, made it difficult to concentrate. To notice anything except him.

'What?' she finally asked.

His left shoulder lifted in a nonchalant motion. 'That dress. Not the kind to get dirty, but I don't know what to expect today.'

'You enjoy not knowing what to expect, do you not, Saleem?'

Keeping his eyes on her, he bent daringly, lifting the hem of her gown to inspect the material between two fingers.

Taking Mustafa's complaint about the city's heat to heart, Elise had picked one of the lightest-coloured gowns in her wardrobe, a soft pink with a beautiful flower pattern throughout. The design was such that a swathe of fabric cinched the waist on the outside as a corset might otherwise do on the inside so that latter was not needed. It was a dress that a body could look the right proportions in without needing the usual embellishments to make it so.

'Was it a bad choice?' she asked.

He nodded. 'It is too beautiful. You are beautiful in it. And Mustafa said it is an all-male event.'

'You should have let me go with him then. Why didn't you?'

He gave her a look that seemed to say *Do not pretend not to know the answer to that question.*

'I will try to push Fareed on to events in order conclude quickly. Kafr el Dawwar is not too far away from the Lodge so we should have a chance to see the city a bit. And perhaps my sister will be there with her husband. I think you would enjoy each other's companionship.'

She looked out of the window, afraid he'd see her disbelief. Or her joy.

Saleem wants me to meet his sister.

She felt his eyes on her, trying to read her emotions, but Saleem couldn't know what it meant to her. What family meant to her. How rare it had been since her mother, that last trip to Greece. Even in the Whitmore home after her father's death, the sense of family had been strained.

A minute later, Saleem said, 'Of course, Lady Olive is likely the companionship you will enjoy more. I am glad for you that she is safe.'

She turned back to him, met his gaze. 'Glad for me? What about yourself? Would not your sister rather meet Olive than me?'

He frowned. 'Why do you think that?'

'Because you are supposed to be wooing her. Introducing her to your family as your intended.'

He nodded contemplatively. 'I am sure they would love to meet her, yes. Will meet her yet. I haven't considered how it would be and suppose that when she and I discuss the note she left before disembarking the ship…that it will clear the confusion between us.'

Elise wanted to hear, but it frightened her, none the less. 'Confusion?'

'I believed that through our letters, I had already met Lady Olive. If that mutual friendship, the *connection* we had in them, was a misguided belief on my part, then… well, meeting her in person will be confusing.'

Guilt squeezed Elise's chest. Olive was safe. She'd run away because she didn't want to marry Saleem, but what if she'd come to her senses? Realised that what Lord Whitmore might want for her was in her best interests. Olive had a romantic view of life. That Elise had felt an instant attraction to Saleem in a falafel queue, before she knew he was a prince, was the sort of story that might delight her, but that did not mean she'd be accepting of her best friend and potential husband having anything beyond an innocent friendship that developed through letters. Letters that Olive herself had encouraged.

'How would you introduce me to your sister, if she is there?' Elise asked

Saleem grinned. 'Carefully. She is one of the biggest gossips at court, I'm afraid. And I don't want to draw the khedive's attention to the kerfuffle with Lady Olive.'

'Very well.' Elise made it a point to smile, but she wondered if it was more than that. She did not want to ponder his response too much, nor think about her feelings on it because if she did, she'd recall that had very much been Gerald's indifferent attitude towards introducing her to his family.

He was a louse who'd tricked her through her uncle, but he was also a man with a title. With a heritage to uphold. Such men did not see futures with women like Elise. Women who had neither the traditional looks nor the lineage of nobility.

Gerald and the man sitting in front of her were decidedly nothing alike in character, but although Elise seemed to forget it often, Saleem *was* a prince.

What larger heritage was there to uphold than the one that came with that title?

* * *

As it turned out, Prince Fareed didn't come with his wife to Kafr el Dawaar, but when Saleem returned from delivering his father's caravan gifts to the city's mayor—the eumda, he'd called him—he had a different surprise.

He knocked on the carriage door. 'Apologies for leaving you while the men deliberated over stinky pipes and tea with sugar. No, more like sugar with a dash of tea.' Saleem sounded especially playful and then Elise heard giggling behind him. She stepped out of the coach and smiled at his dazzling smile, his hands behind his back trying to conceal whatever or whoever was there.

'But I did try to rush, especially when I learned that a certain treat had come with my brother-in-law, Fareed.'

'A treat, good enough to eat?'

His eyes widened playfully. 'I have not told her that you eat anything, please do not scare her! We must satiate you both with cake as soon as possible!'

'*Khaloo,* please get me cake now!'

'Look at your English—the tutor is earning his money, no?' Saleem laughed and then spun, crouching to pick up the girl hiding behind him and lifting her so that he was carrying her. She was a beautiful child, no more than six or seven years of age, with large brown eyes and a button nose. She wore a pink silk dress and her curly auburn hair was done in ringlets and jewelled hair slides.

'Miss Elise Thomas, meet my niece, Miss Maysoon Fareed.'

'This is the most special May? A pleasure.' Elise stuck out her hand.

May was momentarily shy, pushing her head into Saleem's neck until he murmured something reassuring in

Arabic to her. She then faced Elise, pushing her beringed chubby fingers out.

'Hello,' she squeaked. 'Nice...meet you.' Her English was hesitant, out of practice, but Elise could tell that she was an intelligent girl.

Saleem met Elise's gaze, 'They pulled out the *feseekh* with green onions and poor May very smartly felt sick at the smell. Fareed thinks I'm doing him a favour, but I only have a short window. There's a park nearby, for families. A renowned oud player from the area will be performing and I believe we can find cake on the way.'

'*Ya'Allah* then,' she exclaimed.

'I do love it when you say that.'

The three of them started walking, moving along the canal beneath which was a narrow tributary of the Nile. They passed all manner of people, mostly families out with their children since it was a holiday in the city. Most ignored them at first, but when they saw the khedive's guards trailing Saleem, they gave them a wide berth.

Saleem pointed out the church being built, a beautiful white building soaring with dual minaret structures on either side, tall crosses carved into the edifice in the form of tiny windows that must be stained glass from within. 'It is not quite Easter yet, we are early for the Sham el-Nessim festivities, but they say the church will hold its first mass that evening.'

'So the occasion here is not only a Christian one?'

'Sham el-Nessim stems from the time of the Pharaohs. When Egypt was made Christian then it was associated with Easter, but even after the Islamic conquest, the observance on this day remained. Today it is less a religious celebration than a promise that spring is nigh and with traditions that no one thinks too much about—'

'Khaloo!' May addressed her uncle, her shyness gone,

but her annoyance at not understanding everything he was saying apparent. She talked for a few minutes, keeping Saleem's attention on her while Elise watched. She'd seen his charm and ease with many before, but it was his devotion to May, the way he carried her without complaint and patiently listened to all she said, that Elise was sure was her favourite side of him.

Saleem will make a wonderful father.

She scolded herself for the thought, the false hope that accompanied it. She forced herself to be more realistic.

The prince enjoys your friendly company. That does not mean he will be the father of your children!

'May says I'm talking too much English and she can't follow along.'

'You are ever the translator.'

He laughed.

'Well, if you have to go back, she and I can spend time together. May can teach me some Arabic and I can be her English tutor for the day.'

The girl whispered something in his ear, causing Saleem to chuckle before sharing it. 'May claims you are too pretty to be a tutor.'

Elise recalled what Saleem had said about his niece. She stopped, widened her eyes, and made a show of touching his arm to stop him as well. When the girl looked at her, Elise slowed her words, so May would understand. 'Me, pretty? That is a very big compliment coming from the most beautiful girl in the world.'

Elise couldn't decide whether it was uncle or niece who gifted her with the most approving look then.

The three of them spent the next hour enjoying the soulful music of the oud player, seated on swing sets in the park, her in one, May on Saleem's lap in the other.

While the stringed instrument's sounds mingled with laughter of people and bird song, he pumped his legs to delight May. He peppered her with kisses, unabashedly pleased with his niece's joy.

Once, he caught Elise staring and he threw her a charming lopsided smile, one that said he knew exactly what she was thinking: that she wouldn't mind one of those kisses herself.

She flushed, embarrassed because it was absolutely true.

Then, the three of them played a fun game of 'translation' where Elise said one word in English and Saleem and May vied to guess what its Arabic equivalent was. Of course, Saleem let May win every time.

Before he pulled himself away to return to his duties and promised to pick them up with the carriage when all was done, he bought Elise and May two cups of pistachio-and-orange-blossom-flavoured sweet cream churned over blocks of ice until it was a taste of paradise. Perfect for handling the day's hot sun and which they all agreed was better than cake.

'I'll leave the guard to watch, make sure you're both safe.'

He winked at Elise before crouching to bid farewell to May. 'Take care of Elise, she is our guest and cannot speak Arabic so you must be a good host.'

'Hat'her, Khaloo,' she promised.

The next while with just the two of them was as much fun and May helped pass the time quickly. She was a vibrant girl with an abundance of energy which certainly didn't match Elise's persona at that age, but she imagined that it was like watching a young Saleem. May was just as energetic and talkative to the elderly woman peddling her Sham el-Nessim textile crafts—woven bags and cushions with spring-like designs—as she was to the group of boys kicking a ball between them. When language proved a barrier, May engaged Elise in a clapping game.

The chant she recited to go along with it might not have been exactly the same words, but had Elise marvelling at the universality of 'Pat-a-cake, Pat-a-cake, Baker's Man'.

It was almost disappointing when Saleem returned with May's father in tow. *Almost.*

'Baba!' The girl leapt to him while Saleem feigned hurt.

'I give her all the fun things and her father gets that greeting while I get nothing?'

Prince Fareed was older than she'd have expected, but he was distinguished looking with slicked back silver hair and kind eyes. He set his daughter down and said in perfect English, 'Thank you for watching Maysoon.'

'It was my pleasure. You have the loveliest of daughters.'

'Unfortunately, we have a train to catch back, but we will see you and the Lady Olive at court soon, I am certain. The family awaits her arrival and are most looking forward to welcoming her.'

While May gave Elise a farewell hug, she tried not to be jealous of Prince Fareed's comment. The belonging that might be Olive's. A family that would not be Elise's.

It was late afternoon by the time they left the city. 'We will be back before supper, much to Mustafa's chagrin.'

Saleem watched her for a long moment before patting the seat next to him enticingly. 'Join me?'

He held out a hand to lead her across the coach. To sit close to him. And he didn't let go of her hand when she had.

'There was a moment back there,' he said, his breath a whisper because he was so close, 'when you watched me with May. You wished for me to kiss you, too.'

She snorted despite herself. 'You presume, Prince Saleem.'

He shrugged. 'That will be the second time that I have today. Assuming that you would come, that you would enjoy yourself being the first.'

'Well, I am glad to have come.' She stared at him, gathering all her boldness. 'Maybe one is permitted presumptions, if said presumptions are correct.'

He laced their fingers together, slowly, adeptly, as if he were stoking a fire in her blood. They both twisted so that their lips were a breadth apart. 'I was correct, then.'

'You were.'

Her free hand fingered his jaw as his hand came around her waist. She nearly went in first, her anticipation exhausted, her patience spent. No worries mattered then. Not Olive, not what Saleem planned to do when she arrived.

Then came the touch of his lips on hers. Hot, generous. Gentle, yet demanding. Their kiss was fast and hard, while also being slow and worthy of being savoured.

Elise had never experienced such a sensation and she wanted it again. She opened her mouth wider, stuck out her tongue and he entwined it with his. When he made to withdraw, she growled and he let go of her hand to grasp her chin, cupping it so she couldn't move. Saleem's mouth covered her upper lip and then moved to her lower. His tongue tangled with hers, urging it meet his until the two were practically sparring.

She pushed her fingers through his curls, needing to catch her breath. 'Saleem,' she gasped.

He let go of her chin, his lips skirted her jaw, giving her a small reprieve and, she feared, trying to rein himself in.

He gave her one last peck on the lips before taking a deep breath and pulling away. 'Apologies, but that yearning I witnessed had to be settled. I am a man who takes his hosting duties seriously.'

Elise could think of nothing witty to say after that. Indeed, she could think of nothing at all, she could only savour the feel of his mouth on hers.

Chapter Thirteen

Saleem

'I'd like to paint your portrait,' Elise said as they made their way to the archivist's office in the Anglo-Egyptian Bank. 'A token of thanks for a most generous host.'

Saleem stopped before the office door of one *Mr Patterson.* It was the heavy wooden type, the kind that stood in a dark contrast to the lightness of the space, the brightness coming in from the large, open windows and the white-tiled floors and starkly painted walls.

He was glad to be back in Alexandria, but he could not deny the perfection of the day before. How glorious it had been to have Elise in his arms, what it felt like to finally kiss her. And though, out of respect for her, he'd pulled away, it had been one of the hardest things Saleem had ever done in his life.

He wanted Elise. Not just physically, that was a part of it, certainly, but it was more than that. Saleem had watched her yesterday with May. The three of them had laughed and played together. It was fun for him, but more than anything, he'd felt that she was happy for the first time since she'd arrived.

Perhaps the relief over Olive's being found contributed

to Elise being loose and carefree. And though they'd had fun at the catacombs, Saleem believed that the sense of family provided by May and Fareed was the thing that made her enjoy herself best.

It was something he'd assumed about Olive from the letters they'd exchanged. He believed she yearned for a place in a large family—or maybe that's what he'd hoped to see in her. Olive had run from the prospect, but Elise seemed willing to run to it.

She made Saleem happy.

And as conflicted as he might be about his marriage prospects and facing his father over his duties to Egypt, Saleem was sure that he wanted to be more to Elise. Not just her 'host'.

'Unless,' she said, 'you believe I cannot do you justice on a canvas.'

Saleem thought of Olive's portrait, how it had surprised him, but also because the author of the letters wasn't who he'd pictured. He wasn't sure why, but his instincts told him that if the portrait of Olive had looked more like the woman standing before him now, he'd not have been surprised.

She is beautiful.

The hall was empty—Mustafa had cleared it for them—so Saleem leaned in, and playfully tapped Elise's nose.

'My handsomeness *can* be overwhelming,' he joked, 'but you're the painter to most do me justice.'

'What is it, then?' She read him frighteningly well. Saleem couldn't mask his doubts, his feelings, around her.

He hadn't yet knocked on Mr Patterson's door, but it opened then with a jolt before he could pull away from Elise.

'Oh!' exclaimed a voice.

Saleem turned to find it was Miss Stephania. The

shocked look on her face put him on the defensive. His memory of how evasive she'd been with Elise the night of his dinner party was still fresh.

She looked between him and Elise, as if she were trying to figure out their relationship. What concern was it of hers?

'Prince. Elise... Miss Thomas,' she said, nearly with a curtsy. 'What are you doing here?'

Elise smiled stiffly and adjusted the hat she wore, a straw one with a green ribbon bow and silk flowers.

'This is the Anglo-Egyptian Bank and Elise is an Englishwoman after all.' Saleem tried to put humour in his tone, but he'd likely failed in the endeavour.

'And what brings you here, Miss Dimitri?' Elise managed to sound politer.

'Stephania, please.' She took a deep breath and smiled. 'A relative died unexpectedly and I have been trying to *settle* some matters for them regarding an account held here. Even non-Anglos are permitted.'

'I'm sorry for the loss of your relative.' Elise instinctively reached for the older woman's hand and squeezed. Whatever rudeness Stephania had subjected her to seemed forgotten.

The older woman put a hand on Elise's and then, surprising them both, leaned into a hug. 'Thank you, my dear.'

Elise patted Stephania's back. She was as gentle with her as she'd been with May.

'Ahh, I was wondering what was stopping my next appointment from entering.' Mr Patterson had appeared. He was a middle-aged man with flaming red hair and spoke with a Scottish brogue. The suit he wore seemed more like what would be worn by one of his father's intelligence officers than a banker. 'It appears you two are familiar with each other.'

'Yes.' Stephania sniffled as she pulled away from Elise. 'I should let you get on with your meeting, but perhaps the two of you would like to join me after you're done? There will be a play at the Serapeum this afternoon. A small gathering, a youth troupe of actors Portelli likes to support in their artistic endeavours.

'Afterwards, we could have you over to our home. I make a delicious Greek moussaka. Egyptians have their own style of the dish, but mine is a long-held family recipe with fresh oregano grown in my garden. What do you say?'

'Greek moussaka is my favourite. I haven't eaten a good one since my mother passed,' Elise said, tempted perhaps by her own hunger. 'But, alas, I am subject to my host's schedule.'

She looked at Saleem, adeptly putting the decision in his hands. Except, he had not been alone with Elise nearly enough yesterday. Who knew how long this appointment with Mr Patterson would take and how things would change once Adnan and Olive were back?

'It sounds like a great time—unfortunately, today is not free. My guard, Mustafa, is at the end of the hall. Perhaps arrange another day with him or have Portelli send word?'

He made to usher Elise into the office, excusing them as delicately as he could. Stephania seemed not to want to let her go, but it was a nodding nudge from Mr Patterson that finally had her relinquishing Elise.

'Yes, I will do that. Send a formal invitation, have a dinner party. It was wonderful to see you.'

When she had left, Mr Patterson introduced himself and ushered Saleem and Elise into his office, 'Have a seat, get comfortable while I find us refreshments and then we'll start straight away.'

Saleem held out a chair for Elise and settled next to her, bringing his own closer and disliking that they were the sort with armrests.

A double barrier between us.

He reprimanded his own ridiculousness.

'Stephania seems different,' she said.

'Odd that we should meet her here.'

Elise nodded absentmindedly. 'What is the Serapeum, then?'

He chuckled. 'That is not why you did not want me declining her invitation. Admit it, it was the prospect of moussaka.'

'I can appreciate things other than food.' Elise playfully swatted his arm, but Saleem caught her hand, brought it to his lips. Instinctively.

The light moment was trapped in the air between them. Turned to something less playful, more serious. A moment he wasn't sure what to do with.

'Saleem.' Was his name on her lips a gasp or a plea? He could not tell exactly, only that it rippled through his body with a wicked pace.

'The Serapeum of Alexandria is the site of an ancient Greek temple,' he said. 'Only ruins now, but a beautiful spot overlooking the sea. A play there would be grand, but Mustafa would probably need to vet it more. I can, for the most part, roam Alexandria pretty freely, but a prince in a public place for an extended period of time would require planning. Also, I selfishly wanted to spend time with you today, before…well, Adnan and Lady Olive return.'

And I am forced to reckon with my duties as said Prince.

Elise closed her eyes, bit the bottom of her lip and gently pulled her hand away when she heard Mr Patterson's return, his shoes clacking along the tiles of the hall outside the room.

'What do you have in mind for our time?' she whispered.

'We start with a swim at the Lodge. Truly, it is what you should have done that first full day in Alexandria. I will have the kitchens make Egyptian-style moussaka which we call *me'sa'a*, from the root word for "cold", which makes it wonderful beach food.'

'I do not know how to swim.'

He grinned. 'I can teach you if you'd like.'

Before she could answer, Mr Patterson had returned. He apologised for coming with only his own glass of water. 'Your guard insisted I could not serve you anything.'

'He is protective. Do not be insulted.'

'I am not at all. Discreetness and privacy are necessary in my work—which made that wee collision at the door unfortunate.' He brought his office chair around the desk to sit before them. 'What can I do for you both?'

Elise pulled the gold bar from her bag and handed it to Mr Patterson. 'I found this among a deceased...relative's things.'

They'd agreed not to mention her father or uncle, but the way Elise strained on the word 'relative' pained Saleem. He could see how much family meant to her. How devasted she felt at the loss of her father and bereft at not having any loved ones left to call her own.

Saleem leaned forward. 'It bears the mark of the Bank of England, but as we were examining it, we noticed the marking there.' He tapped at the corner and watched as the man's eyes widened. It wasn't exactly the same as the shopkeeper's who seemed to be looking for it—but Mr Patterson's look was not one of surprise either.

'You've seen something like it before,' Elise voiced the conclusion he'd come to. 'Another bar like it, perhaps?'

Mr Patterson glanced at the closed door behind her. He shook his head, but said, 'Yes. I've seen one like it before. Many, many, like it, in fact. I would ask your relative's name, Miss…? And if you have any sort of document proving it, then I will have more to say on the matter.'

Elise looked at Saleem and he could see that she was seeking his advice. She wasn't sure if she should tell Mr Patterson the truth of her identity, but instinct told Saleem that the banker was honest, that he had no ulterior motivation or desire to hurt her.

He nodded.

Elise pulled out her passport, showed him the page quickly first and then handed it to Mr Patterson. 'My name is Elise. *Clifton*. My father is the deceased relative and his name was Thomas Clifton.'

It was natural for Egyptians to take their father's names, but there was an apology in her eyes that put Saleem on alert. Had Elise tried to deceive him by omitting her last surname?

Mr Paterson replied, 'Then, ma'am, I will speak as freely as I am able, but…do hesitate to say anything in the presence of others.' He subtly indicated he did not want Saleem to be there, but Elise felt otherwise.

'I want Saleem to stay. I trust him implicitly and need his counsel.'

Elise *needed* him. He would not disappoint her.

Mr Patterson said, 'All right then. I can confirm that Thomas Clifton did have an account in this very bank, but two years ago, things changed. My understanding is that he did not want his brother or official authorities to know of the account, its contents.'

'I don't understand,' Elise said. 'Investigators checked his holdings after his death. It was the only thing they cared to check rigorously. Papa's lawyer implied they'd looked through all his offshore accounts. Did they miss this one?'

'On official records, Mr Clifton closed the account, withdrew its contents and spent them on his business holdings back in England. In truth, he merely changed the contents and the account holder. That is what I mean by secrecy in the job.' Mr Patterson smiled.

'What do you mean by "changed the contents"?' Saleem asked.

Mr Patterson handed Elise the gold bar she'd found back. 'He turned his money into gold bars, like this one.'

'He was sending them here? I found this single one in our London apartment.'

'I do not know about that one, but he has been shipping them periodically for the past two years in larger quantities to the account holder.' Mr Patterson rubbed the bridge of his nose under the rim of his spectacles.

'Whose name did he put on the account?'

'That I do not have permission to disclose,' Mr Patterson said. 'But if you give me where you are staying in Alexandria, they will likely reach out to you once they learn you are Thomas Clifton's daughter. My belief is that that person has, by your father's wishes, been entrusted to oversee your inheritance.'

Elise collapsed into her chair. Saleem knew she was wondering who her father had entrusted with it, whether they were simply a friend or if, unbeknownst to her, Elise did have family in the city.

Mr Patterson handed Saleem a notebook and pencil.

'If you would kindly write down your address, I will pass it on.'

Elise objected, 'I'd rather Saleem's place of residence not come into the matter.'

'It is not a problem, Elise,' he said.

'Please.'

'Very well.' Saleem returned the writing implements. 'I can send my guard back here in a few days to check you've obtained permission to disclose the name and how best to reach the account holder. Would that suit?'

'Certainly.'

Elise thanked Mr Patterson, but it was her look of appreciation for Saleem that made him believe he'd not need a swim later on.

He was already floating.

They walked down to the beach at the Lodge after the noon sun had lessened. Elise brought her easel and paints. 'You pose; I will try to capture your likeness.'

'You're very demanding,' Saleem teased. He waved a hand over his loose white galabaya, 'Underneath are only cut-off trousers. I have come for a swim and to teach a lesson.'

Elise shook her head and, setting down her materials on the blanket the servants had laid out, she twirled in her summer dress. While the burnt orange skirt of it was full, the capped sleeves and revealing neckline made it so that if he stared too much he'd likely embarrass himself. 'This is a painting dress and underneath are garments *not* for swimming.'

He chuckled to hide his yearning to know precisely what garments Elise was referring to.

'A painting dress would be fine getting wet then,' he urged.

'Maybe, if I've made enough progress.'

He conceded, letting her position him at the best angle. She fussed with his arms and head among the pillow cushions the servants had put out. Her fingers in his hands, underneath his chin, nearly undid him, but it was the way he caught her regarding him that steeled his desire.

Elise finds it as difficult to be around me as I her.

The realisation made him most glad, but also more dangerously tempted.

For a while, he basked in the sun, content to leave Elise to her task and reflect on the contentedness he felt when he forgot what awaited him beyond this place, beyond that moment.

The seagulls swept overhead in a nearly cloudless sky, the sands and blanket with the heat of the sun warm beneath him. Their bellies were full from the moussaka they'd consumed and the sweet tea they'd drunk.

'You're eating like an Egyptian now,' he commented, recalling the way Elise had dabbed at the tomato sauce at the side of her lip with a piece of balady bread. How her eyes closed a tad as she let the aubergine bites melt on her tongue.

That satisfied look she got when she ate, Saleem loved it so much.

'Don't talk,' she reprimanded softly, 'you're distracting me.'

'I quite like being a distraction.'

Her lips curled and her nose wrinkled at his comment, causing Saleem to be distracted.

For a long time after, they were silent. No one was near and he could almost believe that they were the only two people left in the whole of the world. Saleem didn't think he would mind it so much were it true.

'At the bank, my passport. My name. *Clifton*. I'm sorry it was the first you'd heard it.'

'Why didn't you tell me it before?'

'Olive had mentioned that Muslims, Egyptians take their father's names and I...well, my surname is associated with negativity in England. Mr Patterson was discreet, as he said, but Papa's businesses were regarded for a long time as criminal. He'd become legitimate, but none forgot it. I could tell you horror tales of how people treated my mother while she was alive, but worst still was how my father was treated after his death.

'You know a little of the investigation in terms of monies, but the circumstances of his actual death? They basically left him to rot, unburied. Neither I or his lawyer or even Lord Whitmore with his political connections could do anything to expedite the case and, when it was concluded, the coroner only said, "Well, we can't tell if he fell or was pushed."'

'The dead should be buried immediately. It is the right and honourable thing to do. I'm sorry for your suffering, Elise. For your father, the indignity pushed upon him.'

Elise's sad smile tore at Saleem's heart.

'With you being a prince, I did not want to bring you into it. Even my uncle, who was and likely remains the biggest criminal to emerge from the Clifton name, has managed to elude it. People forgot his start...he lives without any hindrances. What if he is here, Saleem? Offering to buy gold bars because he thinks it will lead him to the ones Papa has hidden here?'

'Your uncle would not know that your father trusted someone to hold them in the bank for you?'

'I guess not. To be honest, I wouldn't either. Papa trusted no one—Lord Whitmore with me, perhaps, but his long-time lawyer died a few years ago. He was still with the same firm, but maybe Papa didn't trust them to let them in on this one?'

Elise shook her head, then buried her face in her hands.

Saleem sat up, inched towards her. But he dared not touch her right then. Who knew what his attempt at comforting her would lead to?

'Mr Patterson will contact the account holder,' he said, 'and we'll learn who your father trusted. If your uncle is here, we will find him at the meeting tomorrow, ensure he does not get his hands on any gold bars and find *something* with which to detain him and learn if he had anything to do with your father's death.'

She sniffled, lifted her face and smiled. Thankfully, Saleem's words, rather than his touch, had comforted her.

'You don't have to come to the antique seller either. Mustafa and I can go, now we have the sketch of your uncle. You don't have to face him at all.'

'Can I let you know my decision tomorrow, then?'

'Certainly.' Saleem wondered, 'May I ask, if your uncle was able to escape the Clifton surname, why wasn't your father, despite him working to establish his business legitimacy?'

'My uncle married an English rose of a woman with a title—lovely, fair, but not rich. I think he asked my father for money secretly or even continued to work with him before my father went legitimate. Regardless, Uncle Andrew would hide his money origins from his high society friends. Shower them with his purported generosity. With his respectable marriage, people forgot his beginnings. My father, on the other hand, married a Greek woman, never was good at deception. If he didn't like you, you knew it. Even if they were able to ignore his surname, they never saw him as anything but a lover of a d —Well I cannot say the word, it is a slur but it means someone who is foreign and has dark skin.'

'That's terrible, Elise.' So much about her character, her insecurities, made much more sense to Saleem now. 'Did your father try to shelter you both from the prejudice? Was he a good husband? A good father in that sense?'

Elise met his gaze. 'Thomas Clifton was as good a husband and father as he could be. He loved us and ignored what people were saying about him, about my mother. About us as a family. I understood he didn't want to give them power by acknowledging the hatred outside of our home, but it hurt, nevertheless. I never felt good enough. And then certain experiences solidified the fact that I wasn't.'

She was referring to her suitor. Gerald.

'You are not only good enough, Elise. You're perfect.'

She frowned at his words. 'Maybe, Saleem, a random generous man in a falafel line can say that. But a prince, heir to the throne of a country with a timeless history? No nobleman could ever say that the mixed-race daughter of a criminal is perfect.'

Elise squared her shoulders, before continuing, 'I am not sad about it, however. These last few days have showed me that I am coming to terms with it. Once I figure out if my uncle had anything to do with Papa's death and meet the person in Alexandria whom he trusted, I will be free. My father left me a sum of money that will keep me independent and I can go on with my life. Pursue my art, perhaps. Eat my way across the world. Turn the pages on my next chapter. I can find contentment in my spinsterhood.'

'Spinsterhood!' Saleem scoffed. 'You're hardly a spinster, Elise.'

She angled her head, neither agreeing nor disagreeing. 'Nevertheless, spinsters live by their own rules and that is what I mean to do.'

Elise wanted a family, belonging more than anything, it was plain to see. Why couldn't she see it herself? Or maybe she knew, but had talked herself out of *not* thinking that that was what she wanted.

Saleem could challenge her to know her own truth. 'And what if you dared to fall in love with someone?'

'Would you go back to your position so I can finish this painting?' she asked, completely ignoring his question.

He grinned. 'I'm afraid we will need another session.'

She dropped her eyelids and he touched a strand of her hair as the sea's breeze whipped it around her face. Her most perfect face.

Saleem found himself confessing, 'I long for your same openness towards future possibilities but my father is...*demanding*. I have tried to balance what he wants with what I want. Find a happy medium, but the khedive is a hard man to please. Honestly, I'm not sure I'll ever want to not please him, to not make him proud of me, so I wonder if that means I'll be sacrificing what I want for ever.'

'How is he not proud of you, Saleem?' Elise's angry tone surprised him. And while he'd avoided touching her for fear of what it might lead to, she boldly cupped his face in her hands, made him look at her. Almost shouted as she said, 'You're brilliant and kind, you care deeply for this city and its people. The tram project? The catacombs? Even that queue at the falafel stand? I've seen it, watched your charm, your authenticity. Everyone who knows you, even for a little while, loves you.

'And all you've done for me? My goodness, Saleem, if your father cannot tell your princely merit or see that you will be the best thing that ever happened to Egypt, then he must be a fool of a man.'

'I should set you on him the next time he doubts me.' Saleem chuckled, putting his hands over hers so that they would not leave his face. He was grateful for her. Her friendship. The excitement she brought on when they were together. If he wasn't careful, Saleem would get used to her presence in his life. 'I have faults, too.'

Keeping their gazes locked, Saleem took both her hands from his face and lifted her as he rose himself. When he stepped back, he enjoyed how her eyes roamed over his galabaya, snagging on the place where his trousers began beneath its thin cotton.

'Oh?' she gasped. 'What faults?'

'That I am terribly presumptuous.'

And then he ran them into the sea, dragging her with him, and splashing himself with the ice-cold water that did nothing to curb his desire for Elise. The seawater was waist level when she tugged at his arm so that he stopped and faced her.

'I don't want a swimming lesson, Saleem,' she sputtered.

'What do you want, Elise?'

She said nothing, but the yearning in her eyes was his answer. He was kissing her before he could think straight about why he shouldn't be.

Her arms came around his waist. His pulled her close. With his free hand he cupped her chin so his access wouldn't be interrupted.

Elise tasted like honey dripping from the sun. And he couldn't get enough of her lips. Her wet hair brushing his hands. Her chest heaving upon his.

Her dress soaking, Elise shivered, and it was the thing that finally forced Saleem to stop.

'You'll get sick,' he said when she protested the distance between them. He practically had to drag her out of the water.

And as he placed a towel over her soaking clothes, Saleem tried *not* to hear Elise's petulant demand.

'Come to my room tonight.'

Chapter Fourteen

Elise

Until he knocked, she wasn't sure Saleem would come. She had a hope, could not sleep for want of it being realised. For *want*, more generally.

Would he throw caution to the wind? Dump it in the sea as she had done when he'd dragged her into it?

Olive would be back tomorrow. Who knew what would happen then?

For now, all Elise knew was that her and Saleem's time alone was limited. And that she desired him with every fibre of her being.

She couldn't deny it any longer.

Had it ever been the same with Gerald? He had his nefarious motives prompted by her uncle and had been the first to suggest coming to her room. Despite what her uncle had said to her father about Elise's wantonness, Gerald had had to plead with her, because back then she *was* young and innocent. And he had got to her by understanding that she did aspire to be a lady. To have people treat her with respect.

Gerald flaunted his title, said she would manage his home as the Baroness, be the darling of the *ton*. Even claimed that it would be her revenge against those who'd never welcomed her mother for her skin colour or her father for his business reputation.

When she'd allowed Gerald to kiss her it had been sloppy, disappointing, but Elise's inexperienced mind had been sure their lovemaking would be better. She'd imagined he would sweep her away, that the same sensations she felt during a good painting session would translate to her body. But when he was in her room and he had her naked beneath him, Gerald quickly took his pleasure and did nothing to ensure hers was fulfilled. When she'd tried for more, he'd called her 'a needy tart'.

But Saleem's kiss? She'd never ever before felt like that. It had lit a fire within her that was so hot she thought she'd combust.

I can find his room, go to him.

Nothing mattered except this last night before Olive returned. Not what Saleem would do to appease his father. Not even his title.

She was walking to her door when the light rapping came and she leapt to open it.

Saleem stood there, a plate in hand and a sheepish grin on his face.

But she barely noticed either of those things since he had come bare-chested. With his clothes, she could only imagine the fine form beneath and in the water earlier it had been outlined for her. To witness his smooth bronze chest and his slim waist with the muscles of his abdomen taut was another experience altogether.

Elise fisted her hands and tried to lull her heavy breathing.

'I came, bearing biscuits.' He spoke in a hushed tone, the merriment in his smile diverging from the intensity in his eyes. 'All I could muster from the kitchen without waking anyone.'

'Come in.' Elise angled to let him pass. He'd bathed, his cologne had notes of invigorating lemon. Not that she needed further invigorating.

Saleem inched forward, but stopped before passing the threshold. 'If we do this, I have a condition.'

She sidled close to him so he had to move the plate of biscuits around her back and catch her waist.

'When I am hungry, Saleem, I cannot think clearly. Cannot plan,' she said. 'It is quite the problem, but once I am fed I can handle anything. Take on the world if I must—hear the conditions. But my hunger for you, Saleem, is beyond food and is quite ridiculous. It started in that falafel line—maybe because the single fritter did nothing for me.'

He barely managed a nod, her words affecting him in a way that was empowering for her to watch. Made her bolder, more honest.

'It nearly frightens me, in fact, how desperately I want you. I am rational, level-headed, only freeing my emotions on a canvas. With you, it is as though that paintbrush dances inside of me, awakening body parts which seem to now have minds of their own.'

She touched her left breast as he watched, 'Here.' Then she slid her fingers down the silk of her gown to the heat building between her legs. 'Here.'

'Elise.' Her name was a groan on his lips and Saleem all but pushed her into the room, nearly slamming the door.

She twisted her arm to take the plate from his hand.

He'll need them free.

No sooner had she set it down on the night stand than he used them to grasp her waist, turn her around and pull her close. His mouth dipped to her neck and she pushed back her hair to give him unrestricted access.

'What I am trying to say is that I don't need your biscuits—' she angled her head so her lips touched his '—and I am saying yes to your condition.'

'You don't know what it is.' He peppered her jaw with tiny kisses, too small but achingly close together. 'You are a savvy woman. You would not need to see it in writing before you agree to it?'

'You are an honest man. And I have sampled the merchandise.' She ran her finger up and down his bare chest.

When her index touched the area beneath his navel, the smattering of hair there, he put a hand over it, stopping it from going further downwards. He stepped back, his eyes trailing over her bare legs, snagging at her heaving chest, then finally lifting again to meet hers.

His eyes clouded. 'Fine, we can negotiate later.'

Then he pounced and her insides sang. It was a glorious kiss, better, if it were possible, than the ones that came earlier. Elise wanted more, pulling him close, clinging to his back, refusing to let him end it.

She felt Saleem's hardness, his readiness for her. And her wetness was there, too. It could be quick. Quick would work.

But Saleem's hand wrapped around her neck, his thumb reaching between her teeth, slowing them down. She sucked there and he groaned, his tongue moving to scrape under her ear.

It was as if he was tugging on a string that directly connected to the most sensitive parts of her. She must have growled aloud because he chuckled in her ear.

'You approve?'

In response, her hands came around the top of his shorts,

nearly low enough to touch the top of his buttocks, but he moaned in turn.

'You approve?' she teased.

And then she was trying to pull him towards the bed. It wasn't far, but Saleem resisted, the hand that was at her waist falling to the back of her thigh. There, his fingers weren't as shy as hers had been and they massaged her bottom through the gown. The hand he had on her neck swept to her chest, where he did the same.

Her nipples hardened beneath the material and her skin felt as if it was on fire. She'd never hated a nightgown more.

Regretting that she had to step back from his hands to do so, she slipped it off, shimmying until it pooled at her feet.

'Oh.' Saleem stepped back to examine her nakedness. He took her waist and walked her to where the moonlight came in from the balcony. 'You're beautiful, Elise...but I...'

'No buts. No promises. Nothing but tonight. Nothing but you and me. Elise and Saleem.'

He murmured something in Arabic she couldn't understand, but didn't dare ask for a translation lest it delay the return of his hands. His touch on her bare skin. Everywhere. Roaming, as if she were a blank canvas and he had never seen one.

And the way Saleem looked at her? *Reverent.*

She wanted to undress him and look at him the same way, but when she tried, he held her hands gently behind her back. 'Wait,' he commanded. 'If satiation makes you rational and hunger clouds your mind, I enjoy the *savouring* in either case.'

He lifted a brow and she understood that he would not continue until she co-operated. She dipped her chin in a nod and he smiled. Roguishly.

His lips followed where his fingers had been moments

before. His tongue flicked over her nipples, one and then the other, cupping and kneading between kisses. The more she moaned, the faster he moved.

'Mercy,' she cried.

He stopped and stared at her, waiting until the heaving in her chest subsided and then he spun her around until her palms were flush against the wall next to the balcony door.

He dipped to where her thigh met her buttocks, caressing with his hands while letting his hardness press into her. But then it was gone and she peeked behind to see where he'd gone, but he'd crouched to get better access. Gently he spun her around so that his gaze met hers. So she could see him, watch him as he looked up to her while painstakingly doing his savouring.

Her anticipation threatened to spill.

Two of his fingertips reached the bud of her need and twirled. 'Do you like that?' he asked.

'You're perfectly aware of the answer.' The reprimand came out between gasps and in a huff.

And then those fingers delved deeper. The surprise of it after going so slow had Elise quaking.

She *needed* his mouth on her.

She dug her fingers into his hair, encouraging it. But he laughed at her roughness, pleased.

And when his tongue finally came, she was sure it was because she'd sent out a magnetic signal that it couldn't help but answer.

'Shall I eat?' he teased.

'Yes,' she panted.

He gorged. Nipping and biting and sucking her as though she was a dessert he *had* to finish before it was stolen away.

But Saleem's mouth wasn't even enough, her need ascending. She lowered herself to the floor, made for the waistband of his trousers, pushing them down until she had unfettered access to his manhood. He stood, lifting her with him.

Elise ogled his nakedness and he, in turn, seemed proud to have her witness his unabashed desire for her.

'You are a fine specimen of a man.'

They collided again and their kiss, him cupping her face, she cupping his, was more about them covering one another's moans.

Somehow, she ended up on the bed, sprawled with him on top of her. But he was catching his breath and she wanted him inside her.

Elise was done waiting. She pushed him off and held his arms over his head while she positioned herself, straddling him.

He could have resisted her, but he allowed it. Patient, amused.

And that gave her pause. 'What if I, too, know how to savour?'

She moved her hips over his erection, not entirely giving him access to her, but to tease it, slightly out of reach. Then she pushed back, taking him in hand until his breath became laboured as it pulsated in response.

Elise's struggle was a three-way one. She was torn between wanting to watch him happily squirm, wanting to take him in her mouth so he'd shout her name and wanting to guide him inside her so that she could satiate her own hunger.

Then he decided for her. Grabbing her hips and positioning her over him, he held her there and slid inside her.

They rocked together at a quick and steady pace that

quickly turned hard and fast. Frenzied. And good. Very, very good.

Elise was before a steep drop and nothing in the world mattered but Saleem inside her at this moment. It was pure hunger and need, her emotions combusting as though she'd been hit by lightning.

When they were both finished, he eased her back on to the bed. There were no words between them, only the sound of them trying to catch their breaths as the waves crashed in the distance and the crickets chirped.

Minutes later they were doing it all again. And then a third time.

After, when both were truly and finally spent, his arm holding her close, her happiness was almost too much to bear. It was hope and satisfaction. *Contentedness.* Elise had needed a physical release of her emotions bottled up, stifled. The grief was still there. The constant sense that she wasn't making the right choices for herself was still there. Even the loneliness hadn't entirely disappeared. But as the back of Saleem's fingers gently stroked her arm, Elise thought that all of it could be remedied with more nights like this.

More nights that they didn't have. She couldn't have expectations.

'About that condition,' he said. 'The one I *tried* to make.'

'Hmm,' she purred.

'You were with another man.'

She heard the odd note in his tone. *Was it jealousy?*

'It was not a pleasant experience. Not like how we were. *Nothing* like it.'

'I do not mention him to ask how we compare. I only wish to say that he is not me. My condition earlier—I was consumed with your invitation and wasn't thinking clearly, but it was related to you not letting me or anyone ever treat you as he did. I cannot make promises, but I will try to make it so that this isn't only one stolen night together.'

Saleem sat upright, faced her. Outside, the early morning dawn was nigh, illuminating his sombre expression.

'I want you to stay here. In Egypt. Let me protect you until everything is figured out about your uncle, at least. Don't go back to England, to your town house there. I don't want you to choose spinsterhood for your life, Elise. I want you to choose…'

He stopped short of asking her to choose 'him' or 'us'. Elise guessed that Saleem couldn't bring himself to lie to her, to urge her towards a future that was impossible for them.

'Choose what, Saleem?' she prodded, sliding back. The barriers between them hadn't magically disappeared because they'd been caught up in their desires, in moments of physical intimacy.

'Choose happiness, Elise.'

Chapter Fifteen

⁓⁓⁓⁓

Saleem

Saleem had never found it so hard to make himself clear as when he was with Elise. He wasn't confused by his feelings, he cared for her—their relationship just wasn't as simple as he'd have liked. On the one hand, he believed he knew her, what she wanted from her life even if she hadn't admitted it to him. On the other, he wondered why he should be so adamant knowing that he could not give her what she wanted.

The khedive expected Saleem to marry for advantage. Someone like Lady Olive.

Saleem couldn't give Elise the family or the future she deserved.

Not yet, at least.

Before he'd entered her room, made love to her, he had wished to establish a kind of guideline for their relationship. He didn't want to treat her like a woman he'd get satisfaction from one night and forget the next morning. Elise's friendship had made it so that Saleem could not fathom subscribing to his personal mantra: *Try all things at least once.* Not with her.

'Are you saying my happiness lies in being a part of

your harem?' she asked now. Was it a look of repulsion that crossed her face?

Indignation fuelled his response. 'I don't have a harem and they don't work the way foreigners presume. It is a place of honour, a tradition that dates back in order to protect the women under my father's care. My father actually broke the rules of it when he married Adnan's mother in secret. And his lie, that lie? It devastated us. Hurt my mother and Adnan's. I don't know what lies he told her but…the harem is not what you think it is. It is not a place where indecencies happen.'

'You're saying that what we just did was an indecency?' Elise turned her head to stare out the window.

The sun was rising, but Saleem was preoccupied enough that it didn't restore him as it otherwise might have. 'Are you determined to take everything I say in the wrong way?'

Truthfully, however, Saleem hadn't felt *right* about making love to her—not without a promise on his part beforehand. They were not married. He doubted he could ever get his father to agree to let him marry her—even by her own admission, the Clifton name was associated with criminal activity in England.

Still, Saleem wanted to try. He wanted to find a solution so that he could prove himself honourable to her. To himself. He wanted to fulfil his condition.

But Elise seemed as though that's not what she wanted at all.

'Is it so awful that I wish to take care of you? Protect you? From your uncle's machinations or from unscrupulous men like Gerald? That spinster's life? It isn't for you, Elise.'

'How do you know that? I don't even know it, not yet. I do know I can't agree to stay here. Doing nothing but waiting around for you like a lowly servant to a noble prince.

Maybe you only want me to stay tucked away here at the Lodge for your nightly *needs*.'

She wasn't shouting, but the words were ugly enough that she might as well be.

She moved off the bed, put on her chemise and perused the wardrobe, to emerge covered with a robe.

Feeling too exposed himself, Saleem did the same with his sleep bottoms. He'd not come with a shirt and needed to leave the room before the house woke up and found him here.

The staff wouldn't say anything, but Mustafa would hear of it. Surely his guard already suspected the attraction between Saleem and Elise. He wouldn't hold it against him like his father might because the future khedive was supposed to be following the path the current one set before him, but Saleem didn't want to have to assure Mustafa that his emotions needed protecting in addition to his body.

'You could continue as you have been, get involved with some of the work in the city. Perhaps with Professor Aisha or any other project that strikes your fancy.' Encouraged when she didn't protest, Saleem went on, 'I won't come to your room, Elise, not until things are *settled*.'

'And when you're not here?'

'You'll have the Lodge to yourself. You said yourself it is a paradise. What better place in the whole world is there than Alexandria?'

He cupped her face, tried to make her see his point, but she shook herself free.

'With May the other day, how did you introduce me to your brother-in-law?'

'What?' He rubbed his neck, needing coffee or sleep. Saleem had been trying to wake up early, to spend time with Elise for days now. He'd not slept properly since, telling himself that once things were settled with her uncle, the gold bar, he would.

'What did you tell Prince Fareed about whom he left his daughter with?'

'I told him that you'd come with Lady Olive. Her travelling companion.'

'You said I was Olive's maid?'

'No, of course not.'

'So, then, in what capacity did you introduce me? What title did you give me?' She enunciated every word in that last question and it peeved Saleem.

He wasn't an idiot. He knew where her hurt was coming from in relation to Gerald, but Elise should have given him some credit, too. Some grace. He was trying to be better, but he was a prince. He did have responsibilities.

'Miss Thomas. Fareed isn't the type to ask details.'

Elise's face hardened. 'And what will you tell your father, the khedive of Egypt, about who I am to you? Would he ever agree to let his son play house with the orphan daughter of a man who was considered a criminal?'

'I will take care of my father.'

Elise's chin lifted. Her tone unwavering, she said, 'I don't agree to your condition, Prince Saleem. As soon as the business with my uncle and the gold bars is solved, I will be leaving Egypt. I'm grateful for your hospitality and aid.'

Saleem faltered. 'You promised.'

'I promised?' Her scoff sounded almost cruel. 'Are you a boy in a schoolyard game?'

The insult sounded like one his father might hurl and the nerves in Saleem's body went on alert. He rarely got angry, but years of feeling as though he couldn't measure up to his father's expectations bubbled in his throat. 'I was sure we were of the same mind on this! That it wouldn't be a problem for you to stay here after—'

'Mind or bodies, Saleem? Bodies desire pleasure and we had that, for sure,' Elise lectured, circling him as if he were an errant child who needed punishing, 'but it cannot be more than that. Nothing more than this one night when we let our bodies overrule our rational brains. Do you know why, Saleem? Because you are a prince by title, a gentleman by nature.

'My father loved my mother and cared nothing for his reputation, he defied his family, his business associates, even society for her and she had to suppress her unhappiness with how he suffered silently for it, until it made her ill. I will not make my mother's mistake, pretend as though all is well. And you cannot bear sadness. You are a happy man. Sunshine in a handsome vessel.'

It should have been a compliment, but it wasn't. 'You think of me as only shallow and undecided? You're wrong, the fact is that you make me happy, Elise.'

She quipped, 'Don't you see, Saleem? You are the easiest man to make happy! If Olive had come as she was supposed to and not abandoned ship, you'd be saying that to her. The difference is that it would come with a proper wooing and marriage proposal for the delicate and pure Lady Olive!'

'I thought matters would progress with her, yes, I thought I knew her from her letters but... I was wrong.' Saleem's head pounded, 'Is that what this is about? That I didn't woo you properly? I'm not saying it isn't a possibility, only that I need—'

'No! You are not listening to me, Saleem. I don't want to tie myself to a husband and certainly not one with a title.

I cheapened myself for Gerard in the expectation that he was going to marry me. I won't make that mistake again.'

'Cheapen?' He didn't know if he should be insulted on her behalf or his own. 'You invited me to your room, Elise. A man, a stranger. One with a title. All I'm saying is that you *think* you know what you want, but you are wrong.'

'I invited you to my bed not knowing any ridiculous condition that you wanted me to remain here and you weren't a stranger!' She swiped at the angry tears that fell from her eyes. Salem moved to her instinctively, he didn't want her to cry. But she held up her hands, stopping him.

'You weren't a stranger,' she said, her voice turning soft, 'because it wasn't Olive writing you all these months, it was me. You said I reminded you of a hibiscus rose. That I am hardy, a survivor, that I can grow and flourish anywhere.'

Saleem believed he'd written that line to Olive.

Elise had been lying to him? All this time? Since she'd arrived? All that opportunity to confess? She'd not mentioned her surname, but had been honest about why—but to pretend to be Olive back in England? To let Saleem believe he'd been jilted by a woman he thought he knew?

'Does Lady Olive know what you did?'

'Lady Olive?' Elise repeated.

Saleem's mind raced.

What things had he said to her when he'd thought he was writing to someone else? What had Elise said in return?

'Oh, Olive knew. She asked me to write them, couldn't be bothered to do it herself! You saw her note. She'd rather disembark in a city she never heard of to avoid meeting you!'

'Perhaps hers is a wholesome conscience. An innocent

one that prevented her from lying so easily.' Saleem really needed to get out of the room. He felt as though he was being boxed in, his head pounding in a way he wasn't accustomed. He was saying things that were surprising himself. That didn't sound like him.

Elise marched to the door, held it open for him, 'Will you leave now? Tomorrow I will find a hotel, book passage back to England as soon as my work in the city is concluded.'

He walked past her without meeting her gaze and, as soon as he stepped across the threshold, she slammed the door.

Saleem barely found his way to his room before collapsing on his bed. He didn't think he'd be able to sleep, but his body thought otherwise. He'd never made love like that to anyone before. That must be it. He'd watched Elise climax multiple times, felt her quivers, her racing heartbeat. Yes, there was passion between them, in the way she'd looked at him, the sentiment in her eyes but...

Elise had lied.

That was all he knew. His father had lied. Saleem had promised himself he'd never stand for a lie from someone he cared about.

Elise had lied.

And that was the truth that chased him until he fell into the clutches of a deep, dark and troubled sleep.

'My Prince, is'ha.' He was being shaken gently, but persistently, by Mustafa. His guard never woke him up.

Saleem noticed the keys dangling from this belt. It was the large set that opened and closed the gate.

'Is Elise gone?' he asked, the recollection of their argument last night flooding his mind.

She'd fled to London, begun her next life chapter without him.

Mustafa frowned. 'She hasn't left her room since the morning. Khayria was waiting on her to go painting or come down for breakfast per her norm, but she has not.'

Saleem sat up, noticed the brightness of the sun streaming through his curtains, the breakfast tray that had been pushed aside. It was early afternoon. Late, even by his standards. 'What is it, then?'

'Miss Stephania, Sinjur Portelli's woman. She's at the gate, demanding entry, saying she needs to speak to Elise alone. I wouldn't let her in, but she was insistent, belligerent even. Says she knows things about her parents, but that is all we could get from her without Elise present.'

'Elise's parents are deceased. What could she possibly know about them?'

Mustafa lifted a shoulder. 'What would you have us do?'

'Let her in. I'll be down shortly, but keep her away from Elise—in case she is dangerous. I will talk to her first, coax out what she wishes to say before giving her access.'

Only when Mustafa had left did Saleem realise how strong his instinct was to protect Elise. The woman who'd lied to him for months in her letters and then to his face. The woman who refused him when he made her an offer to take care of her, when he asked her to stay.

Saleem sighed. Maybe his father was right about him being a fool for leading with his heart and instincts instead of his mind. If Saleem wanted to be seen as equal to Adnan, he should have remained focused on his potential marriage to Lady Olive rather than think he needed to befriend her through letters first. Look where that had got him!

Now he had neither Olive nor the woman who'd been pretending to be her.

Still, he made his way to where Stephania sat. Not sat, rather, she was pacing. Mustafa had led the woman to a smaller parlour, reserved more for guests of the servants than for those looking to meet the Prince. Mustafa stood guard outside the door and had brought the gamekeeper with him, too, taking no chances when it came to Saleem's protection.

'We searched her,' Mustafa said, in Arabic. 'She's not carrying any weapons but she's fast for a middle-aged woman.'

'A middle-aged woman who has been in Egypt long enough to understand Arabic,' Stephania shouted from behind him. In Arabic.

Saleem put a hand on Mustafa's shoulder to reassure he'd be fine.

'Miss Dimitri, it is nice to see you again so soon.'

Saleem sat in the lone armchair, a massive one that took up almost as much space as the adjacent chesterfield. He pointed to it. 'Please have a seat and tell me what we can do for you.'

'What you can do for me is call Elise.' The woman remained standing.

'Miss *Thomas* is otherwise occupied. If you'll let me know the nature of your visit, we can take your message to her.' Saleem recalled how he'd written Elise the note inviting her to the dinner party that first night, how natural it felt.

Now he knew why, the memory irked him. 'Mustafa, have one of the servants bring us paper and a pen—'

'What I have to tell Elise must be said face to face.' Stephania's dark eyes were stormy, volleying between him and Mustafa. She was not intimidated; she was challenging them to defy her. She pointed an accusatory finger between them. 'Why are you and your man keeping me from her? Do you lock up your guests during the light of day, Prince? At the bank yesterday, you were the one to spurn my invitation to Elise. She wished to come. See if my moussaka was comparable to her mother's.'

It was not in Saleem's nature to scold people when they'd erred and though his father and brother had tried to impress upon him that it was necessary at times, he rarely had cause to do it. But now he leaned forward with scarcely a second thought. 'You were rude to her the other night. And your behaviour yesterday, quite the opposite. How are we not to think that Elise must be shielded from a woman with such varying moods?'

Stephania scoffed, not at all insulted. 'You think her soft, delicate. Elise comes from sterner stock, I assure you. You do not know her at all, Prince Saleem.'

That part was likely true and it gave him pause, but then Mustafa demanded from the doorway, 'That evening, you specifically asked the servants about the guest from England. You insisted on an invitation through Sinjur Portelli beforehand. You seemed to be *expecting* Elise. Why? What do you want from her? What are you hiding, Miss Dimitri?'

Stephania scowled, answering him, 'I have nothing to hide. I only want to protect Elise.'

Her stance softened when she turned back to Saleem. 'I concede you have her best interest at heart, but this is no matter for a prince. Your involvement may hurt her. Her uncle could twist it against Elise. Andrew Clifton is a very dangerous man.'

Chapter Sixteen

Elise

She had cried bitterly since letting Saleem go, but knew that it was the right thing to do. Only when Khayria knocked at her door, checking in on her with pity in her eyes, but no English words to express it, was Elise forced to fathom all that had happened.

Elise had purposely divulged her role in the letters. That look of betrayal on Saleem's face would haunt her for the rest of her life. And though she might blame Olive's absence on how long it took for her to tell him, Elise knew it was her fault. She'd not said anything about it because she was scared. And then, when she did tell him the truth, that, too, was motivated by her fear.

Saleem had gleaned much about her over the months—read between the lines of her words to know her desire for family and belonging. And he might be right about her not wanting to be a spinster, alone for the rest of her life, but he certainly underestimated the effect her experience with Gerald had had on her. How adamant she was to never be made small by a nobleman again.

As sad as she might be over how it ended, Elise had revelled in their lovemaking—believed it to be a meeting of equals. Her body was utterly content and her lusting over his since that very first day had been satisfied in a most fulfilling way.

Even now, she touched herself in the places he'd touched.

I don't need suitors like a lady might. Like Olive. I could take lovers, without giving up my heart, without the need for family.

Saleem had given her clarity. He'd been generous and good, astute and honourable.

Things had got complicated between them, the friendship they'd fostered might irrevocably be damaged, but Elise would learn from this lesson as she had with Gerald. She'd protect her heart better in future, not allow a lover to know her weaknesses and try to fulfil them. And who knew? If he weren't a nobleman and he wasn't otherwise after her inheritance, she might one day find a husband, have her own family.

Perhaps Saleem's optimism has rubbed off on me.

'You need to stop thinking about the Prince,' she reprimanded herself.

Elise picked at the food tray Khayria had left. Although she tried to find sustenance and enjoyment in it, she couldn't help but think of how attentive Saleem had been with her meals. If food normally helped clear her head, this was mindless chewing that served only to turn her stomach.

'Miss Elise.' Mustafa's voice came from behind her door. 'Please open. It is concerning your uncle.'

She sprung to do as he asked, bothered by the urgency in his tone. 'Is Saleem all right?'

She'd forgotten today was Saturday. The meeting arranged by the antique seller was set to happen later. Olive was returning today as well.

Mustafa blinked. 'My Prince is fine. He's downstairs with Stephania Dimitri. She showed up at the gate today. She *knows* about the gold bar and your uncle, but will say no more until she speaks with you.'

'All right. Give me a minute to make myself present-able, I look a mess.'

Elise did her best to clean up and style her hair, but no amount of powder or rouge could hide the redness in her nose, the swelling around her eyes. She wasn't eager to face Saleem in such a state. He'd see that he'd got to her, that she'd not callously set him aside. She knew he would not revel in her misery or feel vindicated, but Elise did not want his pity either.

Plus, there was the matter of her finding a different place to stay until things were settled with the gold bars and the bank.

'I'm ready now.' With Mustafa at her side, his revolver on display near his belt, she felt stronger. Perhaps when she left Egypt, she'd get her own personal guard.

Maybe I can steal this one away from his Prince.

Although she was determined to avoid Saleem's gaze, she couldn't help but be drawn to it when she entered the salon. He sat in the room's lone chair, one leg casually crossed over the other, wearing a beige short-sleeved shirt that nearly matched the skin of the muscles beneath. Elise's traitorous body clenched, her chest constricting with the memory of what it had felt like to be held in those arms.

He vaulted to his feet, the innate action of a gentleman, and acknowledged her entry with small smile, but Saleem wasn't oblivious. He saw what she'd tried to hide with a splash of water and too much rouge.

His brow furrowed at her appearance, the worry ex-pressed on his face weakening her. She wouldn't renege on her stance, or apologise for rejecting his offer to care for her and speak to his father about their relationship.

Stephania came to stand before her, 'Elise, daughter of Thomas and Valia. Surname Clifton. Is it you, truly?'

'How do you know my parents' names?'

The woman marched towards her, the dangling earrings she wore swinging enough to make Elise feel dizzy.

'Because I was the one who first introduced them. Twenty-five years to the day, in this very city. Thomas was an…associate of my father's and Valia was my first and dearest cousin, my best friend, more than any sister. She'd come to spend the summer here with me from Greece.'

Elise hadn't eaten enough. She was confused by the tears in Stephania's eyes. What she was saying.

'We are family, *Frangosyka*,' the woman continued. 'You were young and might not remember it, but I was there that last trip.'

The nickname quaked in Elise's core. Hearing it aloud broke down any defences she had put up before entering. She clamped both hands over her mouth so the gasp wouldn't escape.

Mustafa led her to the chesterfield, while Saleem looked on, concern clear in his face—but it was Stephania who crouched before her. Loving, patient.

Mama. Her vision blurred with the resemblance between the two women. Memory was a fickle thing, hopeful and despairing all at once.

'Papa called me *Frangosyka*,' Elise whispered, 'but he never had the right accent, only tried to emulate how Mama used to say it. You say it like Mama did.'

Stephania's tears were as unabashed as she had been that first night.

'You were rude to me.' Elise hated that she sounded like

the little girl of that summer, the one who lost her mother and lashed out at everyone who tried to be nice to her. 'The questions you asked.'

'I was taken aback, Frangosyka, that it was you who had come rather than... *Lady Olive,* whom I'd expected. It has been a dream to reconcile with you, a dream I have been working towards, but I did not foresee, did not plan, that it would happen here. Did not plan that your father would be gone...'

Elise realised, 'It's you. The person Papa entrusted the gold bars to. He meant to send the one to you, here in Alexandria.'

Stephania gave a quick nod before turning to Saleem, 'May I speak to my Elise without an audience now?' she said huffily.

'I apologise, not knowing the familial connection, but I am pleased for *you.*' The intensity in Saleem's stare beckoned Elise's. 'Perhaps you would like privacy in the larger parlour? I'll have tea brought in and lunch.'

Stephania took the seat next to Elise. 'This room is sufficient. Especially if you kindly close the door on your way out.'

Mustafa cleared his throat, not ready to leave, 'You have not informed us about the threat Andrew Clifton poses.'

Stephania's hands tightened over Elise's. It was a reaction to Mustafa's question. There were secrets there and Elise, having been reared amid some unsavoury business practices, knew what protecting them looked like.

'He is a dangerous man who should not be provoked in any way. Not until he is resolutely brought to justice for his crimes and behind bars.'

'I believe we are supposed to meet with him later tonight,' Saleem said. 'At the antique seller's shop.'

'You cannot do that,' Stephania protested. 'You've no idea how dangerous Andrew is, all he has done to get his hands on Elise's inheritance. Suffice it to say the meeting cannot happen. Elise cannot be there. She is not safe.'

'She is safe here,' Mustafa said, his face twisting in distaste.

'As she is with me,' Stephania snapped. She turned to Saleem. 'Her father did his best to protect her and in his stead, he entrusted me with her inheritance here in Egypt. With due respect to the Prince, I've been in Alexandria longer even than he has. I know this city, the best places to "hide", if necessary. I thank you for your hospitality, but your interference is not needed in a family matter. If you could tell your guard the same.'

Saleem bristled at Stephania's bluntness but tugged Mustafa's arm. 'Let us give the ladies privacy.'

He made for the door, but Elise suddenly felt it wasn't enough that she had broken it off with him. Whatever Stephania had to say, the truth was that Saleem had work in this city that he loved. Projects that could be damaged by his association with her family name.

Elise would make no assumptions about the depths of Saleem's feelings for her or how he would reconcile his father's expectations when it came to Olive, but all that aside, his genteel nature would not stop until he ensured her safety. Until she was out of his house. Out of his care.

Saleem was the most gracious of hosts, after all.

One day he would fill this place with family and love. She could not be a part of it and, though it hurt Elise's heart to do so, she knew she had to sever all ties now. And permanently.

'Wait.'

Saleem's hopeful look nearly took away her resolve.

'The mystery of who the gold bar was meant to be sent to is solved and Olive is on her way back with Prince Adnan.' Elise evaded Saleem's questioning frown and turned to Stephania, 'I had planned to ask for a hotel later today already, but would it be all right for me to stay with you?'

Stephania's face softened. 'Yes. More than all right.'

'We can leave now, talk at your place? Send for my things later.'

Stephania rose, took her hand so that she would go with her. 'Absolutely.'

'No.' Saleem insisted as if he were Mustafa, 'There is no better protection in all of Alexandria than within the confines of the Lodge. However dangerous Andrew Clifton may be, he cannot get to Elise here. Where do you reside, Miss Dimitri? It cannot possibly be safer?'

'With all respect, Your Highness, and appreciation for taking care of my cousin's daughter after the abandonment of Lady Olive, this is not a matter for royalty,' Stephania insisted. 'Our home is safe. Portelli ensures it.'

Saleem's expression seemed to implore Elise to reconsider, but this was not only her chance to connect with family, it was a way to forget about what had happened between Saleem and her.

He stalked to the door's threshold, called for Khayria. While they waited for her to retrieve the bag, Stephania hugged Elise's shoulder, lovingly pressing their heads together.

She was as affectionate as her mother had been and Elise easily leaned into the warmth, realised she'd long been denied it.

'Portelli's home?' Saleem interrupted the moment, his

voice tight. 'The two of you are not married. It is not respectable.'

Elise knew he was talking about the two of them. 'You needn't insult my mother's cousin.'

'I'm not so easily affronted, Elise. But the Prince shouldn't be too quick to judge who is or is not respectable or who does or does not live up to reputations that shift depending upon who tells the better story at any given time.'

Elise wondered how she'd ever considered Stephania negatively.

She is a wise woman, like Mama.

Before Saleem could respond, Khayria entered, satchel in hand. Elise gave Stephania the gold bar and it felt like a weight off her shoulder. She could have cried with relief at having done what she'd come to do. Papa's unfinished task fulfilled.

'It is yours, darling. It always was.' Stephania locked arms with Elise. 'My carriage is outside the gate. Do you need a minute to say any goodbyes?'

Perhaps it was the stifling nature of this particular parlour or the prospect of being alone with Saleem, but Elise was eager to get out, 'Actually, I think it is better if we leave that for another time. I will return when Olive arrives.'

'Yes, please,' Saleem answered, calmer now. His regular, gracious charm returned. 'I'll leave word at the gate to let you in any time of day. Or night for that matter.'

Mustafa returned, carrying a tray with a note. He saw their stance. 'What is happening?'

'Elise has decided to stay with Miss Dimitri,' Saleem explained with a sigh.

The Prince might be sorry to see her go, but she longed to tell him that this was for the best. That, perhaps, by him associating the letter writer with Olive and her noble title, he had already made a decision about the kind of wife he wanted. And what he wanted and what his father wanted might not be far off.

Elise would have never lived up to what his expectation of a wife would be.

But she didn't want to start crying anew, reuniting with her mother's cousin was something grand to celebrate and she would not let what had happened between her and the Prince put a damper on it.

'I wish you well, Mustafa, and thank you for all you've done for me.'

She meant to shake his hand, but the guard held out the tray, his gaze bouncing between her and Saleem. 'It is a telegraph from Adnan. Your man at the tram office delivered it now.'

'I'll take it,' Saleem said.

Mustafa shook his head, 'Actually, it is for Miss Elise.'

Elise frowned, opened it. Skimmed the words. 'Adnan is asking me to come immediately to Rasheed. Says I am the only one he can think of to convince Olive to return with him. She's refusing to leave.'

Chapter Seventeen

Saleem

He could not let Elise go. Not from the Lodge. Not from his life.

'I will accompany you to Rasheed,' Saleem insisted. 'My brother didn't say anything about me joining, but he knows that that's what I will do.'

Elise shook her head and Stephania vocalised the refusal. 'I will go to Rasheed with Elise since Lady Olive was in fact the woman I'd expected the night of the party. I want to meet her, discuss a few things with her.'

'You know of Olive?' Elise asked.

'Never met her, but, yes, your papa wrote to me often, Frangosyka, about your adventures, the people important to you.' Stephania looked lovingly at Elise.

Whatever animosity he might feel towards the woman for taking Elise away, Saleem was happy for their reunion. He knew what family meant to Elise, how she believed herself alone in the world.

'We should go now if we are to catch the last train of the day.'

Saleem wanted to insist on joining them, but Mustafa's

look stopped him. There was something the guard wasn't wanting to say in front of the ladies.

'Very well, we will send a message to Adnan later, telling him you're on your way.'

Mustafa said he would accompany them to the gate.

And with a final goodbye, gaze lowered, Elise left.

Saleem sat alone in the parlour, sniffing the air for the scent of hibiscus that hadn't left him since that first night. But there was only the slight mustiness of a room without windows that was rarely used.

Saleem had said the flower reminded him of Elise and thought he was speaking to Olive. Was it a wonder that he felt the rapport, the attraction, the sense that he should be wooing Elise above all others since his arrival?

The knock on the parlour door brought Saleem from his thoughts.

Khayria had brought the requested tea tray much too late, but she set it before him anyway.

'Thank you.'

She wiped at tears she must have thought he did not see.

'Why are you crying?' he asked.

'Is it true Elise is gone?'

'She will return for her things, but you know she was only ever a short-term guest.'

'I know that, my prince, and I promise not to be so emotional about other guests, but it will be easy next time since none can be as much of a lady as Elise.'

Saleem took the cup of tea she'd poured for him. 'What did you like about her?'

'Her generosity and humility are unlike any I have seen.' Khayria put a finger on her lapel, indicating a cameo brooch, the ivory silhouette of a lady's head encased in gold. It fastened her hijab to the apron she wore, so Saleem didn't want to take too close of a look, but his sister had a similar item. 'She put this on me when I admired it and refused to let me take it off. As though it meant nothing to her.'

Saleem guessed the brooch was worth at least a few months of Khayria's salary.

'Miss Elise owns jewellery, beautiful gowns, shoes. She is clearly wealthy, but chooses simple dresses and makes her own bed in the morning. My mother used to work at the Raseltin Palace, experienced the foreign guests, how they treat us Egyptians like dirt. "The wealthier, the stingier" she used to say. And cruel, too. Miss Elise was upset in the morning. I heard her crying before her guest arrived. W'Allah, her tears felt as though they belonged to my own sister. Do you know what was wrong with her?'

'Khalas, ba'aa.' Mustafa entered with a reprimand towards the girl. 'I know our Prince is a kind man, but you do not need burden him with every issue big and small, Khayria.'

She left, reprimanded, but Saleem was glad he didn't have to answer her question. Or dwell on the fact that she was crying.

Mustafa scratched at a spot beneath his chin. His guard only did that when he was afraid to incite him into taking an action that could put him in harm's way.

'What is it, Mustafa? You didn't want to mention it in front of the ladies.'

'When I left you alone with them, we had another visitor. The guard we posted outside of the antique shop.'

'He saw Elise's uncle?'

'No, but he saw someone he thinks may be working with him. Maybe a man hired by Andrew. A very belligerent younger Englishman.'

'Why didn't you want to mention it in front of Stephania?'

'Because the young Englishman was seen with the shop owner and Sinjur Portelli.'

'Portelli? Stephania's lover?' Saleem's heart hammered. He'd let her take Elise, having been assured that she was safe with her mother's cousin, if nothing else. His instincts were usually right, but what if he was wrong this time? What if his feelings for Elise had clouded Saleem's judgement? She could be in danger.

'Yes.' Mustafa sighed. 'I know that I always imagine the worst, but that exchange with Miss Dimitri now, how she says she knows where to "hide" in Alexandria and that Portelli keeps their home safe? It got me thinking about my contact in the police station. He was the one who suggested Portelli for the dinner party. He was the one who said there was nothing dangerous about him bringing a lady friend.

'When I heard that there was an Englishman buying a specific sort of gold bars, it wasn't through him. I'd overheard other officers discussing it. In fact, when I wanted the list of names of people who'd arrived in Alexandria, he was the one who mentioned that they were having trouble with officers taking bribes at the harbour.'

'Did you ever see the manifests?'

Mustafa shook his head. 'No, my contact delayed, but what if it was because he was paid off by Portelli? The man is rich, but to have the police in his pocket—that needs to be amended!' Mustafa stared at Saleem. 'This is your city, my Prince. And whoever is the Englishman who was seen speaking to Portelli in relation to Andrew Clifton, he needs to be reprimanded immediately.'

'Why?'

'Because he was heard threatening to burn Alexandria to the ground unless he got "the gold bars".'

Saleem gripped the armrests. He cared about Alexandria, but that didn't mean he wasn't worried about Elise. 'It is a good thing she is on her way to Rasheed.'

'It's why I gave Adnan's message to her and not the other,' Mustafa said, his voice soft. 'She's an innocent in all this, I am sure.'

'The important thing now is to figure out what is going on with this henchman of Andrew Clifton,' Saleem decided. 'Go to the police station, the top of whoever is leading it, not your bribable contact. Telegraph Cairo if you must. Use any and all the royal privileges I'd asked you not to. Tell them the city is under threat and that you demand to see the manifests. Maybe have Portelli and the shopkeeper arrested so that they will point us to the man in question. He must be deported. Alexandria and all her neighbourhoods must be kept safe.'

Mustafa rose. 'I'll go now since the gold bar is with Stephania. I'm relieved you aren't going to that meeting later.'

Saleem nodded, but something was still bothering him about Portelli's connection with the henchman. If Stephania was going to take Elise back to live in their home, maybe she wouldn't be as safe there as she'd believed. 'Did our man happen to hear what Portelli said to the Englishman's threats in response?'

'No, my Prince. He only gave a description of the man, I would have asked Elise to sketch him according to it, but…she was eager to leave, it seems.'

'A sketch would have been good to give to the police.' Saleem ignored the concern in Mustafa's last comment. 'Ship manifests might not help if we do not have the man's name and we do not find Andrew Clifton on there.'

'Well, we do have an overheard first name, my Prince.

I hope it will be enough to find the rest of his name and travel documentation. That it isn't a common English one.'

'Oh? What is this belligerent Englishman's name who is threatening our city?'

'Gerald, my Prince. His name is Gerald.'

Chapter Eighteen

Elise

Elise needed to eat, but she didn't think any amount of sustenance would help her deal with all that had happened in such a short time. Nor could she plan for what was to come.

Before coming to Alexandria, she'd been wandering in London, aimless, trying to get on with her life, waiting for letters from a man who wasn't even writing to her. A prince she would end up giving her body to, but who she knew would never be hers, heart and soul.

And Elise couldn't help but feel Olive was partly to blame for what happened between her and Saleem. She'd answered Adnan's call, but the truth was that Elise was wary of facing Olive. Her friend *had* abandoned her.

The train car was mostly empty. Stephania kept sticking out her head to look up and down the aisle, her right knee bobbing impatiently. 'If there are not enough people, they cancel trips. No warning, never mind any schedule or operators who need to be paid.'

'Perhaps we should buy more tickets?' Elise suggested. She'd no idea how much money her mother's cousin carried, nor had she needed funds what with Saleem's generosity.

Stephania's knees stilled, her face softened. 'Valia was like that, always wanting to throw money at situations. "Why does it exist except to make lives easier?" she would ask.'

'It sounds like her, yes.' Elise didn't remember Stephania specifically. That summer in Greece had been fraught and she'd been amid too much extended family she didn't know and would never know since the single connection between them had been severed. 'The older I get, the less connected I feel to the parts of me that are hers. Not in my face, of course, the skin tone, eyes, hair, frame. It is all her and I see it in the mirror.'

'How lucky you are. Valia was the most beautiful of women. Your father was immediately smitten.' Stephania winked. 'Not dissimilar from that Prince of yours.'

'Whatever is between Saleem and I—it is done. Cannot be.'

Stephania said nothing, but when a pauper boy passed selling apples and wrapped sandwiches, she waved him down and bought the lot. She spoke in Arabic to the pleased boy and he skipped along happily.

'Hungry, I hope? It will not be delicious, I am afraid, but I hope it will be enough to convince the train. I also mentioned to the boy that we have a large, very important family to pick up in Rasheed. And that I will need him to get more goodies for the way back.'

'Then you, too, like to throw money at things.'

'Blood lines, I fear. We cannot escape them.' Stephania winked. 'But I am smarter with my money. Buying seats is more expensive and I have had to adapt to life as a woman largely on my own.'

'You and Portelli are not...' Elise didn't want to be judgemental, but after her own fight with Saleem, she couldn't help wondering if her and Stephania's life would follow the same path. 'I don't know what I'm asking.'

'We have a unique arrangement that works for the both of us. We don't live together full-time as the Prince accused, but Portelli offers me a way that I, a woman mostly on her own in a foreign land, have needed in order to navigate life here. And I *compensate* him for his services.'

Thankfully, the steam engine rattled awake then, a few stragglers running on the platform to find their cars.

Elise unwrapped one of the sandwiches. Plain cheese, soggy and too salty, but it would have to suffice. She handed her one, but Stephania bit into the apple instead.

'I don't understand why Papa didn't tell me about you. About the gold bars?'

Stephania nodded wearily. 'Do not be upset with your father. He wanted to shield you from harm. You'd suffered the loss of your mother and he'd made her the promise to go clean.'

Elise swallowed. 'Papa couldn't hide much from me. I knew how he'd made his fortune. The illegal items he shipped in his containers while he profited and all but made a mockery of Scotland Yard. When he died, they had their revenge, delaying the coroner's report. Keeping his body so that it was too late to bury him beside Mama in Greece as he would have wanted.'

Stephania closed her eyes for a minute before continuing. 'Law enforcement has always been against us, Frangosyka. It's why I didn't want to involve Prince Saleem in all this. As a royal, he'd be torn between his feelings for you and his duties to his country.'

'He wouldn't be torn.'

'I saw the way he looked at you.'

'He's kind, optimism is his nature—and, yes, maybe he feels a *kinship* with me but Saleem would choose his family, the country above all else.'

Stephania creaked her neck, then slid to the seat directly opposite Elise. The train had moved past the sea so that the cooler breeze that blew in earlier was somewhat muggier. The houses that neared the tracks were further and further apart, farmlands or empty terrain filling the spaces between.

'Your father and Uncle Andrew were once close brothers. Thomas was the older, smarter, but Andrew, he had ambitions. Had gone to a fancy school your father paid for and got these ideas of grandeur in his head. Getting a title.'

'He married someone with one.'

She nodded. 'But there was no money. Andrew was all right with pretending, his and his wife's lifestyle being secretly supported by his brother's wealth, but when your mother was pregnant with you, he said something that angered your father.'

Elise recognised the unsavoury look on Stephania's face as she recalled how she'd felt when she heard her uncle that night. 'He called her a "d—." I cannot say the slur.'

'You needn't, it is one I know all too well. He implied that you'd be the same.' Stephania nodded. 'Thomas always had an inkling about Andrew's racism—he'd never invited anyone to meet his wife and her family. He had hidden his background, all the money that Thomas had spent on him, putting him through the finest schools and furnishing him with all the luxuries money can buy. Andrew manipulated his "good" society acquaintances so that, if they happened to learn of his past, they'd thought it admirable how he'd escaped his crime family.'

Elise hadn't known that it was Papa's money that had made her Uncle Andrew who he was. She fumed, 'He scorned the hand that fed him.'

'Not only that, he wanted to take everything that hand possessed. Your father should have cut Andrew off, but he kept saying "he's my brother" and we all understand what value family held.'

Elise swallowed. 'I heard Uncle Andrew fighting with Papa a week before he died. He threatened him over the gold bars. Do you think he killed him over them? That he knows they're here in Egypt?'

Stephania took Elise's hands in her own, bringing them to her lips and kissing the left, then the right. She basked in an unfamiliar sense of belonging, grateful that she could have it, even if it wasn't with Saleem. Even as her heart still hurt over what happened between them.

'Andrew does want the gold bars,' Stephania agreed. 'And, yes, he found out they're here. That's why Mr Patterson was careful with your identity, insisting on seeing your passport, not giving out my name at the bank as the account holder. There was a mistake somewhere—somebody answered a query in England and it led Andrew to finding out what Thomas was doing with his money. It's why I was called into the bank.'

She took a deep breath before continuing, 'It was a complicated process Thomas designed, but the only way he knew to protect your inheritance from his brother. The gold bar you found was meant to be a sign between us, engraved with a symbol to indicate that this was the last of his monies.'

Saleem had found it that first time he'd examined the bar, thought it odd.

'The drachma.'

Stephania nodded. 'But it never arrived and then Thomas died. One awful article in the English papers is all the word I had.'

Elise winced. 'The one about me and my lover being responsible for Papa's death?' She could almost laugh about the ridiculousness of it now.

'Yes. I'd known about Gerald and the debacle at the races the year before. It was why your father decided to transfer his money into gold bars in the first place. He thought Andrew's law degree, tactics like going to the papers, would hurt you.'

Of course Papa had told her about Gerald.

Elise knew her mother's cousin was spent, exhausted from telling it all. 'Thank you, Stephania, for bearing the burden.'

'Anything. Always.'

They watched the passing scenery in companionable silence, how the sun swathed the farmlands in shades of soft orange and burnt pinks. She'd have loved to paint it, how different the sky seemed to look depending on where you were viewing it. Saleem would have something to say about it. Bask in it.

She missed him.

Elise had said that their attraction was only one of bodies but that had been a lie, too. The truth was that they wanted to spend time together because they had fun. And even if it was only his generous disposition and thoughtfulness at play, Saleem's presence made her feel secure. Cared for. *Cherished.*

'You're thinking about your Prince.' Stephania had been watching her.

Elise didn't argue with the 'your'.

'We were supposed to be at a meeting now, to sell the gold bar. Draw out the buyer.'

'At Antikalar? You were going to show up unexpectedly?'

'How did you know about it?'

Stephania grinned. 'Portelli, too, likes to throw money at everything.'

Elise sighed. 'I'm glad Saleem will be safe from my uncle. This whole debacle. You see, it is why he can never be "my Prince". He will marry a noblewoman. He was intending to woo Olive…their fathers wanted the match.'

'Egypt struggles financially. The khedive must believe that Lord Whitmore is rich and powerful and his daughter comes with a nice dowry, but *I* saw the way Saleem looked at you that first evening, Frangosyka. He's only increased in his admiration.'

Elise shook her head, denying; Stephania patted her knee, reassuring.

'It's good that you two didn't go to Antikalar, because you would have run into Gerald. He's who your uncle sent to do his dirty work.'

Stephania had stressed that there was nothing to worry about, that Portelli had managed to bribe the antique seller to not disclose anything. Elise put Gerald out of her mind. Saleem knew all about the cad, his role in Elise's life. Meeting him in the flesh would have been awkward at the very least.

'Gerald will leave Egypt empty-handed,' Stephania said as the train came to a stop at its final destination. 'And then we will go to the bank and I will hand over your gold bars, as your papa planned.'

They disembarked to a wide, flat plain, dusty and nearly abandoned save for a kiosk to purchase tickets.

'Why is there no one to meet us?' Stephania wondered.

Elise realised they'd left in a rush. If they'd not been in the situation they were in, with her desperately trying to get away, Saleem would have ensured Elise was taken care of. That the trip would not leave her stranded. He would have come himself. 'Prince Adnan might not know that we are on our way.'

They started walking along the only road and soon came across a stable of horses and a number of coaches. A sign in large white letters and multiple languages above a small building next to it indicated they'd arrived at the Rosetta Carriage Company.

'Here.' Elise recalled the conversation Adnan and Saleem had had at the harbour that first day. 'It's a friend of the Prince, probably where the telegram came from.'

The bell over the door jingled when they opened it, but the man in attendance barely heard them. His face was buried in a book.

'Hello.'

'Yes?' he answered in English, lifting his face to reveal a youthful, intellectual face.

'My name is Elise and this is my mother's cousin, my… aunt, Stephania.' It occurred to her that for the first time since her mother had died, she had a woman who could act as her chaperon. She wasn't about to promenade in London's prestigious neighbourhoods or have a debutante's ball, but the thought brought Elise some joy. 'Prince Adnan's telegram?'

Stephania took out the telegram to show him, but there was no need. He was nodding in recognition, though he'd never before seen either of them. 'Lady Olive's friend from England?'

'I am.' Elise didn't add *for my part at least.* Would she be able to contain her disappointment when she saw Olive again? Olive had abandoned her. And what would happen if she were able to convince her to return to Alexandria?

Yasser said, 'Adnan has been having…er…*trouble* with her. When I asked him what Saleem would do, he thought of sending for you.'

'The Prince is an insightful man,' Elise said.

'Saleem often surprises and inspires me with his insights—his comprehensive vision,' Yasser added with a smile.

Stephania probed, 'What sort of trouble are you referring to with Lady Olive?'

Yasser closed the book he was reading. Elise caught the title, an English one, *El Naddaha: Nymph of the Nile*, before he answered, 'You'll soon see. Come, my carriage is out front.'

But before they could leave, another telegram came through. 'It's from Mustafa, Prince Saleem's guard. For Adnan.'

He took it without reading his contents. Elise said, 'It's probably just him informing Adnan that we're on our way.'

'Late. Someone should have been waiting for us,' Stephania muttered.

When they were finally on their way, they had a nice ride through the quaint village. It turned out that Olive had let out a villa, one of a row at the edge of a field of palm trees and cotton plants.

'"Ezzbah",' Yasser identified it. 'It's not yet the time of year when the rich family who owns the land would be here to oversee production, so the city's mayor has the authority to rent out its houses to those who ask. We were taken aback that a young English woman *knew* to ask. And in Arabic, no less.'

'How do you know this?' Stephania queried.

'The mayor is my grandfather,' Yasser said with an earnest, almost embarrassed chuckle. He politely averted as his eyes as he helped them dismount this carriage.

Elise warmed to Yasser. He was well mannered and intellectual and she could see why Saleem had made him a friend. From that first dinner party guest to Professor Aisha and this grandson of a mayor, none of Saleem's contacts were nobles necessarily, but he treated all of them with the same ease. They, in turn, would do anything for him. And if Elise didn't know better, she'd have gone as far as to say that Saleem had strategically surrounded himself with those who could benefit the country.

Not only was he the charismatic and generous man she'd first met in a falafel queue, he was, indeed, a very capable and forward-thinking, *noble* leader.

'Finally, the cavalry has arrived!' Adnan met them after they'd descended from the carriage. They walked to the stone gate of the ezzbah house. 'Where is my brother?'

Stephania answered, 'He sent us instead.'

'And you are?' Adnan likely didn't mean to sound so gruff, but his mannerisms were different than Saleem's, less refined.

Stephania, however, wasn't a shy young woman. She, too, was tough. She snorted, ready to challenge the Prince.

Elise stepped forward. She'd learned a thing or two from Saleem, about how a little softness and understanding of people's natures, reading their moods, could serve.

'She is my mother's cousin, Stephania.'

He asked no questions of it. Perhaps Adnan still thought

of her as Olive's maid. Rather than upset her, however, the thought now made Elise marvel at how different he and his brother were in dispositions. 'Saleem has been busy in Alexandria and when your telegram arrived, I said I could come with Stephania as chaperon.'

Adnan's brow relaxed and he turned to Yasser. 'Did you tell them how stubborn Lady Olive has been?'

Yasser lifted his hands in mock surrender.

He handed him the telegram from Mustafa and while he read it, Adnan walked Elise and Stephania to Olive's door. 'The khedive is on his way to the Raseltin Palace in Alexandria. Lord Whitmore is arriving tomorrow. You didn't know?'

'It must have been after we left,' Elise said.

'We can take Olive to her father,' Stephania said. 'Leave us with her and we'll take the next train out.'

'*If* you can convince her.' Adnan huffed, 'She's an insolent woman, but she needs to be where her *father* expects her to be. Daughters ought to listen to their fathers.'

He knocked on the door for them. A quick rapping that the person inside was clearly familiar with.

'I am not going anywhere with you. Give it up, *grumpy*!' Olive shouted in an ironically grumpy tone.

Adnan threw them a look as if to say *Good luck with that one.* 'I will arrange a train car to Alexandria within the hour. We'll be there before night fall. Be at the Raseltin Palace to welcome her father as if nothing was ever amiss with Lady Olive. Tell her to be ready.'

It wasn't exactly a suggestion as Saleem might make. Adnan didn't give them a choice, he just said what he said, then left.

'Well, he's pleasant.' Stephania chuckled, watching him march off. 'Knock again, gentler this time.'

She rapped on the door. 'Olive, it's me. Elise.'

In seconds, she heard the bolts being released and the door was swung open and the sight of a woman, her blonde hair frizzy and piled high, her frock a plain green kaftan a few sizes too big, her feet in slippers, was shocking.

Elise almost didn't believe it was Olive—she looked nothing like the girl she'd known most of her life with her pristine English ways, always ready for a stroll along a promenade, matching her parasol with her shoes, her silhouette perfectly corseted.

Olive threw herself on to Elise. 'I am ashamed and unmitigatedly sorry! It was selfish leaving as I did. And though I'd planned it and wanted desperately to tell you, it was cowardly of me not to…to leave you the burden of telling the Prince I wanted nothing to do with him.'

The familiarity in the hug gave Elise pause. She thought she'd buried her upset towards Olive for abandoning her, but what kind of a friend did that to another friend? Not just any friends, but ones who were like sisters. 'Why then?'

Olive stepped back. She opened her mouth, but then caught sight of Stephania and promptly shut it.

'My mother's cousin, like an aunt to me,' Elise explained. 'Stephania Dimitri, meet Olive Whitmore.'

Olive's eyes widened. 'Oh, my goodness, Elise. You found family here, too?'

Too? What did Olive mean?

Before she could ask, Stephania was the one ushering her inside and shutting the door behind them. 'Yes, Lady Olive. Elise's mother and I were cousins but closer than sisters.'

The home was akin to a cottage, the floors were a cool marble, only parts of which were carpeted with straw-like mats, the walls bare save for Qur'anic verses, done in a kind of gold embroidery. In the sitting area, rather than a proper set up, there were cushions on the floor and a short round table. Nothing at all like the Lodge.

Nothing at all like anything the Lady Olive Whitmore was accustomed to.

Stephania went into her 'blunt' mode to ask, 'Are you experimenting with how the poor classes live, Lady Olive?'

Olive took it in her stride. 'I wanted the true Egyptian experience and you must call me Olive. Any family of Elise's must think of me as family, too.'

As they took their seats, she rushed off to get them something to drink. A thick orange drink, cold and tart.

'Kamar al deen,' Stephania called it.

'The mayor sends around people offering meals and cleaning services, so it hasn't been too bad.' Olive looked at Elise. 'How have you been? How have you liked Alexandria?'

Elise's tongue was stilled due to a combination of disbelief—how and why was Olive here?—and disappointment—how and why had Olive abandoned her? It wasn't as though she could tell her about what happened with the Prince who should have been wooing her.

'Fine. I accomplished what I set out to do.'

'Oh, what was that?'

Was Olive as infuriated with this conversation as she was? 'I know we didn't talk much since Papa died, but I came to deliver a package I found of his. It was meant for my mother's cousin, after all. Saleem helped me with that.'

'Saleem?'

'The Prince.'

'Ah, yes.'

'What is wrong with you, Olive? Why did you abandon ship? Lord Whitmore doesn't know, but he must be worried about you, the state you left in! He's arriving in Alexandria momentarily—a full two weeks before he was supposed to.'

Olivia burst into tears. 'He's here? Already? I won't see him. I can't see him! It's too soon!'

Stephania stopped Elise before she could scold her. 'Your friend is under duress.'

'I was under duress! I have been for months, Elise. Ever since your papa died.'

Elise steeled herself. She'd felt it then, needed answers now. 'Why? Was it because you had a father and I didn't?'

Olive sniffled, shook her head. 'No, nothing like that. I'm not ready to talk about it yet, but… I just need you to forgive me for my neglect, Elise. It's the only way I'll be strong enough to face Papa.'

'*Your mother and I always wanted a sister for you, Frangosyka.*'

Papa had said it that first day when he'd picked her up after the initial meeting with Olive at the Whitmore estate. Olive had been so vibrant, welcoming. Running in the wild flowers outside their manicured gardens. She'd had a lifetime of living without her mother so maybe she didn't know that suffering, but looking at her now, Elise knew that was no longer true. She looked like a woman who would have a lifetime of suffering ahead of her.

'I forgive you, Olive.'

Chapter Nineteen

Saleem

Saleem nearly missed the Antikalar building. The potted plants from the first time he'd been here had been destroyed, their clay broken into pieces and left in a pile on the pavement.

He climbed the steps, knocked on the shop door and window, but no one answered. He tried again, louder when he heard something coming from within. Shouting. In English. A meek response. Glass shattering. Mustafa would seethe, but Saleem pounded further.

If Gerald was inside and this behaviour was the kind he'd use against the rest of the city—or if he meant to hurt Elise in any way—Saleem had to stop him.

Finally, the nameless shopkeeper appeared. He looked as though he'd not slept since the last time he'd seen Saleem, didn't bother to search if Elise was with him.

He rasped a rushed, 'We are closed.'

'We had an appointment for this time. I was supposed to meet your buyer.' Saleem lifted up the sack he'd bought, fitted with bars of soap to mimic the gold bar.

The shopkeeper put one foot out of the threshold, pushing Saleem back. His eyes widened in warning, 'You're mistaken. We have no appointment.'

Saleem insisted, 'I was here with my...*wife*. You gave me this time.'

The shopkeeper leaned forward, hissing, 'Tell Portelli I told Gerald what he asked me to, but that is it. No more. You better go now.'

He made to shut the door, but Saleem threw out his arm, preventing it.

'What did Portelli ask you to do?'

Before he could answer, the man who was in the shop with him growled with disdain. He had a gun and it was pointed at the shopkeeper's temple for a split second before he slid it inside his jacket and pushed out of the shop.

He barely looked at Saleem, dismissing him as though he weren't there. But Saleem studied him with more than a simple passing curiosity. This was Elise's suitor. The man who'd been her lover. He wasn't jealous, but he was... *angry.*

Gerald was average height, but his thickness made him bigger. His skin was ruddy and his thin hair a shade of blond that was nearly white. His looks might be pleasant enough, Saleem supposed, if his sneer didn't make him so abominable.

'I entrusted you to get me the gold bars,' he growled at the shopkeeper, 'now I learn they're in the Anglo-Egyptian Bank? And the account owner is here, in the city? Once I get my hands on Elise, she'll give me all I want.'

The shopkeeper slinked back, closing his shop door. The sound of him bolting it from the inside was loud but meek, nevertheless.

Gerald's thick shoulder crashed into Saleem as he stormed past, but he didn't feel it. Gerald knew Elise was here.

She's in danger.

Stricken at the realisation, Saleem dropped the pretence of the sack, the gold bar that wasn't there, tossing it near where the plants had been. He ran after Gerald.

'Sir, sir. You are an Englishman, have you had the tour of Alexandria?'

The fellow was taken aback by Saleem's English, but not enough to be bothered by it. 'I don't need a lackey guide. Not much to see or drink in this city for that matter. And they call this the European quarter? More like a desert.'

'Because you do not know it like the locals. There is an underground gentleman's club a few steps from here, hard to find except for those who've frequented it before. The best of cigars, imported from Cuba. The hardest of whiskys, and—' Saleem nearly gagged with the effort, but managed to wink suggestively '—if we're lucky, the most entertaining of the fairer sex.'

Gerald was intrigued, but he wasn't an idiot. 'I'm buying, eh?'

Dank smoke filled his lungs, hazing Saleem's surroundings. He had to keep his head clear despite the hookah pipes and alcohol. A belly dancer twirled around him, the *tabla* drum beating to the shaking of her hips, pounding in his head.

Gerald's meaty hands were reaching for them as if they were fruit on a tree.

After they'd made love and he'd presented his condition, Elise believed Saleem jealous of Gerald. But he'd only evoked him so that he could make his motivations clear. That he would care for her. Saleem hadn't met the man, but now he had, it should be vindicating how right he was. It was hard to fathom how such a cad, a womaniser, could have ever tempted Elise by promising to care for her. Be her husband, no less!

Had Gerald ever declared his love for Elise?

Saleem noted the belly dancer's worried expression. 'Hands down. No touching.'

Gerald growled in response and put down his glass to paw with both hands.

'They will kick us out.'

'Let them try.' He made a show of pulling the gun from his jacket pocket and sliding it into his belt.

Saleem pushed a few *qurush* into the woman's grip. 'Go,' he told her in Arabic.

'Shukran,' she said, scrambling away.

'Why'd you do that?' Gerald hiccupped. The drink was finally taking effect.

Saleem didn't want him too drunk he couldn't answer his questions, just inebriated enough he wouldn't pose a threat to anyone here. Saleem needed to get him arrested before he sought out Elise in his bid to get her gold bars. Thankfully, she was safe in Rasheed. Far from Gerald and any threat he posed.

Saleem thought quickly. An unregistered weapon was cause enough, but it was rarely enforced and police often let underground places like this operate because of the bribe money they brought in. 'These places talk to each other. If you're banned from here, you'll be banned from the next.'

'Don't matter, I'll be back in England soon.' The last bit came out like a song.

Saleem should have taken it as his opening to ask what he came for, but instead he found himself questioning, 'You got a woman back there?'

Gerald cackled. 'Several.'

'A wife, I mean.'

'Who needs one of those? Unless she's filthy rich.' Gerald took a long puff of a cigar, the exhale that followed fanned the flames rising in Saleem's blood. 'And then, you only want to take her in the dirt.'

He cannot be talking about Elise.

Saleem leaned forward. He had to change the subject.

Get him to talk about Andrew. What he has done to his brother. That's the resolution Elise needs.

'Sounds as though you had an experience.'

Gerald laughed. 'You could call it that.'

'What happened?'

'You lot might not know the difference, but in England, I'm a gentleman. Turns out, I was using her for her money, she was using me to get a title.'

He cannot be talking about Elise, he thought again; this time, Gerald noticed Saleem's frown.

'You don't believe me.'

Saleem itched to punch the pout off Gerald's face. 'I was just thinking about the fathers of such girls. Can they not keep them under roof?'

'No worse father than Elise's.'

Saleem tensed, struggled to hold in all his emotions. 'Elise?'

'That was *her* name. Her dad was a criminal. Oh, he tried to go legal, but it didn't matter. He was always angry, uncivilised. After I broke it off with Elise, he came at me one night. Would've killed me if I weren't younger and stronger.'

'You shot him?'

Gerald reached over to snuff out his cigar in the sheesha bowl. He followed Saleem's pointed look to the gun. 'I didn't have this then, but it's why I carry it now.'

Saleem's mind fired with all Elise had said about her father. His death was inconclusive, that the English authorities didn't investigate it enough. If he could get a confession from Gerald now, he'd testify to it later. Go to England for the trial if he had to. His father wouldn't like him getting involved in a murder case, but what did that matter if justice was served? If Saleem could give Elise solace and put her mind at rest?

'How did you do it, Gerald? How did you kill *Elise's* father?'

Saleem thought he might have given away his deeper interest in the matter when he said her name, but Gerald didn't notice.

Around them, night had fallen proper and all the oil lamps had been turned on, but, in the light, the man's eyes darkened with a memory.

'Whitby's Cheesemonger. It's a shop in London with an alleyway next to it. Behind their awning, they keep old rocks, use them in their cheese making. I led Thomas there, bashed his head against 'em in the dead of night, a rainy one. Then I dragged him to—'

There was a commotion outside the club that seemed to be pouring in, but it wasn't that which made Gerald stop. He was staring at Saleem. Maybe the fool could see the horror in his face that Saleem could no longer hide.

'You knew my name,' he said. 'I didn't say that my name is Gerald.'

'I think you did. How else would I know it?'

'What did you say your name was?'

Before Saleem could answer, Mustafa shouted, 'My Prince!'

He'd come with the shopkeeper. Police officers. And Elise.

What was she doing here? She was supposed to be in Rasheed! *Safe.*

Saleem, she mouthed, her eyes sad. Not scared, like they should be.

She didn't know that the man next to him wasn't just a past suitor. He was a murderer.

The next part happened in a flash.

Mustafa was frantic that Saleem not be harmed. His guard's instincts were always alert. But Saleem was frantic that Elise not be hurt.

But when Mustafa pulled his gun on Gerald, with an eye on his Prince rather than his target, Saleem realised. This was no dog chasing a cat. Gerald had a gun, too. And he would not hesitate to use it.

Saleem leapt forward to stand before Elise, confusing Mustafa.

He heard the shot. The screams.

And then came the acrid smell of gunpowder mingled with the smoke in the air before everything went dark.

It was one thing to *feel* bruised and bloody, another to have a swell of emotions at seeing both his brother and Elise. The concern in their faces. And dare Saleem believe it?

The *love.*

'You fool! What were you thinking going alone, running from your guard?' Adnan reprimanded him in Arabic as Saleem struggled to sit up in his hospital bed. He ran a hand through his hair, one eye on Elise as she hung back near the room door, letting his brother fuss over him.

His brother rushed through an explanation of how Gerald's bullet had caught him near his ribcage, right under his heart. It had been taken hours of surgery to remove it because it was such a sensitive area, but he would recover quickly and with only a minor scar. The doctor said Allah had blessed him—even a quarter of an inch difference in the bullet's trajectory would have been disastrous.

Saleem was embarrassed to see the gown they had him in was an awful grey frock and that his lips felt dry and chapped. And for the first time in a long time he disliked the abundance of sunlight for it brought the pain he'd suffered into full relief.

'Fool or hero?' he said in English, reminding his brother that they were not alone. He smirked. 'Depends on one's perspective, Brother. What do you think, Miss Clifton?'

At the mention of her name, Elise ran to him, leaping on the bed. But Saleem didn't care as his arms came around her waist and she buried her face in his shoulder. She couldn't talk for a minute, couldn't answer because she was crying. His body ached, but the weight of her was a good kind of pain. The smell of her soothed him as well as any medicine when he inhaled.

Saleem looked up at his brother, crooked his neck towards the door. Adnan took the hint that he wanted to be alone with Elise, but not before casting him a quizzical look. One filled with warning.

Hearing the door shut behind him, Elise sniffled and muttered, 'Foolish, foolish hero. What did you do to yourself?'

'I couldn't let Gerald hurt you.'

She pulled away and met his gaze. 'I still cannot believe that louse is here.'

Saleem ran two fingers along her jaw, watched the sadness in her eyes. 'He did more, Elise.'

'He killed my father?' she guessed.

'I heard his confession with details. I will testify to it. Justice will be done.'

She must have heard the rawness he felt when he said it for she gasped quietly, clapping her hand across her mouth. She cried then, long and hard, her shoulders shaking, her chest quaking, and all he could do was hold her close, stroke her hair and whisper over and over again that he'd see to it: 'Justice will be done.'

Saleem didn't know how long they remained that way, but when a nurse entered to change the dressing on his wound, Adnan had gone and Elise made to do the same. He grabbed her hand, wanting her to stay, but feeling as though he could not make demands of her.

She smiled. 'I'll be back soon.'

'When will I be released?' he asked the nurse.

'One night for observation, Prince Saleem, that is what the doctor insists upon. Your brother said he would arrange it so your schedule would be free.'

Adnan was concerned for him, but... 'I have a home with all the amenities.'

The nurse scolded, 'This bed, this room, is the best we have.'

'It is not that it isn't a fine one...' Before he could finish the thought, the room began to spin and the nurse rushed to bring him a bowl. He was glad Elise hadn't seen him being sick.

Vindicated, the nurse said, 'The doctor says that if you sleep well for one night and are able to keep down a meal, you can be discharged and we will send someone to check on you at your home.'

As if on cue, Adnan brought in a tray with a bowl of adz soup and dried balady bread.

'I've come to feed my brother.'

When the nurse had left, Saleem watched Adnan crumble the bread into the lentil broth and wait for it to soak. 'They did not have any of the palace fare, but this looked healthy enough. My mother made it often, fatta style. It'll make you stronger, help you feel better.'

Adnan made to feed him the first bite, but Saleem could manage that alone. 'I may be younger, but I am not a baby.'

His brother gave up the spoon with a chuckle.

The taste of toasted garlic was pungent, slightly burned. 'Your mother makes it better, I am sure.'

Adnan got the faraway look on his face. 'I used to fuss about the lack of meat, but she worked hard to make this perfect. Her pride didn't allow her to take the khedive's money and I didn't know it.'

'I've kept you away from her for too long.'

'She is doing well, expects me to be a bit late. Your friend in Rasheed is a good man. Yasser sent her a note on my behalf that first day, through contacts he had in our neighbourhood in Cairo. The fellow takes his wife to check on her every day and gives me an update by the end of it. Immediate communication is quite the blessing.'

'It is.' Saleem nearly finished the whole bowl of soup before he set it aside and remembered at last the note that came from Rasheed. Adnan had found Olive Whitmore. 'Was Elise able to convince Lady Olive to come to Alexandria?'

A soft look crossed Adnan's face, one that Saleem didn't quite know how to decipher in relation to the words that came out of his mouth. 'That insolent, stubborn woman? Not sure if it was Elise who convinced Olive or the fact that her father is arriving in Alexandria today and I threatened her that the khedive would invade Rasheed if she wasn't there to greet him.'

'What? Lord Whitmore is coming ahead of schedule?'

'Yes,' Adnan answered. 'Our father is on his way, too. They're preparing the Raseltin Palace. No need to worry about it or plan anything. Mustafa has arranged everything. The khedive won't know you were shot unless you want to tell him.'

Saleem asked, 'How did Mustafa manage it?'

'Mustafa was at the police station when he saw Lord Whitmore's name on the manifests. He sent the telegram to Rasheed as soon as he learned and called Cairo to inform the khedive on your behalf. Acting as if it was all prearranged. He said it was what you would have done.'

'So you booked the train back the same day Elise arrived?'

Adnan lifted a brow. 'You worried she didn't get a break in between, Brother? She was fine.'

'She could have been killed!' Saleem didn't want to get angry, not with his brother.

Adnan nodded. 'Alhamdullilah, she is safe. I'm sorry I wasn't there. When the four of us arrived at Raml Station, Mustafa met us, but didn't want to say anything in front of Stephania or Olive. He pulled me and Elise aside. Said you'd gone missing, but didn't want to alert anyone else because of Stephania's lover? I don't know the man's name. Anyhow, when Mustafa mentioned a Gerald had threatened the city and he believed that you went after him, Elise insisted on accompanying him to find you.'

'Did Stephania have anything to do with Gerald?' It hurt Saleem to think Elise might have been betrayed by the woman. She didn't need to suffer the loss of yet another family member.

'All I know is that Mustafa insisted there was cause to watch her with Lady Olive. I offered to deliver them to the Raseltin Palace, but had to pretend as though nothing was amiss. When I did that, I went to the police station. If Gerald wasn't already badly beaten by those who'd tackled him after he shot you....' Adnan gulped before cupping his brother's cheeks in his hands. Kissing his forehead. 'Don't ever do something like that again.'

'At least not with you there to save the day?' Saleem tried to make light of the emotion that surged from his brother, rare as it was.

'You don't need me any longer, Brother. I can see that now. You're all grown up, ready for your future.'

Now it was Saleem's turn to swallow his emotions. It's what he'd always wanted to hear from his brother, but talk of the future made him seek Elise out.

Adnan followed his gaze to the door. 'Elise left. Mustafa took her to the Lodge for a bath and change of clothes.'

'Really?'

His brother suppressed a smile. 'Her and Mustafa both, blubbering all night about you. It was *something*.'

'What did they say?'

Adnan teased. 'Mustafa blubbing, "I am supposed to be *his* guard." Elise countering with, "Why does he always have to prove himself?" There was a lot of "He's charming and he's smart and he's good-looking." Actually, maybe not that last one.'

After a good chuckle, Adnan sobered. 'In truth, and despite the anger over what happened to you, it was nice to be free of Lady Olive Whitmore.' Adnan shrugged nonchalantly, but the timbre of his voice told a different story. 'Olive is the most stubborn of women! I cannot imagine how a nature like hers might ever be wooable, even if she had been loyal to her itinerary.'

It had not been that long of a time ago, but the prospect

of wooing Olive felt as though it belonged to another life-time. 'It turned out Elise was the one writing her letters.'

'Olive mentioned it to me, yes.' Adnan shook his head. 'You told her I was pining over her?'

Adnan sighed, pulled out the portrait Elise had done of her friend from his coat. 'Remember this? I believed you were, as you say, pining. And I do not appreciate a woman who would do that to my brother. Little did I know you were very much *not* pining.'

Saleem laughed. 'I *was*, for the most part, having the best time of my life.'

'You forgave Elise for the deception?'

'You hate lies as much I do…but something of her suffering, of why she did it and how she admitted it gives me pause. I didn't say I forgive her, we fought. When she went to Rasheed, I know it was mostly to get away from me.'

Adnan nodded solemnly. 'I'd wondered why you didn't accompany her.'

'I'll go from here to Raseltin rather than the Lodge as soon as they release me. I'll welcome Lord Whitmore but then have to disappoint our fathers that Olive and I do not mean to marry.' He suppressed a yawn, exhaustion hitting him like a punch to the face.

Adnan fluffed his brother's pillow, helped ease him down and cover him with the blanket. 'Do not worry about it now, Saleem. You need rest.'

What I need is to tell the khedive that I care for Elise.

He had to make his father listen to him.

Chapter Twenty

Elise

Elise was afraid to have her heart broken. She was grateful for many things: all that had happened since arriving in Egypt, all she'd gained.

Her mother's cousin.

Closure on what had happened to her father.

Saleem. Alive and as beautiful as he had always been.

But, last night, she'd barely slept at the Lodge after she'd left him at the hospital. Remembering the things she'd said to Saleem after they'd made love. She almost wished she could take it back, agree to stay here for ever with him.

Elise thought she had a plan for her life, thought that spinsterhood would suit her just fine, but travelling back and forth to Rasheed, only to return to him standing next to a man with a gun in his hand, had put in her heart a kind of fear she'd never before experienced. What if she were to go back to England and something happened to him while she was gone? Assassination attempts—or worse, completed ones—were a common thing with royals. If something happened to Saleem, she'd not survive it.

With him and in this home, she'd had a sense of belonging, tasted its sweetness in her days here.

Stephania was family, yes. Olive a friend, still. But in a few ways, Saleem had come to mean more to her than either family or friend.

Elise didn't want to give that up even though he did have a title. Even though his father might never accept her to share his life.

She'd chosen to wear a gown of pale yellow silk with crimson ribbon detailing. Its collar was high, but didn't cover the length of her neck. A fact that was thrown into relief when she knocked on Saleem's hospital room door and his gaze was drawn to it.

She was sure he wanted to kiss her there. 'You're up.'

'And you are a vision,' he said.

'Khayria served me a filling breakfast.'

'She cried, you know. When you left.'

Elise didn't know if Saleem meant it as a reprimand for her leaving, but it wasn't the time to discuss what happened with him. She was satiated certainly, but her feelings were, understandably, fraught.

She ignored the comment and took in the simple shirt and trousers Mustafa had brought over for him. 'And you are looking better, I am glad to see.'

'Alhamdullilah. I am feeling better.'

Mustafa entered and held up a cane. 'The doctor insisted.'

Saleem took it, but asked, 'Is it really necessary?'

'Unless you'd rather I carry you, my Prince,' he teased.

'No, that is fine. But I will need to drop it when we get to Raseltin. Adnan just left…said he is off to Raml Station to catch the train to Cairo. He assures me that nobody suspects anything. Of course, I cannot hide being shot, but the news can wait until we're sure Lord Whitmore's trip ends successfully.'

'You wish to go to Raseltin?' Mustafa asked.

'Now?' Elise added.

Saleem looked between them. 'I should have already been there to welcome him, yes. Do you not want to, Elise?'

Did she? 'It's fine. Everything happened so quickly yesterday, I just didn't think about it. But if you are going anyway, then yes, certainly. I'm happy to accompany you.'

'Adnan said Stephania stayed the night at the behest of Lord Whitmore.'

Mustafa stiffened. He'd apologised to Elise about doubting Stephania, told her that it turned out that Portelli was working on her mother's cousin's behalf to have Gerald arrested. He'd misunderstood the man's intent and felt guilty for working Saleem up so much he'd gone after him. He told her that if it wasn't for his hyper-attention to anything and everything that threatened the Prince, Saleem would have been safe at the Lodge.

She put a hand on the guard's arm. 'Stephania wants to thank Lord Whitmore for his care of me. When she learns what happened last night from Portelli, she'll thank you both for your help in keeping me protected even more. She is, as I am and will be eternally, grateful.'

Elise said no more, afraid that she'd burst into tears with the depth of gratitude she felt, but also the grief.

As much as she had found in Alexandria, that loss was still inside her.

Her father had been killed by Gerald. The knowledge of what happened didn't make the pain go away.

'You're quiet,' Saleem said from his seat across the carriage, when they were en route to the presidential palace.

'Sorry.'

'Don't apologise. I'm happy to stare at you as you think. Happy you are here. We need to talk, Elise.'

'I know.' For the first time in as long as she could remember, Elise did not have a plan and she was sure that no amount of food would clear her head. 'Not yet, but soon. I promise.'

It was her turn to watch Saleem as he looked out the carriage window. After a few minutes, he turned back to her, locked his gaze on hers. Her stomach leapt as it did that first time. Elise hadn't finished his portrait and she wished she could go back to that moment at the beach. Him posing, her painting.

Saleem asked, 'Have I told you about my maternal grandfather?'

She shook her head. 'No.'

'He was a sweet man, had a host of daughters and a wife who passed early so that he had to raise them mostly on his own. My mother was the youngest so he was quite old by the time I was born. He died when I was too young.'

She put a hand on the one he had gripped around his kneecap. Her reactions with regards to Saleem were becoming instinctive and she feared she'd not be able to hide her admiration in front of the khedive. Or anyone else who might be watching.

He twisted his hand upwards so he could cup hers in his palm, never taking his eyes off her. The way he scraped his lower lip with his upper teeth as if holding back his desire for more nearly undid Elise. A carriage ride in Alexandria didn't usually feel this hot. 'I am sorry.'

'For what?' he asked, shooting her a look that told her he noticed her flushing.

'That you lost your grandfather!'

He chuckled. If he didn't put his hand on his ribcage

where the bullet had grazed him, it would be as though nothing had changed between them.

'He was old and bed-ridden and hated having become a burden to anyone. This despite the fact he'd spent his whole life serving others. His daughters fought his long-term servants for the chance to nurse him. All felt indebted to him, committed to his care not because they were duty-bound, but because they loved and admired him for who he was and how he'd served them. I wanted what he had, wanted to have his life, to be thus loved at the end of it.' He scoffed at himself. 'Strange, I know, for a boy.'

'You must have been a very wise boy.'

He cocked an eyebrow. 'I am not wise even now. But my grandfather did tell me something that has stayed with me.'

Elise was teary-eyed before she could even ask what it was. Saleem's emotions found a way to seep through his words, delving deep, despite the seeming shallowness of outward-projecting optimism. She'd already perceived as much from his letters, but being in the presence of him, hearing him speak the words, was akin to delving naked into a steaming bath. Or a frigid one.

'What did he tell you?'

'*Altoyur al askhaliha taqah*. It literally translates to "birds fall upon those who are alike to them". I think the English have a similar saying: "Birds of a feather flock together." My grandfather explained that we admire those whose qualities we ourselves possess and that's why connections happen on a soul-to-soul level. He said it is not a matter of arrogance that because one person thinks they have a good quality, they will only admire others with that exact same quality. Rather, it is about understanding the values that make us who we are. If we know and understand ourselves, we can find and immediately recognise who we are meant to be with. Our bird. Our flocks.'

Elise fretted, 'We are very different, you and I.'

Saleem agreed, 'You are reserved, cynical. Measured.'

'And you are open, charming. Undiscriminating.'

'You are an artist.'

'You are a visionary.'

'You are earnest and loyal. *Loving.*'

'You are earnest and loyal. *Loving.*'

Saleem chuckled and the sound made her heart feel light. 'What do you think, Elise? Do our souls belong together?'

Their carriage had come up to the wall of the presidential estate: a bright white high brick that was much less inviting then the homey gate at the Lodge. A host of uniformed security men stood on high alert, long rifles strapped with white leather belts across their bodies.

Elise watched Saleem's expression. She wondered what he was feeling at the prospect of meeting Olive for the first time, but her feelings were too muddled with all that had happened since discovering her friend's note to broach the subject with him now. She would just have to watch him and see for herself.

Before she could determine it now, however, the carriage was met with a few of said men eagerly greeting Saleem.

He was gracious with them, shaking any hands that found their way inside the carriage and sticking out his hand to shake others who did not. If the gatekeepers noticed her presence, they did not address it at all.

'They are not intentionally being rude,' Saleem explained. 'They are used to women of the harem being veiled in their presence because they are considered to be on the outside of the palaces. Servants behind the walls are deemed "worthier".' He stressed the word with a flick of his wrist. 'They speak English, however, and know proper protocols without needing to be advised.'

'I quite prefer those at the Lodge. Their work ethic and devotion is most admirable.'

Saleem teased, 'And what of their employer? Do you admire him?'

With my whole heart.

'The architecture here, as you'll see, is much more re-fined than at the Lodge. There have been changes over the years, but it remains wholly in an Italianate architectural style. This is the East Gate, built in 1847.'

Elise stuck out her head to count six huge granite pillars that looked very much as though they might have come from the Renaissance. Towering above them were green plaques, coats-of-arms that represented the khedives that had come before. 'And there are lines of Quranic verses etched into the wall with copper.'

'Breathtaking.'

When the carriage finally came to a stop and the door was pulled open, Elise expected Mustafa, but it was an-other man. One, who grabbed Saleem from the carriage almost angrily. He spun him around and spoke a fury of Arabic before giving him a half-hug and a rough pat on the back.

Elise would have thought it violent, but both men were grinning.

And when she emerged from the carriage with Mus-tafa's aid, grabbing the cane Saleem had left behind, she took it all in.

The magnitude of where she was and how small she felt in it.

Elise had forgotten how she often felt ill at ease in London, as though she didn't belong. In Alexandria, at the Lodge, that feeling had all but disappeared. She'd begun pulling out the dresses her father had bought her, the colours she'd never wear back there, lest people treat her as they had her mother.

But standing there now? That feeling came back to her. *I don't belong here.*

There were at least thirty employees of the house, the uniforms they wore, the rigidness of their stances flustered her. She fretted with her gown, adjusting it every which way, thinking that she really should have asked for Khayria's help with a corset—picked something else besides the yellow she thought would please Saleem when picking him up from the hospital, but which seemed garish now.

If only she could remove her hat, Elise was sure her head might not feel so heavy. She might not feel so hot. Even though they were surrounded by the sea's breeze, there was a tautness to the air that seemed to hold it back.

Saleem turned back to her. 'Meet my father, the khedive. Baba, this is Miss Elise Thomas Clifton.'

Elise didn't know if she should curtsy, barely even remembered how to do it from when she and Olive used to practise when they were girls, but she did it then. The khedive allowed it and when she rose, she caught the slight wink Saleem threw her way without his father's knowledge.

'It is a pleasure, Your Highness.'

He smiled, but while she could see a slight resemblance between father and son, the khedive was not as effortlessly handsome as Saleem. The bridge of his nose was rounder, his moustache too thin, the arch of his eyebrows sharper. Nor was he as tall as Saleem and his outfit, though not full regalia, was much too formal.

He bobbed brusquely, but he was Saleem's father and she knew how important family was to him. And, according to his grandfather's theory, how important to her, too.

'We are pleased to welcome you to Raseltin.' The khedive's English was measured, each syllable enunciated. 'Our dear friend, Lord Whitmore awaits you within, I only wished to ensure my son was in one piece.'

Saleem winced. 'You heard.'

The khedive stared pointedly at his son. That was the only response he gave.

As she wondered if he blamed her for what happened, Saleem angled to her side, inserting himself between them protectively. And tossing his cane to Mustafa, who stood apart, nearly shame-faced.

'As you can see, Khedewy,' Saleem said. 'I am fine. 'Twas only a minor incident.'

'Sounds like what Adnan would say.'

'And when have you *not* preferred to listen to what he says instead of me?'

Elise noticed the slight sink in Saleem's shoulders. She stepped forward, would have taken all the blame, but then Olive was calling for her, running towards her from the palace door. Lord Whitmore and Stephania followed close behind.

Olive looked a vision.

When she'd seen her state in Rosetta, Elise couldn't help but feel sorry for her. Now, seeing her as Saleem would, she couldn't help but feel jealousy. She wore a baby-blue gown that seemed to perfectly match the colour of her eyes. Her face was made up with a light hand, but with a kiss of sun in her cheeks and her golden hair perfectly coiffed, she was stunning.

Mustafa must have had her things brought here, part of

the preparation for her father's arrival. Meanwhile, Elise's wardrobe had been untouched at the Lodge.

Olive hugged her warmly. 'You look beautiful!'

She was open with her compliments, as Saleem was. Which brought to bear the conversation they'd had in the carriage. Would he see that Olive was more obviously like him? That she would be worthy of wooing after all and as he'd planned?

'Lady Olive,' the khedive said, his voice sweetening in a way that wasn't there when he spoke to Elise moments ago, 'may I present my son, Prince Saleem Ahmed Ali.'

Olive turned her attention to Saleem, demurely batting her lashes and curtsying in a practised manner, her hand outstretched for him to take and kiss as if they were meeting in a ballroom.

'Prince Saleem Ahmed Ali,' she repeated his full name flawlessly—as if she herself were an Arab and had always known the language. And then she followed with an Arabic phrase that Elise couldn't quite understand, but which brought a smile to the khedive's face.

She resisted examining Saleem's face for his reaction to it, but he had graciously bent to accept Olive's hand and bring it to his lips.

She is not wearing gloves, Elise fretted.

Saleem did not carry on the conversation in Arabic. 'Only Saleem, please.'

'It *was* a mouthful.'

Saleem smirked. 'Adnan mentioned you preferred nicknames.'

Olive shielded her eyes, playfully acting embarrassed. Elise had seen her flirting before, but she couldn't be certain if that was what she was witnessing now or if it was Elise's jealousy that made her think so.

She didn't have much time to dwell on it, for Lord Whitmore appeared in tow. 'Elise, darling. How wonderful to see you and I am so glad you've met your mother's cousin here, too.'

He embraced her as warmly and then turned his attention to meeting Saleem.

Stephania took Elise's hand in greeting. She wore the same clothes she'd worn on their trip, as if she'd not gone home and rested. Still, the relief on her face surpassed her haggardness. 'It is over, Frangosyka,' she whispered.

Then to Saleem, she said, 'Thank you for all you have done for my family.'

He nodded graciously. 'I trust it will all work out. That there will be justice.'

Adnan must have impressed upon Stephania not to say anything in front of the khedive. 'I believe so. Now, I do think I should be heading home, finally to get some rest.'

'Mustafa can take you,' Saleem offered.

The guard nodded happily with the reprieve. 'It will be my pleasure.'

Elise walked Stephania to the carriage. When they were out of earshot she said, 'I know I was supposed to move to your home, but with what happened to Saleem and between Gerald, I think—'

'Do not think anything now, darling. There will be time for that later.' She shook her satchel, 'This last gold bar needs to be deposited and the name on the account switched. I suspect you'll need to accompany me for that in the coming days. For now, Lord Whitmore will explain to you how your inheritance can be transferred to England, or whatever you wish. He has things to say to you. And I suspect your Prince does, too.'

'He's not my Prince,' Elise repeated but it was weaker now, sadder then it had ever been.

Stephania kissed her cheek before stepping into the carriage. 'You'll always have a home with me, but you should not think of it as a means to run from your real home.'

When she'd gone and Elise returned to where the others were, Saleem met her gaze and smiled. Had he been worried she'd leave with Stephania?

Lord Whitmore was saying, 'I remember you as a boy, Saleem. You're quite the young man now. Your father had brought you, your mother and sisters to London. It was the year before Olive was born.'

The khedive added, 'I'd quite forgotten that trip to your estate. We had afternoon tea with your wife. God rest her soul, a lovely woman. My wife raved about how wonderful she was with our children. She was most pleased to hear of Olive's birth, saddened, of course, to hear about your wife's untimely death. As we all were.' He looked meaningfully between Olive and Saleem, then suggestively said, 'A strange thing destiny is, how it spins and comes around.'

'Alas, I was a bit too young to recall that trip,' Saleem said to Lord Whitmore, then effortlessly changed the subject. 'Speaking of which, I trust yours was enjoyable, sir?'

'Rushed, but some news came to light and I knew I had to deliver it in person.'

Lord Whitmore took Elise's hand and then Olive's. 'I think the three of us need to have a conversation immediately. The khedive has graciously offered his study for privacy.'

Olive tugged her hand free from her father's. 'Elise and I have spoken and I deduced the rest of it from Stephania.' She smiled at Elise without even looking at Lord Whitmore.

Her father scratched at his ascot. 'Very well, where will you be, Olive?'

The khedive answered, 'Saleem can find a way to entertain her. Would you like a tour of the grounds, Lady Olive? The fig trees for which the palace is named will be starting to bear their fruit.'

Elise's heart sank, but she dared not look at Saleem or Olive. Would not show she was worried they'd be left alone like those courting might.

Saleem wondered, 'Perhaps Miss Clifton would like me there with her, since—'

'No! It is not necessary.' Elise didn't know what possessed her to refuse so vehemently save for the look the khedive threw her way when Saleem offered.

His father clearly didn't like her. And would he be so wrong in not wanting anything to do with the Clifton name to sully his royal son, a man destined to lead Egypt?

Seeing Saleem hurt in the hospital, knowing what he'd done for her in facing Gerald had made her forget the impossibility of hers and Saleem's relationship, but it hit her then again. She'd been foolish to ever hope for the possibility they'd find more than friendship.

Their company parted ways, Olive and Saleem in one direction, the khedive leading Lord Whitmore and Elise in the opposite. It was hard not to notice the majesty of the palace and the surrounding complexes as they watched over the pristine lines of the garden spaces. The spaces between the lines glimmered with a cleanliness that made it hard to believe that this was the outdoors.

There were flowers within the pathways, but they looked almost manufactured, false—too arranged. The trees that existed were carefully arranged, their branches and leaves manicured so that there was no difference in height or breadth or branch between them. And though the sea was at their backs, it might as well have been a river for it was deathly silent. There were no seagulls singing, no peacocks squawking.

The servants, too, stood rigidly, not trembling as the khedive marched ahead, but Elise caught their exhales of relief when he passed. He was nothing like Saleem, who put people at ease, went out of his way to be of service to them. Saleem made others, in turn, fall over themselves to serve him. Like his maternal grandfather.

Saleem would be a wonderful leader. Strong, yet kind. Focused, yet flexible. Smart, yet humble.

Lost momentarily in the memory of their time at the catacombs, she nearly bumped into Lord Whitmore who'd come to a halt behind the khedive.

'Have your meeting,' the latter said, 'but do not delay, it is nearly lunch, and the staff are preparing a delicious one we will take soon.'

'Thank you, Your Highness.'

Lord Whitmore shut the door behind them. 'I'm glad to see you're all right, Elise. Your mother's cousin told me Gerald was here. When I put you and Olive on the ship here, I thought I was keeping you safe until we dealt with your uncle once and for all.'

'You were building the case against him, using your connections,' she said, 'but said nothing to me all along.'

'I'm sorry. I was waiting for it to be concluded.'

Elise collapsed into the leather couch, put her hands to its coldness in an effort to hold back her tears. 'It struck me, you know, the first time we visited after my mother died. I asked Papa "what do a lord and his daughter want with a nobody like me" and he said, "The lass lost her mum too." Because I was desperate for belonging, I found a home with you and her, but if he threatened you in some way, forced you to take me in, then....'

Lord Whitmore sat next to her. He put a comforting hand on her shoulder. 'I won't lie to you, Elise. Thomas did threaten me—he knew something I didn't want to get out. But even then, I knew he was forced to do it only out of his love for you. Desperate men left alone to parent the daughters they love and without the wisdom of their wives have done worse. Yes, we were different in rank and did not have a typical friendship, but we had much in common. I mourned Thomas like a brother.'

The tears she would have spilled flowed anyway, but they were quieter ones. Bittersweet.

'And you, darling Elise? From that first visit it was clear that you would be the loveliest friend to Olive. The best, most sincere. Remember what I used to say?'

She sniffled, 'That I was the fulcrum to Olive the see-saw.''

He chuckled, before offering her his pocket handkerchief. 'We needed you more than you needed us.'

'Olive ran away. Slipped off the boat with a note, left me in the lurch.' Elise wasn't sure why she said it. Was it a lingering anger at her friend for abandoning her or jealousy that the khedive clearly saw Olive as a bride for Saleem?

Lord Whitmore wasn't surprised at the news. 'Olive is upset with me. Don't worry about her or be upset with her. She's a good girl who'll remember who she has always been soon. We'll get her back.'

Elise nodded, but she wasn't so sure—the Olive she'd known seemed as though she'd been gone for months. 'If she'd talk with me, maybe I could help?'

'I'm sure she will when she feels ready to.' Lord Whitmore smiled. 'I actually brought you in here to convey some good news. Your Uncle Andrew was arrested in London. Your father came to me after that whole debacle of yours with Gerald and said he had a plan for protecting your inheritance, but told me nothing of your mother's cousin and what he was planning through the account here.'

'What did he want from you, then?'

'He believed Andrew might be involved in criminal activities that he covered with his noble connections. Thomas thought that if he could sully his name, expose him utterly, it would protect you from Andrew's schemes in future. Your father had managed to sell his assets and cleanse his money, but his brother was unrelenting and learned that Thomas had been turning his money into gold bars. I don't know the details of that, but it was a kind of legal loophole that Thomas found and entrusted Stephania with here. Or that is what I assume.'

'Papa always kept his secrets on a need-to-know basis.'

Lord Whitmore sighed. 'Your father was not a very trusting man. Daring in business endeavours, but afraid perhaps to relax in the company of those who cared about him.'

It was true. Papa had been betrayed by his own brother and, though her death was no fault of hers, abandoned by his wife. It was no wonder that Elise wanted family and belonging. For so long, it had only been him and her.

'I couldn't find anything on Andrew and then, of course, your father's death delayed matters. But I was angry when your uncle talked to the papers, even feared he had something to do with Thomas's death. The police were terrible in that investigation, as you know, but I didn't fight them because I was using it to look more into Andrew.

'We found out about his involvement in a horse-race

cheating scheme. Stephania spoke to Prince Adnan when she arrived and I understand that they want to keep Prince Saleem out of it as much as they can, but if he testifies what he heard Gerald say, then we may be able to link it back to your uncle's involvement as well. The point is that this will all be over soon, my dear.'

'Saleem will testify, but I fear it will harm his reputation. The association to my name.'

'If there is one immediate thing I noticed about the Princes of Egypt, they are both men of integrity. And integrity cannot, by definition, ruin a man's reputation.'

'Thank you. For everything.' She stood from her seat and hugged Lord Whitmore. 'Will none of it harm you?'

'Not in the slightest. It will likely go down as the crowning achievement in my political tenure: to have uncovered a horse-racing scheme. We can soon return home, Elise. All of us. Heads lifted high.'

Chapter Twenty-One

Saleem

He stared at the door of his father's study, wondering if he should interrupt the meeting happening behind it.

'You're very different from Adnan,' Olive said. His father had suggested a game of chess, but the woman could not play to save her life. Saleem, usually quite good at it, was distracted by thoughts of what could possibly be taking Elise and Lord Whitmore so long. There was, it seemed, a limit to how long Saleem could be without Elise's company.

'He is a grouch, reprimanding and judgemental.'

'Who?' Saleem asked.

'Your brother.'

Saleem would have reprimanded her for speaking ill of Adnan or taken a moment to ponder the *interesting* dynamic he sensed between Olive and his brother, but then the door he was staring at finally opened. 'Perhaps we can finish the game later, Lady Olive?'

Saleem crossed the hall, happy to see that Lord Whitmore had his arm wrapped around Elise. It was strange that it made Saleem so happy to see her being treated with tenderness.

That he should, in turn, feel tenderness towards that person.

It was why his father's cold shoulder towards Elise earlier had angered Saleem. He needed to talk to the khedive, warn him that whatever he thought was going to happen with Lady Olive was impossible. That Saleem had feelings for Elise and would...*what*?

He wasn't quite sure how he'd inform his father about his intentions in that department. He would, of course, at the first opportunity. Being shot had solidified what Saleem knew must happen, but had not allowed him time to plan it in a way as to ensure his role in Egypt's future would not be compromised. He would honour his responsibilities as heir, whether his father trusted him to or not.

'All well?' Saleem asked, his gaze snagging on Elise's for a beat longer than it should have. But Lord Whitmore didn't seem to notice, his focus on Olive, likely still at the table they were playing chess at. She was not a fast mover.

Too practised she was in her daintiness, not like Elise who might have raced him. Saleem was eager for their walk earlier to conclude, not only to get back here but because, well, Lady Olive had a tendency towards blabbering.

'Yes,' Lord Whitmore said. 'I thanked you earlier, Prince Saleem, but did not want to say too much in front of your father. Tomorrow, when we leave for Cairo, I'll go to the embassy directly to begin the extradition process for Gerald. He has been indicted in another crime back home and along with Andrew Clifton, but this new information about his role in the death of Thomas Clifton will surely expedite the matter.'

'I can testify to it. Come to England if necessary.' Saleem chose his next words carefully, lest he upset Elise with details. 'Sir, he mentioned the Whitby Cheesemonger. A pile of rocks they keep there in an alleyway next to their awning. It is where Gerald did his dastardly deed. Perhaps investigators will find *evidence* there.'

Lord Whitmore nodded. 'That is helpful, thank you. I will pass that on to the proper authorities. If they find something, you likely won't need to be involved at all. In any case, a deposition from here should be enough. Though we would be happy to welcome you in England.' He turned to Elise. 'Would we not, my dear?'

'Certainly.' Elise smiled politely, but he couldn't tell what she was thinking. Surely they had passed that stage in their relationship: her, returning to England, ever leaving Saleem, must be unthinkable.

When Lord Whitmore moved to join the khedive who announced that lunch was being served, he'd have said as much to her. Olive intruded before he could.

'Did I hear that right?' she hissed. 'Does *he* mean to take us back with him?'

Elise reprimanded, 'Your *father* wants to ensure your safety, Olive. He knows what you did, how you ran from me. If I cannot manage your recklessness, then better to be where his servants can watch you.'

Saleem felt caught between them, but did not think it was his place to interfere between the two friends. In fact, he quite enjoyed seeing this side of Elise.

She would be a good mother. Not at all coddling, as he was sure to be as a father.

'There must be a way for me to stay in Egypt, I am not ready to go back!' Olive grumbled. 'I wish I were you, Elise. Independent, outside the rules of society.'

Elise was bothered, he could tell, but she gave a quick shake of her head. She didn't want him to say anything in her defence and so Saleem kept his mouth shut.

He was glad he did because by the time they reached the dining room, Olive had stuck her arm in Elise's, whispering something or another, and pulled her away.

Hadn't Saleem seen his sisters behave in much the same way?

It was an intimate setting, despite the opulent dining room. Their feet sinking in the plush oriental carpets, they were surrounded by burgundy-painted walls gilded with gold ornaments. The windows were large, but hindered by the crimson-coloured tasselled drapery even as they were pulled back. It was the gigantic chandelier overhead with its diamond crystals that captured most of the sunlight from them.

Raseltin was not the Lodge. Saleem had never judged its pompousness, their main palace in Cairo was even more so with its harem. And he'd thought he preferred the Lodge for its manageability as he was in Alexandria mostly on his own. Now he'd returned to the lap of extreme luxury, however, Saleem found himself judging their surroundings by what Elise would think. If she were made uncomfortable by the formality.

Saleem was placed next to Olive at the round table set for them, but Elise was across from him and he was quite glad to have the view. He enjoyed watching her eat and wondered if he could ever again enjoy a meal if she were not there to share it with.

And it seemed her pattern was a bit more haphazard than it used to be, which was very satisfying because it meant that he had had some influence on her.

Next to him, Olive picked at her plate.

'Do you not like the food, Lady Olive?' Saleem asked, trying to be polite, though she looked as though she'd been deep in thought. 'I'm sure the kitchen can prepare something else you'd prefer.'

'No, this is fine. Not all of us girls can eat like Elise and remain svelte.'

Saleem straightened. He wasn't sure if she meant to compliment or insult Elise, but he was miffed either way. His brother had warned him about Olive's nature, but something in the way he'd spoken about her had Saleem guessing that Adnan actually admired her.

Saleem had no idea *why*.

Olive turned to him. 'So, Price Saleem, what is your favourite food?'

'I'm partial to falafel, actually,' he said, loud enough for Elise to hear. He was joyous when she tried to hide her knowing smile.

The khedive reproached, 'Falafel? Where did you eat that?'

'When in Alexandria, Khedewy...'

Olive declared, 'Everyone in Rasheed said the falafel is delicious here. I will love to sample it.'

'You must do it quickly, then, for I'm afraid we're set to sail soon,' Lord Whitmore supplied.

Olive set down her fork. 'Actually, Father, I've been doing much contemplation and have decided I should like to stay in Egypt indefinitely.'

Lord Whitmore patiently asked, 'And how do you propose to do that, my dear?'

Saleem did not care for their father–daughter drama happening out in the open—better it was discreetly rendered in the study where he'd spoken to Elise.

Saleem was much more interested in thinking about the ways he'd have liked to sample the speck of bechamel sauce which had affixed itself to Elise's upper lip.

Then, he was jolted by Olive's hand on his own and the declaration that followed.

'By asking Prince Saleem if he will have me for his wife.'

Elise coughed and Saleem frantically shook his head. 'You must be joking—'

The clapping of his father drowned out Saleem's objection.

'It is fate!' the khedive shouted happily. 'We can arrange a quick wedding before your father returns to England, perhaps have a small ceremony here. Tomorrow! Give the house a day to arrange a nice party. Get the shaykh that leads the Abu Al Abbas masjid to perform the ceremony. It is not a big hoopla in our tradition. Just a witness from our family and a witness from hers. At the end of the summer, we will do a grand wedding in Cairo. Invite dignitaries from the world over. Make it a few days long. Or as many days as dresses Lady Olive cannot decide between.'

Who knew his father's party planning would one day rival his mother's? This excitement was unlike him. Unlike anything ever to do with Saleem and that gave him pause.

'Khedewy…' Saleem thought the more formal title would quell his father. 'I have not asked anyone to marry me.'

His father shot him a warning stare, the same one he often gave him when he was a little boy before hissing, *'Be a man!'*

Saleem was a man now and he could make his own decisions. Especially when it came to deciding with whom he wanted to spend his life.

'Then, perhaps you should take the Lady Olive to the study. You can ask her, without pressure from us.'

Saleem shook his head with a narrow eye on Elise, but

she refused to look up at him. Refused to look up at all. 'Lady Olive, may I ask why the rush? You were not at all eager at the start. In fact, I was given to believe that you didn't want to marry me at all.'

He said nothing about the note when she abandoned ship, but he wasn't sure she'd heard his question anyway. She was looking at her father, as if her entire reason for wanting to stay was most about punishing him.

Lord Whitmore asked, 'Olive, are you sure this is what you want?'

Saleem thought he would put his foot down, demand she behave. But when Olive answered, 'Yes', he merely nodded.

Stunned, Saleem watched as Elise stood.

She rounded the table, hugged her friend. Her jaw set, her shoulders rigid, she maintained a cold decorum that made Saleem want to scream and kiss her right there, in front of everyone.

'Congratulations, Olive,' she said. Then, without meeting his gaze, she offered a blunt, 'And to you, Prince Saleem, the same.'

It was almost as if there had never been anything between them. Why wasn't she as shocked as he was? Was it that she was putting up a front, as he was struggling to contain his own emotions?

'Thank you for a lovely lunch, but may I borrow one of your carriages to return to the Lodge?' Elise asked his father. 'My things are still there and the activities, the *travel*, of the past few days has taken its toll and I wish to rest.'

Saleem would have offered to go with her, but he needed to solve this.

'Of course, my dear.' His father was suddenly nicer to Elise. He called one of the servants to take her and then, without looking back, she was gone.

Saleem didn't know if he should run after her or berate his father for what he'd done to embarrass her.

The awful position he'd put Saleem in.

He wanted to shout that he would not marry Olive. That even when he believed his feelings for her were growing, it had been Elise all along. He'd spent too much time of his life trying to please his father, to balance what Saleem wanted with his duties. Elise had walked out now, but in their time together, he'd learned that he should trust himself more, that his instincts were good. He'd be a good leader, serve his country well, whether his father believed it or not.

But it was the gratitude on Olive's face that stilled his tongue.

Saleem wouldn't marry a woman he did not love, but he had always had a sense of when someone was hurting and would not, *could not*, add to it.

And Olive? That look? Desperation mixed with recklessness, yes, but more than that, it was hurt.

He'd not seen it earlier, so eager was he to ensure Elise was well, but Olive had had the opportunity to talk to him, ask his thoughts on marriage. At the very least, reveal a hint that she would surprise him like this. Instead, she'd barely spoke beyond complaining about Adnan and his pestering of her in Rasheed.

Although Saleem would allow that Elise loved Olive as a sister, the truth of the matter was that Elise had left without Olive the wiser for her feelings. Elise never would have done the same to Olive.

'I suppose I should go, too, find a gown that would be suitable,' Olive said now. 'Or did you still want to ask me, Prince Saleem?'

'No! I did not want to ask you.' But rather than take it

as a rejection, she flitted from the dining room, misunderstanding. 'Very well then, see you at our wedding.'

'You do not wish to marry Olive.' Lord Whitmore had been watching Saleem. He proved more observant than his daughter, his blue eyes soft, his long grey sideburns were dishevelled with his scratching of them. He couldn't be much older than Saleem's father, but he looked as if he had decades on the khedive. It looked as if he'd spent a lifetime holding his *emotions* inward and that it had taken its toll.

Before Saleem could answer that he did not, his father rose. 'Now we are unencumbered by the presence of women, let us talk marriage details over a good cigar, no?'

He called for the servants to clean and led them to the parlour he kept for his favourite smoking guests. It had been a while since Saleem had been there and he could not remember it being so dank.

Stifling.

Perhaps the memory of humouring Gerald had got to Saleem more than he cared to admit.

Saleem would not humour his father. He'd get what he wanted.

'I was caught off guard,' he said, looking between the khedive and Lord Whitmore, 'but surely you both understand that there can be no marriage between Lady Olive and myself.'

Lord Whitmore said, 'Olive stunned me, too, but I cannot disappoint my daughter.'

From his perch, the khedive tsked. 'You were exchanging letters with her, Saleem. Your mother told me you were *moved* by them.'

Saleem saw his opportunity. 'I since learned that Elise was writing those letters on Lady Olive's behalf. In fact, Elise and I have grown *close*—'

'Walad,' his father hissed the word for 'boy' in Arabic, used it in warning. 'Ma'tibash homar.'

He was telling him not to be a donkey, but Saleem was reminded of a donkey that fell through a hole and discovered an entire underground world.

'Abi,' Saleem spoke in proper Arabic, called him by his 'father' title, 'I will not marry her.'

He didn't mean for Lord Whitmore to understand, but the man seemed to, regardless. He added, 'You wish to marry Elise?'

Saleem knew that that was the only way forward. 'I do, yes.'

'Apologies for my son, Lord Whitmore. He is young, foolish, but since me and you are indeed friends, I don't mind saying he is also my heir and needs to marry for the good of the country. He has ambitions for it, projects here in Alexandria. He needs a woman by his side who will support him at home and on international stages. As pretty as Miss Clifton may be, Olive is a true English beauty. One with a title and a dowry.'

Now it was Saleem's turn to hiss angrily in Arabic, 'What kind of defeated mentality is that? Elise is not white enough or blonde enough for you?'

The insult to Elise felt as though his heart was being squeezed. To have it be his own father was preposterous.

'What's going on here?' Adnan came breezing in, like a cooling wind, breaking the stare his father kept on him and drawing it to his older son.

The one he respected.

'Shouldn't you already be in Cairo?' the khedive asked.

Adnan threw Saleem a concerned, quizzical look before answering their father, 'They made us wait for hours and then they declared that the public trains would not be running today because the khedive was travelling on them tomorrow and they needed to clean them. Can you imagine the irony?'

'You should have listened to me and stayed. A father knows what is best for his son.' The khedive meant it as a jab at Saleem.

Rather than engage with it, Adnan sank in the seat next to Saleem, a show of support. He smiled at Lord Whitmore. 'So, there was no need for our goodbyes earlier, my Lord. How have you enjoyed the day with your daughter?'

'I think Olive is not pleased with you for wrenching her from Rasheed to meet me.'

Adnan said, 'Then I shall suffer her wrath gladly for it was not prudent for Lady Olive, as a maiden, to remain in the city unchaperoned.'

'Adnan, you missed the event of the afternoon,' the khedive announced. 'There is to be a wedding after all. Late summer, perhaps. But we will need to seal it before heading to Cairo. Saleem will be doing his katib kitab tonight or tomorrow.'

Adnan blurted, 'Katib kitab? With Elise?'

'To Olive Whitmore!' The khedive sounded sick of repeating it.

'No. I am not.' Saleem enunciated. 'I hate to upset her or Lord Whitmore but, sir, I cannot marry your daughter, not when I care for Elise.'

'Of course not,' Lord Whitmore agreed, 'but I fear she will run away again with this news.'

It was Adnan's muttering in Arabic that confused Saleem. He couldn't make out what his brother was saying but the look on his face was blank, his eyes wide. As if he were flabbergasted to hear the news. He asked him, 'How did the "event" happen?'

'She surprised us at lunch by asking me and our father was—'

Their father was answering Lord Whitmore. 'Then do not give Olive the news. Saleem will agree to the marriage. I will see to it.'

'I will not.' Saleem stood. He was done talking about it. He had to find Olive, let her know and then he had to grovel before Elise.

'Think of the dowry, what it can do for Egypt.' The khedive's face reddened with crassness. He rarely lost control of his temper, his poise. But if Saleem might have been guilty before for not putting the country and his duty before his heart, those words worked wonders to vanquish that guilt.

'Father, you cannot believe me so pathetic I do not have my own investors. My own monies. My ideas, my projects will improve Egypt, bring her wealth without a wife's dowry.' By now, Saleem was shouting at his father and his brother had to hold him back.

'I think this is my fault,' Adnan said. 'I was the one who told Olive that if she wanted to stay in Egypt, she shouldn't have written that note. That she should have married you when she had the chance. Her desperation, it—'

Lord Whitmore tried to play the peacemaker, 'If it is the dowry you seek for Egypt,' he said to the khedive, 'you should know that Elise is extremely wealthy. The sum of money she inherited in England was substantial enough, but the rest for a number of reasons had to be converted into gold bars. The amount of which is…well, let us just say that if her father *were* alive, he might not agree to the match thinking *the Prince* was only after her wealth. In comparison, Olive's dowry is actually a paltry one.'

Mr Patterson had not mentioned the amount of gold bars

in her account at the bank and Elise had not said much about her inheritance. She dressed simply, acted humbly. When they fought, she'd implied she'd be comfortable living as a spinster in her London town house, but Saleem had had no idea of *how* comfortable.

'Does this change your feelings about Elise?' Adnan asked.

His brother was worried that she'd lied to him about it, but Saleem didn't think she'd lied. All he thought was that her money was the reason why she didn't like titles. People like Gerald, like his father, would use it to their own ends.

The proof was in the khedive's face, how it had relaxed. Although Saleem was glad that there would not be more of a fight between his father and him, they were two very different men. Saleem had never been and would never be the sort of man who married for a dowry.

'It does not change my feelings about Elise, it only emphasises the need for me to protect her more. From anyone, including myself or my country, any who would take advantage.' He stared pointedly at the khedive.

Lord Whitmore patted his father's shoulder and then shook Saleem's hand. 'Then you have my blessing, dear boy. Thomas Clifton, Elise's papa, used to say that is what he wanted most for his daughter. *A protector.* That is what I most want for Olive, too.'

'What are you saying about me?'

None of them noticed Olive had entered the room. She looked around, took in the scene.

She stiffened when her eyes landed on Adnan. 'I thought you would have already been back in your precious Cairo.'

'The train was delayed.'

There was a tension between them, one that was exasperated by Lord Whitmore approaching his daughter cautiously. She stepped back, flinching at his hand on her arm.

Adnan had come to stand by Saleem and he bristled, too.

Olive marched towards Adnan. She stared at him for a long minute, examining, questioning, but rather than his brother flinching under her scrutiny, she shuddered. It was the strangest encounter and Saleem was sure that he saw some spark there. 'Is it your fault, Grumpy?' she asked. 'Were you the one to turn your brother off our marriage?'

'It wasn't me. Saleem and Elise are in love. Any fool can see it, why didn't you?'

She clasped her hands on her mouth, looked at Saleem for confirmation. 'Is it true?'

'Yes.'

'But Elise said nothing. Oh, I am a horrible friend,' she lamented. 'I'm so sorry!'

She collapsed in the seat closest to her and buried her face in her hands. It was quite the sight to behold and with the tears in Lord Whitmore's eyes as well, the way he held back even though he clearly wanted to comfort her, made it sad all around.

The man patted his coat, looking for the handkerchief that was missing.

Saleem did feel sorry for them.

Not enough, however, to stop him wanting to make a quick exit and get back to the Lodge to declare his love for Elise.

It was Adnan who produced a handkerchief. He held it out to Olive and she gave him a soft look before accepting it.

'I only wanted to stay in Egypt,' she whispered.

The khedive offered, 'We could host you at the palace. The harem accepts guests.'

'The harem is restrictive,' Adnan answered for Olive. 'The lady has already declined that offer. I made the same days ago—anything to get her to leave the ezzbah. She said she wishes to come and go as she pleases.'

Olive sniffled. 'And you were the one who told me only married women had such freedom! Your bad advice led to me making a fool of myself, hurting my best friend!'

'Maybe it was a bad choice to seek a marriage to a man already in love with another.'

Saleem objected, 'Adnan, you don't need to defend me.'

But neither he nor Olive was listening to him now.

'Then, perhaps you can find me another man to marry so I can stay!'

'Olive,' Lord Whitmore said, 'I must insist that this is untoward behaviour. You are embarrassing me.'

She barely heard him, her gaze locked on Adnan.

Saleem had never seen so many emotions cross his brother's face in such quick succession. Anger. Annoyance. Frustration. Exasperation. Empathy.

The khedive nudged Saleem, for the first time seeking his help with Adnan. 'Stop him before he embarrasses us.'

Instead, Adnan shocked them all.

'You want a husband, Olive?' he said, his tone a ragged whisper. 'Marry me!'

And if Saleem and the rest of the room weren't surprised enough with his proposal, Olive's nod came next. There was defeat in it, but something else Saleem made out as well.

Hope.

'All right, Adnan. I accept. Yes, I'll marry you.'

Chapter Twenty-Two

Elise

Elise had had the most restless of sleeps, but Khayria had brought her the best of breakfast trays. All her favourites, including what she now knew as "kibda."

'Liver make you strong for wedding.'

The girl had learned some English for her and Elise smiled approvingly, but thought that she would not need it for much longer.

Once Olive was mistress of the Lodge, she could speak with her in Arabic.

That thought made her sadder still, but she was glad Khayria wasn't around to see it.

Besides, she was Elise Clifton and she'd always been pretty good at thinking clearly on a full stomach and having the ability to devise good plans.

Today, it was a singular task: watch the man she loved marry her best friend.

Because, yes, somewhere along the way—likely from his first letter back to her in England—Elise *had* fallen in love with Saleem. She could admit it now, when it was too late. That was part of any good plan: seeing the truth of things.

She told herself that Saleem and Olive would fit. He

would make a good husband, riding the waves of her reck-lessness with his sunny ways and generous heart. They'd go through life unburdened, have lots of children.

There was, of course, the unsavoury matter of what had transpired between Elise and Saleem. Their very intense love making on this very bed, in this very room. They'd been lost in the moment, swept away by the intense need their bodies had for one another.

Elise couldn't think about it without blushing at the things they did.

How very good they felt.

Would Olive care that her husband had been with her friend?

Elise wouldn't tell her, because Saleem most certainly would. He demanded honesty. Because of what his father had done, Saleem wouldn't tolerate a marriage based on a lie.

But it is their concern, not mine.

It wasn't as though Elise was Saleem's first lover, but Olive didn't think to investigate that. Which was odd for her, considering that she used to say that she did want a virgin husband.

'Is it so terrible that I want to be his first as he will be mine?'

But Olive was a changed woman and she hadn't shared why with Elise.

Maybe she'll tell Saleem. Let him help her.

As sad as Elise was about the whole ordeal, she did love her friend.

Elise could be happy for Olive, she didn't need to plan for that. And when the ceremony was done, she would get on with her life, too. She had a few ideas about what her next chapter would be. A visit to Greece with Stephania was her top priority.

Saleem had given Elise closure by getting Gerald's confession, but he'd also inspired her. He was a model of goodness, using one's talent and privilege to serve. To better the lives of others. Elise would consciously follow his example and do the same.

When she'd eaten the last of the kibda, she downed the glass of milky tea and took her tray out to the corridor, where Khayria would usually sit, waiting. Today, oddly, she was nowhere to be found.

Elise heard the buzz of folk below—it seemed as though there were a number of people—but she didn't think she was ready to face Saleem getting ready for his wedding.

She'd expected him to knock on her door last night or this morning, braced herself for his apology or his excuses.

Listed them in her head.

You said it yourself, Elise, our stations are too different.

I wanted a future with you, asked you to stay here with me. To let me protect you.

You said you wanted to be a spinster, go back to England. That I was wrong about you and you didn't want a family. Belonging.

And Saleem would be right. Elise had no rebuttals to anything he might say.

But in the end, he hadn't come to see her. Maybe he thought that avoiding her was for the best. Or maybe he'd not come home last night, spent the time at Raseltin, finally getting to know the woman he should have been wooing all along.

I will not feel sorry for myself.

She sniffed the air. It smelled like honey and roasting nuts.

And something else. Roses. No, not roses.

Hibiscus.

She followed her nose down the staircase and saw the work being done. All the flowers.

Seriously, she'd never seen so many of the same variety of flowers indoors.

They were being hauled in by the staff, Khayriya and Mustafa arranging them in every nook and cranny of the room.

She searched for Saleem, but he wasn't there, no Olive either. But it looked as though they'd decided to have their wedding here.

Elise steeled herself, stepping back before anyone caught her there, solemnly stalking the scene.

'Sabahel Khayr.' Saleem's voice greeted her. He stood behind her, not exactly sleepy, but looking as though he'd had a restful-enough sleep. Which, were she being honest, made Elise a little bit angry.

Better angry than sad, at least.

'Good morning yourself,' she managed to say. 'Happy wedding day.'

'I'm hoping.' He smiled.

'You've decided to have it here?'

'The Lodge is home, do you not think? Is not "home" a perfect place for a wedding?'

She nodded, but had to look away. Elise decided she would have to cut off her friendship with Olive after today. She would not be able to be in Saleem's presence without wanting to ogle him, touch him. Love him.

She moved to brush past him. 'I need to get ready,' she said when he stood in the way.

He put his hands on her shoulders, slowly lifting her chin to face him. His touch enflamed every inch of her, her head clouded. His lips hovered over hers.

Saleem is getting married today, her mind blared a warning.

'I need to get ready,' she repeated.

'But your dress hasn't arrived yet.'

She had no idea what that meant, but Elise couldn't allow this to continue. The temptation that Saleem posed.

'You're sad,' he observed.

She met his gaze. Let him bask in exactly how sad. Perhaps then he would do something to finally end his pull on her.

'I have always hated feelings of sadness,' he said. 'In myself certainly, but in others, too. The burden of sadnesses was something I did not want to bear. Sadness feels heavy in my chest and my chest basks in lightness. And so, I did my best to avoid any sadness.

'But at the hospital when I saw you were sad to see me hurt, something shifted. For the first time, I felt that I would gladly take all your burdens, Elise. Claim your sadness in my heart if it meant you didn't have to be sad, ever. And thus, knowing that I had succeeded in the endeavour, my sadness would be erased. I would be kept happy.'

The emotions that came with his words burst forth, reminding her of his letter where he'd said that the hibiscus reminded him of her. How she'd sobbed that day for the first time since her father had died.

'I know I drove you to this,' Elise cried. 'Pushed you away from me. But you were right about it all, Saleem. About me. About the future we could have had. I was too afraid, too insecure. Too spurned. I thought myself unworthy of a nobleman and could not see that you were a nobleman first—and that it wasn't your title that made you so.'

He kissed her head. Peppered her cheeks with more to

wipe away her tears. And he held her, letting her sob until she'd quieted. Until she felt better.

'I will be strong for you today,' she said. 'I owe you that much.'

'I did get justice for your father's murderer,' he teased.

'And you took a bullet for me,' she added.

When she heard Stephania's voice calling from downstairs, Elise grew suspicious. Surely she hadn't spent enough time with Olive to warrant an invitation to her wedding?

Perhaps Stephania's come to take me to her home, as planned before we set off to Rasheed.

'What's going on, Saleem?'

'Sounds to me as though your dress has arrived.'

And then Stephania was in the hallway with them, eyeing Saleem's casual pyjamas with her typically blunt glance. 'You're still here? One thing about Egyptians, they're always going to be late.'

'It is hard to plan a wedding in a day,' Saleem said.

'Olive had to do it before Lord Whitmore left for England,' Elise added, feeling the need to explain on Saleem's behalf.

Saleem clarified, 'Lady Olive is getting married next week, Elise. You left early yesterday and, well, things took an odd turn. She is marrying Adnan.'

'What? How?'

Stephania understood the look of confusion on Elise's face to accuse Saleem, 'Have you even asked her yet?'

'I wanted to make sure she had her breakfast first! The last time I asked her something important, she downright refused me and I suspect it was a little bit because she was hungry. I'm not taking any chances this time.'

'What on earth is happening?' Elise wondered, her heart beating faster, her nerves more scattered than they'd ever been.

Olive was not marrying Saleem?

He wanted to ask her something?

Saleem ignored her question and pointed out Elise's room to Stephania. 'If you can lay out the dress and give me a bit of time?'

Stephania pressed her lips together and shuffled away, the dress in question hidden from view.

Elise had an inkling now of what was happening—yet she couldn't believe it.

'Will you come to my room for a minute? I don't believe you've seen it yet and this is a high traffic area. I don't want us to be interrupted before asking what I mean to ask.'

'Saleem,' she whispered, but it was all she could muster. She nodded, let him take her hand in his. Lead her to the opposite side of the floor. His room wasn't too far, but it was like entering another world when they crossed the threshold of it.

It was breathtaking.

The walls seemed longer than in her room and the window was so large, it looked as though a wall was missing. Everything was a beautiful cream colour and, with its unencumbered view of the sea, it was as though Saleem's room was an extension of the beach.

He watched her taking it in, then stood behind her, laying his chin on her shoulder. Elise wasn't cold, but she shivered with his closeness. How much it wasn't enough.

'Do you like it?' he asked.

'It's gorgeous.'

'I wanted to make the master bedroom a part of the tour that first day you arrived, but thought better of it. I didn't know why then, but seeing you here now, I can see why.'

She shifted gently so that she could face him, take in his beautiful smile. 'Why?'

'Because I knew it wouldn't be mine any more. That you would belong here. That my room would be yours.'

He kissed her then and she melted into it. Would his lips on hers always make her feet curl? He cupped her face between both hands, deepened the kiss so that she was overwhelmed with both emotional and physical yearning for him.

'Wait.' She put her hands to his chest, pushed him away. Not too much, just enough to give his mouth room to talk. And lest he got any ideas about stopping for too long, Elise lowered her hands, wrapped her arms around his waist and pushed herself closer. 'Is it true that Adnan and Olive are going to get married? Olive can be reckless and your brother seems much more rational. There was tension between them, but it was more as though they wanted to make war rather than make love?'

Saleem grinned at how she held on to him, but Elise didn't care, especially when the hands he'd cupped her face with were now engaged in tender play with her hair. 'It *was* strange between them and shocking. But…whether they actually get married is up to you.'

'Me?'

Saleem's lifted brow made it so that Elise didn't know whether or not he was teasing her but seeing the doubt on her face, he lowered it. 'It's true. You see my father set a condition. He said that the spare cannot marry before the heir. Even though Adnan is older than I am and cannot, alas, ever sit on the Egyptian throne, the khedive was adamant on that point.'

'What?'

'It is why there was such a rush after you left Raseltin yesterday. Planning a wedding before my father and brother, Olive and Lord Whitmore must return to Cairo was quite a feat.' Saleem chuckled. 'Of course, this is just the "official" required to obtain a licence. We call it a *"katib kitab"* and we can do something bigger and fancier in the Cairo palace—with my mother and whole family. I suspect we'll have to. Perhaps, with Adnan and Olive if you'd like. Knowing you, I guessed that a big fancy wedding is not what you would want. That's why I wanted to do it small and intimate here, first.'

'What are you saying, Saleem?'

'That if you do not love me enough to marry me, perhaps you will agree to because you do not want to stand in the way of Olive marrying Adnan.'

'If I do not love you enough? Saleem, I love you with all my heart and body. My *soul* loves yours.' She stood on her tiptoes, pulled his face down to hers so that their gazes were locked. She stared at him and he at her for a long minute before he pulled away.

'Wait here.' He rushed to the table next to his huge bed and ran back with a letter in hand and a small jewellery box. 'I wrote it last night, thought to stick it under your door for you to find first thing in the morning, but I selfishly wanted to watch you read it. The letters we've sent before today might have been under *circumstances*, but this is a new start for us. And I want to bear witness to it.'

Elise struggled not to cry when she opened the familiar paper, recognised the familiar script.

Read her name there. And the words meant for her.

Dear Elise,

I love you and promise to honour and protect you for all my life. I promise to write you better and longer letters. Will you let me? I dare you to love me, too.

> *Marry me, please.*
> *Yours,*
> *Saleem*
> *PS You haven't finished my portrait. I hope it will*
> *be a favourable one, but if it is not, at least we'll have*
> *something to discuss.*

At that last line, her tears fell back and a joyous laugh came instead. A laugh that felt like a harbinger of a lifetime of them.

When she looked up from the note, Saleem had bent on his knees. He held open the jewellery box. Inside was a beautiful emerald ring. 'My mother sent it for me with my father, said she was sure that the woman that moved me in her letters would be needing it for a proposal by now. That when I love, I am committed. My mother knew even before I did or maybe at the same time. I love you, Elise. Your words. Your beauty. My soul *absolutely* loves your soul. Will you share your life with me? Will you marry me?'

'Yes, Saleem. Yes!'

He swept her in his arms and they laughed and kissed and danced to the music and joy in their hearts.

Until the knock at the door reminded them that they weren't alone on the beach. Mustafa and Adnan were there. 'We're here for Saleem,' the latter said. 'And I believe your room has women waiting for you too, Miss Elise.'

She nodded and Saleem offered to take her back, but Adnan shook his head, 'We'll never get started then.'

Mustafa did the honours. 'A thousand *mabrooks*, Princess Elise. I will look forward to serving you alongside my Prince.'

'Did you know that I thought once of hiring you myself? Stealing you away from Saleem to be my guard?'

She marvelled at the irony of it. How quickly conditions could change if people took a chance and allowed optimism and love to reign.

Saleem had showed her that.

Inside her room, Stephania was there with Olive.

'Congratulations are in order, I hear,' Elise offered.

'It's not about me today, it is your day. This is your story and what a beautiful one it is!' Olive hugged her tight, 'Oh, Elise, forgive me for being so oblivious to you and Saleem. Your love. I was foolish and selfish, but if I'd known—'

'Never mind it now, you're forgiven and I want my sister with me.' She took Stephania's hand. 'And my cousin— aunt.'

She looked at the dress laid out for her. 'Is that...?'

Stephania lifted it reverently. 'It was your mother's, Frangosyka. Saleem came to me last night. That Mustafa is tricky and found out my address that I like to keep secret, but anyways Saleem said that he had Lord Whitmore's permission, but wanted mine too, to ask for your hand as a gentleman would. It reminded me of your papa, Thomas's and Valia's rushed wedding. And then I remembered that I had the dress your mother wore, tucked away to give to you one day. You don't have to wear it, but—'

'I want to! More than anything.'

The white dress was embroidered throughout, but they were thin beads over an ethereal lace. The homage to her Greek roots was in the laurel patterns of the lace, the draping cut and the wreath-like silver tiara that came with the veil.

It fit her perfectly.

And while Olive and Stephania offered many compliments, filling the room with their 'oohs' and 'ahhs', Elise had to see it for herself.

In the mirror, she glimpsed her reflection, felt that her mother was there with her. *In her.* And her father as well.

You look beautiful, they seemed to say. And Elise believed them.

She floated down the stairs to where Saleem stood, waiting for her. His charming, handsome smile was as large as his good and open heart. She'd never been happier.

She'd found love. Family.

The most princely of Princes.

Elise Clifton had found belonging.

* * * * *

*While you're waiting for the next book in
Heba Helmy's Princes of Egypt miniseries,
why not let yourself get swept up in her previous
charming historical romances?*

The Earl's Egyptian Heiress
A Viscount for the Egyptian Princess

Harlequin® Reader Service

Enjoyed your book?

Try the perfect subscription for Romance readers and get more great books like this delivered right to your door.

See why over 10+ million readers have tried Harlequin Reader Service.

Start with a Free Welcome Collection with free books and a gift—valued over $20.

Choose any series in print or ebook.
See website for details and order today:

TryReaderService.com/subscriptions